Hattie's Preacher
The Outlaw Series, Book 1

by

Sherry Derr Wille

Published by
Melange Books, LLC
White Bear Lake, MN 55110
www.melange-books.com

Hattie's Preacher ~ Copyright © 2013 by Sherry Derr Wille

ISBN: 978-1-61235-667-9 Print

Cover Art by Lynsee Lauritsen

Hattie's Preacher
Sherry Derr Wille

David Long gave up a promising law career when God called him to preach the word. Little did he know the red headed pianist at his church in Mortonville would capture his heart.

Hattie Fairchild knew the only proper place for a proper maiden lady to play the piano was in church. Even though she didn't believe, she found she could ignore the minister's words by staying hidden away in the balcony and reading her novels during the sermons.

When David Long came to town. Not only did he move the piano from the balcony to the main floor of the sanctuary, he also decided to restore her faith in God. In the process she found herself falling for the man who looked more like a black smith than a preacher.

* * * *

What reviewers are saying...

HATTIE'S PREACHER is a beautiful story about a woman who's lost her faith in God because of the sins of one man. But it's also the story of redemption - faith restored and true love coming to show the Lord's mercy to the lonely and broken-hearted. You'll definitely want to find out what happens to Hattie, her preacher and her family in the next two books in the OUTLAW SERIES. Sherry Derr-Wille, an author who has written in many genres has found yet another niche in Christian historicals. Bravo!

Karen Wiesner, Award winning Author of Waiting for an Eclipse.

Prologue

Philadelphia 1881

"Gentlemen of the jury, have you reached your verdict?"

"We have, Your Honor."

"How do you find the defendant, Willard Palmer?"

"We find him not guilty."

David Long looked at his client. He'd defended Willard to the best of his ability, even though he knew the man was guilty as sin. Being the youngest associate in the firm, David had no other choice.

"You did it, David!" Willard exclaimed, slapping him on the back. You saved my sorry hide. My father will see to it you get a well-earned bonus."

"Tell your father to keep his money. I know you well enough to know there will be more legal fees in the future."

"Then I'll make you a wealthy man."

"Not me. This is my last case. I wish you well."

Without waiting for Willard to make further comment, David shoved the papers littering the defense table into his briefcase and stalked out of the courthouse.

In the weeks of preparation for the trial, as well as the proceeding itself, David sensed an uneasiness settling into his being. It hadn't been until the reading of the verdict that it struck him.

Above the voice of the foreman of the jury, David heard another, a softer more powerful one. *"You are mine, David Long. The time has come for you to serve Me."*

David knew he'd heard the voice before, but then he'd been asleep. In his dreams, God told him of a life spreading the word of the Lord. Upon awakening, the dream was always vivid, its meaning always clear. It was only the weakness of his own flesh that kept him from acting upon it. What did he know about spreading the word of God? He was a lawyer; the son of a blacksmith, even though he went to church on Sunday and participated in evening devotions with his family, he wasn't a preacher. He had neither the training nor the ….

Nor the what? He was a lawyer. He certainly wasn't afraid of facing a packed courtroom to argue the innocence of a man he knew to be guilty. Surely, he would have no trouble facing a congregation to spread the word he knew to be the truth.

Hearing the voice as well as the words while he was awake frightened and yet exhilarated David. God wanted him, David Long, to spread his word. In his entire life, David had never heard of God speaking to a modern day man. God talked freely to men like Abraham and Moses, but not to someone in the nineteenth century.

Outside of the courthouse, David pushed through the crowd of people anxious to hear the verdict. Once away from the crush of the mob, David hurried to the building that housed his law office.

"How did it go, my boy?" Raymond Saunders, David's employer inquired.

"We won," David replied, flatly.

"You did a great job. There's a raise waiting for you. I knew we made the right decision when we put you on this case."

"Keep your raise, Mr. Saunders. I won't need it. This is my last case. I'm leaving the law. I'm sick to my stomach over the miscarriage of justice in that courtroom today. Willard was guilty. The only reason he's free is that I convinced the jury he was innocent."

"Do I have to remind you that was your job? Mr. Palmer paid us handsomely for your services."

"From now on, he'll have to pay someone else. I will no longer take money to lie so a guilty man can go free. I have no other cases pending.

I'm certain you'll have no trouble replacing me."

David turned from his astonished boss and made his way to the office he'd called his own for the past eight years. It took only minutes for him to stack neatly the papers from his briefcase on the large mahogany desk. It amazed David how quickly he was able to pack up eight years of his life.

When he arrived home, his father, like his boss, was less than favorable

"You did what?" William Long demanded.

"I quit the firm. I've given up the law?"

"But why?' his mother said, wringing her hands. "Being a lawyer has been your dream."

"It was your dream, Mama, yours and Papa's. God wants me to do His work now."

"My son hears the voice of God," his father lamented, thrusting his hands into the air. "Whoever heard of the son of a blacksmith talking to God?"

"Whoever heard of a shepherd boy killing a giant? A boy with the same name as mine slew Goliath with a rock and a sling. He did it because God guided him to do so. Today God decided to guide me to spread His word. Can I do less than obey?"

* * * *

David sat in the parlor of the parsonage. Around him, the shabby hand-me-down furniture denoted the life he would be embarking upon.

Did he know what he was doing? As a lawyer, he'd never want for money. He could easily afford a home in a fashionable neighborhood. Did he want to spend the rest of his life living in the poverty the ministry demands?

The answer came back as an overwhelming Yes.

"David," Reverend Kanter said, as he entered the room. "What brings you here today?"

"I...I want to find out how I go about becoming a minister."

Reverend Kanter looked over the top of his spectacles. "I thought you were well established with a good law firm. Why have you had this change of heart?"

David swallowed hard. How did he even begin? "I don't know if

3

you will believe this, but God has called me. He wants me to spread His word."

Reverend Kanter leaned back in his chair, his hands clasped before him. The gesture made David more than a little uneasy.

"Have you given this matter sufficient thought? The young are often impetuous in their actions. They do not always think beyond the moment. Have you thought beyond the moment, David?"

"I'm hardly what you would call young, Reverend Kanter. You must know I've passed my thirtieth birthday. I would imagine by the standards of many this would seem like a sudden decision, but I have prayed about it. I started having the dreams weeks ago. Then, in the middle of a trial, He spoke to me while I was awake. I know you must think I am doing something I might regret, but I don't agree."

Reverend Kanter began to smile. "I'm inclined to believe you, but I want you to take a month to consider your decision. While you do, I want you to read some books. When you finish them, come back and we will talk again."

David left the parsonage feeling more than a little disappointed. He'd expected Reverend Kanter to welcome him with open arms. Instead, he'd filled David's arms with books.

"What did Reverend Kanter have to say?" his mother greeted him when he returned home.

"He wants me to read these books," David replied. "I thought…"

"You thought he would give you a church. It takes more than a desire to spread the word of God. If Reverend Kanter says you should read, then you should read."

David reluctantly agreed with his mother. Without further conversation, he went to his room, put the books on the table, and began to pour over one of the volumes he carried in his arms.

The first book in the stack was the Bible. Although he'd memorized the verses as a child, now he read the words as a man. Among the other books, he found explanations to the passages he did not understand.

Over the next month, David left his room only for meals. The more he read the more he wanted to know. A new world opened to him.

* * * *

"It's been a month, David," Reverend Kanter began, once they were seated in the parlor. "What have you learned?"

From the moment David started talking, the words tumbled over one another in an attempt to be heard. Before he knew it, two hours had passed, and he'd talked non-stop the entire time.

When he finally exhausted what he had to say, Reverend Kanter smiled broadly and then laughed out loud. To David, the gesture seemed humiliating. How could this man he had sought guidance from make fun of him to his face?

As he started to get to his feet to leave, Reverend Kanter motioned for him to remain seated.

After the man regained his composure, he reached across the short

After the man regained his composure, he reached across the short space separating their chairs and clasped David's hand.

"Please don't misinterpret my joy, David. I expected you to see what path God intended for you to travel. Instead, you found an extensive map for your entire life. You are indeed blessed. During this time, I have contacted the church officials' here in Philadelphia. They have assured me you should require no further schooling. In fact, they want to meet with you on Monday morning. I am to bring you to their church so they can question you before they give you your first call."

David could hardly believe his ears. Instead of the ridicule he'd heard from his father since leaving the law, he'd found acceptance. Within a few days, his life would take a new path. The disappointment of a month earlier turned to the anticipation of his new life.

"Where do you think this call will be?"

"I have a friend, Reverend Jonathan Hill, in Mortonville, Illinois. His health is failing rapidly. I'm afraid he must give up his church. It will be a perfect first call."

Chapter One

Mortonville, Illinois

"Did you hear the news?" Gertie Kellogg said when Hattie Fairchild met her on the street Wednesday morning.

"It's no secret Reverend Hill is leaving, Gertie. Even I know that."

"Well, of course you do. I mean, with you playing the piano at church and all, you'd be one of the first to know. I wasn't talking about him. I was referring to the new minister. I hear he's very young, very handsome, and very single."

"So? Why would this information be of interest to me?"

"Oh really, Hattie, everyone in town knows there isn't a single man your age within fifty miles of Mortonville. The new minister might be your last chance."

Hattie rolled her eyes and hurried on her way. She refused to dignify Gertie's comment with a reply. She'd never been considered a great catch and the fact she was fast approaching her thirtieth birthday didn't make her any more attractive.

Her sister, Laura, had been the beauty in the family, and what had it gotten her? From the letters she wrote, Caleb Tyler was an abusive husband who had turned four of their five sons into ruthless killers and bank robbers.

Even her mother had been considered a rare beauty in her youth.

There was no denying her life had been hard. As a farmer's wife raising two girls to adulthood and four boys barely past infancy, the hard life stole whatever beauty she had, whatever youth she possessed. Hattie's father spent much of his time in the tavern playing cards and drinking. He left the work of running the farm to Hattie and her mother who died long before her time.

After seeing the disastrous marriages of her two closest female relatives, Hattie swore she would remain an old maid rather than endure a loveless and abusive union.

Five years earlier, her father died of a heart attack, leaving Hattie with a farm she could not run alone. After selling the land, she sent half the money to Laura and invested her portion with an old friend, Abe Levens, the local tailor. For years, she had done piecework for him, so it seemed only logical that they become partners. With Abe's death two years ago, Hattie became Mortonville's only seamstress and tailor. The decision to become a businesswoman had been a good one.

Hattie looked around the shop that doubled as her home. Often she missed Abe. He'd taught her more in the three years they worked together than her parents had over the entire course of her life.

Abe Levens was a widower in need of a partner as well as a housekeeper. Hattie had been more than delighted to fill both positions. He became the kind of father she had longed for all her life. Not only was he patient when he was teaching her something new, he was also a loving man. Never having children of his own, he was more than happy to take on the role of foster father.

Then, to her amazement, Abe insisted she accompany him to church on Sunday mornings.

"But, Abe, you must know I'm not a church goer. I can't even say I'm a believer."

"You may not be either, but you will go to church with me. My Marta and I came here from New York over twenty years ago. There is no synagogue in Mortonville. If I wanted to fit in the community, I had to do as my neighbors did. In my heart, as well as my home, I am Jewish. If you want to be successful in this town, you will make the people think you believe as they do."

At first, going to Sunday services had been a chore, but Hattie soon became adept at allowing her mind to wander to things other than the scripture reading and the sermon.

When she was asked to play the piano for the services, Hattie was delighted. Music she understood and loved. She found she could concentrate on the black dots that dominated the lines and spaces and not have to worry about the words of praise the congregation sang. With the piano in the balcony at the back of the church, Hattie could come and go unseen, the only evidence of her presence being the sweet strains of the music coming from the balcony.

Over the years, the façade she'd built did exactly what Abe said it would. None of them had any idea their dedicated church pianist carried the classics in her music bag and read them during Reverend Hill's lengthy sermons.

This day, the merry jingling of the bell above the door to the shop diverted Hattie's attention from her thoughts of Abe and the life he'd given her. Putting aside the sewing she held in her hands but hadn't worked on, she turned her attention to her customer.

"Good morning, Hattie," Reverend Hill greeted her. "I wanted to stop by and have a talk with you before I leave."

"Please, do come in. I have a pot of coffee on the stove. Can I get you a cup?"

"Don't bother. Much as I'd like one, I'm afraid this old body of mine wouldn't be as appreciative."

Hattie nodded. Instead of making room to sit in her cluttered shop, she put the closed sign in the window, pulled the shades and ushered Reverend Hill back to her private living quarters.

Very few people visited Hattie, yet she kept the backrooms company ready at all times. For too many years, she lived in her mother's filthy home. As a child, she'd cultivated no friends because she'd been too ashamed to have them at her home.

"As you know, we will be leaving here soon," Jonathan Hill began.

Hattie poured herself a cup of coffee. "Where are you and Mabel going?"

"We have a son in Ohio. He has a large congregation there. Once I'm gone, Mabel will be cared for by him."

Tears prickled behind her eyes. The thought of this dear man dying saddened her.

"Don't cry for me, my dear. I welcome death and the chance to go Home."

His words caused her tears to flow even harder. He so easily talked about a better life after death, yet she doubted it. For Hattie, you lived and then you died. Once you died, everything ended.

In comfort, Jonathan covered Hattie's hand with his surprisingly frail one. "I didn't come here to talk about the life I'm anticipating."

Hattie looked into the eyes of her friend. "I ... I know." She choked back her sobs. "You came to say good-bye."

Jonathan began to smile. "That too. My real reason for coming is to talk about you."

"Me?"

"Yes, Hattie, you. I'm afraid I've let you down. When you first started attending services, I selfishly thought the word I was spreading had taken root. Over the years, I've watched you come to church on Sundays and hide away in the balcony. I have not ministered to you, and you have not fully accepted the Lord."

Hurt radiated from her heart to the very core of her being. The expression on Jonathan's face made it clear the man felt he had failed.

"It's nothing you've done," Hattie said, the words coming almost too quickly. "I consider you and Mabel two of my best friends. I'd never knowingly do anything to hurt either of you. My faith, or lack of it, has nothing to do with you."

Jonathan sat quietly for a moment, as though contemplating her words and then continued. "I understood Abe's motives for going to church, but what are yours?"

Hattie shrugged. "In the beginning, I think they mirrored Abe's. When I was asked to play the piano, it was a dream come true. Where else could I do something with music and still remain a proper maiden lady?" For me, what started as something to promote my business has become the joy of my life. I love my music."

"Dear, dear Hattie. My wish for you is that your love will become the road to your future. I will continue to pray for your redemption."

"Will you tell the new minister about me?"

"You know I won't. If David learns about you, it will be by his own perception."

"David?"

"Reverend Long. He grew up in a church where an old friend of mine is the minister. He tells me that even though David is close to, if not over thirty, this is to be his first call. In Philadelphia, he was a lawyer. I think the two of you will enjoy a great battle of wills."

Although Hattie had work she knew must be finished, she sat in her parlor long after Reverend Hill left. She thought about what he said and drank the remainder of the coffee in the pot.

The fact Jonathan saw through her carefully planned façade was upsetting. When the new minister came, she would have to be careful. The last thing she needed was to be exposed. Not only would it be disastrous for her business, but it would also be the end of being the pianist at the church. She could survive without her sewing. She had enough money set aside to live comfortably for quite a while. Her music was something else. The only joy she could remember in her life centered on the piano and the music she could coax from its keys. To give up the one thing that made her happy would be devastating.

"What am I going to do, Abe?" She spoke as though her old friend stood beside her.

When her question remained unanswered, tears rolled down her cheeks. It had been a long time since she'd indulged in a soul-cleansing cry. Since Abe's death, she'd been alone. Until today, it hadn't mattered. She had her music, and that made her happy. What if Reverend Long forbid her to play once he realized she didn't believe in his God?

* * * *

David passed the time on the trip from Philadelphia to Mortonville absorbed in one of the many books Reverend Kanter suggested he read. Along with his other belongs, his father insisted he take his law books.

"I'll never use them again," David had protested.

"Maybe you won't, but what will it hurt to take them with you? I realize God has called you to spread His word, but He also gave you the mind to be a lawyer. There may come a day when the minister will need the lawyer. When it does, you will be prepared."

David looked back down at the book he held in his hands. These were his books now. He loved the law, but he loved the Lord more. Even though he might never use the law again, it was a comfort to have his law books with him. He thanked his father for insisting he make room for them in his new life.

"Mortonville, Illinois. Next stop Mortonville, Illinois," the conductor called as he made his way through the passenger car.

David put the book in his traveling bag. As soon as the train came to a stop, he was on his feet. After sitting on the moving train for so long, his legs felt as though they wouldn't support the weight of his large frame.

He stepped from the train to the platform and inhaled deeply. The sweet smell of summer in the country told him he'd made the right decision. Having grown up surrounded by the odor of smoke from his father's blacksmith shop mingled with that of horses in need of shoeing, he knew he would have never been content to spend his entire life in the city, away from the wonders of nature God provided. Within the walls of the courthouse, to say nothing of his office, he missed the reminders of home.

Across the platform, David noticed three men fidgeting nervously. They certainly looked out of place in their Sunday best on this Wednesday morning.

"Excuse us, sir," the eldest of the trio said, as he crossed the wooden structure. "Did you see anyone else getting off at this stop?"

David smiled. He knew what was coming next. Just as no one believed a man of his bulk was a lawyer, it would be harder to comprehend him being a man of the cloth.

"Are you expecting anyone special?" David was unable to resist the chance to have a bit of fun at the expense of the men he decided must be the members of the church council.

"We're supposed to be meeting the new minister for our church," the second man to approach him explained.

"Then I think you've found him. I'm Reverend David Long. I'll be ready to join you as soon as my horse and carriage are unloaded."

"You're our new minister?" The youngest man in the group gaped.

"I was the last time I checked. Now, if you will excuse me, I see my horse being unloaded. I'll be with you shortly."

David left the group to stare after him as he hurried to where two men were leading David's high-spirited black-stallion from the train. From the next car, the carriage his father gave him upon completion of law school was being unloaded. It was all he could do to keep from cautioning the men to be careful with his most prized possession.

Behind him, the horse nickered, as if trying to get his attention. David turned and then stroked the horse's nose. "Did you have a good trip, Thor?"

The big horse nodded his head as though saying he was happy at last to be out of the cramped quarters of the car where he'd been stabled.

"Is all of this baggage yours, Reverend Long?" said the man he would soon come to know as Edward Harmon, the town's barber and president of the church council.

"Yes, it is. Don't try lifting any of it, though. Most of the crates are filled with books. I wouldn't want you to hurt yourselves on my account."

After hitching Thor to the traces, David effortlessly hefted the crates and trunk to the storage area behind the seat of the carriage.

"We didn't know you'd have your own transportation," Ed commented, nodding toward David's horse and rig. "Herman here brought over his wagon, but it looks like you won't be needing it."

David extended his hand to the man referred to as Herman. "You must be Herman Kellogg. It's a pleasure to meet you."

The man with a ruddy complexion, at least the part that showed beneath his full beard, smiled. "Don't know where Ed's manners are. He should have introduced the rest of us right of."

David knew where the man's manners were. They'd gotten lost when he realized someone who looked like a blacksmith was their new minister.

"This here is Ed Harmon, President of the council," Herman continued. "The youngster over there is George Ransom. We didn't know if you'd have transportation to get to the parsonage, so we brought along my wagon. Since we don't need it, George can ride back to town with you. We don't want you getting lost on your first day here."

If the three men who greeted him hadn't been so downright serious, David would have burst out laughing. The expression on the faces of the illustrious church council was priceless. If he lived to be a hundred, David knew he would never forget the disbelief he'd seen mirrored in their eyes.

Once David was assured all of his belongings were present, he climbed onto the seat of the carriage. He smiled as George scrambled up to sit next to him.

"Herman called you the youngster," David observed. "Do I have to guess what he meant?"

"I doubt it. I'm the youngest member of the 'Good Old Boy's Club', otherwise known as the church council."

"The 'Good Old Boy's Club?" David said.

"Herman and Ed as well as my dad and Ralph Mason have run the church for the past twenty years. When my dad died last year, I inherited the position. I have a feeling you're going to shake up more than Herman and Ed."

"You mentioned another man, Ralph Mason. Why wasn't he here today?"

"He had a run in with his new bull last week and it stove in a couple of ribs. Doc's got him confined to bed. I feel sorry for Edna having to put up with him. He can be as grouchy as an old bear."

"Let me get this all straight. You're the youngest member of the church council. Are there any young families in the congregation?"

"Lots of them. They just don't have much say in things. Reverend Hall was older than my dad, so he didn't have a problem with the things that were going on. In other words, he didn't suggest things be done in a different way."

For the first time David found he could contain himself no longer and laughed out loud. "I'm afraid the church council is in for a shock. I'm not exactly what they were expecting. You might as well know, I'm more experienced when it comes to trying a case in court and shoeing a horse than I am about preaching the word of the Lord. What I do know is God spoke to me. He told me to leave my life in Philadelphia behind and do His bidding. My ways may be different from Reverend Hill's, but I pray they will be just as effective."

The smile on George's face said more than words. David was certain he'd made his first friend in Mortonville. George was close enough to David's age that they could easily become close. If nothing else, the man knew where all the skeletons in town were buried.

"So, when you're not meeting new ministers at the station, where will I find you?" David prompted.

"My wife, Ruth, and I run the general store. I'm sure you'll be seeing a lot of me, since I'm also the postmaster. Everyone in town shows up at the store at least once a day six days a week."

David had little trouble visualizing the small town country store George described. Back home the general store in their small town outside of Philadelphia had been the hub of activity for the entire community. Old men went there to play cards and checkers, young men to talk about the weather, and women of all ages to share the things women had shared with each other since the beginning of time.

At George's direction, David turned Thor onto a tree lined residential street. Ahead of him, David saw the spire of a white clapboard church. Somehow, he'd envisioned his first call would take him to a country parish surrounded by cornfields and dairy farms. He certainly hadn't expected close neighbors.

"What do you want to see first, the church or the parsonage?" George said, once David stopped the carriage in front of the white two-story house next door to the church.

From the wide veranda style porch, David concluded his predecessors had large families. He could almost see children playing beneath its sheltered roof on rainy summer afternoons.

"I'd like to see the church. It doesn't matter what the house looks like. Without a family, it's just a place to sleep." From the look on George's face, David knew the man had anticipated his answer.

After getting down from the carriage, David stood staring at the building in front of him. This was his church. The people who worshiped here would look to him for spiritual leadership. He wondered if he was up to this calling.

"Shall we go in, Reverend Long?"

"Yes, of course."

George led the way up the steps and opened one of the double doors. David gasped with pleasure as he stepped into the bell room, which doubled as the narthex of the church. Instantly, he knew this was where he belonged.

It took only a few steps for him to move forward into the sanctuary. Inside, two rows of divided pews were painted a pristine white and stood in direct contrast to the highly polished wood floor made up of wide cut boards. Two steps of a darker wood led to the raised area where an ornate altar and pulpit stood. For a moment, he silently stared at the area where he would spend his time, where he would preach his sermons and read the words of the Lord.

"It's not what I expected," he said. "How long has this congregation been established?"

"Officially about twenty years, at least that's how long ago the church was built. Before that they met in the homes of the parishioners for an additional twenty years."

David nodded. This was not some struggling congregation. It was made up of affluent farmers and merchants who took great pride in their church.

He wondered why God, had sent him here? Was it to teach him or somehow to help the people who worshiped here?

Chapter Two

By noon, Hattie was more than ready to close the shop. Saturday mornings were reserved for people to pick up the sewing she'd finished over the past week. Since no one had been in for the last hour, whatever was left hanging on the rack would remain there until she reopened on Monday morning.

After eating a light lunch of fresh lettuce from her garden and cold chicken from the night before, Hattie donned her bonnet and left the house. The walk to the church would take less than ten minutes. Once there, she would take on her other tasks for the week. She would polish the piano and pick up the songs for tomorrow's service.

As usual, the church was deserted. The solitude reminded her Jonathan would not be the one giving the sermon tomorrow.

She'd heard, from Gertie Kellogg and Ruth Samson about how shocked the council had been when they met the Reverend David Long at the train station. If anyone asked Hattie, which they didn't, it was about time someone shook up Ed Harmon, Herman Kellogg, and Ralph Mason.

Hattie's thoughts continued until she found herself seated at the piano. From her music bag, she pulled a soft cloth and lovingly dusted the keys. Although someone came on Thursday and cleaned the church, she knew they never made it to the balcony. It didn't matter. Hattie loved the piano Ralph sent for all the way to Chicago five years ago.

Once she finished with the keys, she concentrated on the fine wood of the cabinet. From her bag, she produced a bottle of lemon oil. Even if the oil was expensive, Hattie didn't care. When it came to caring for such a fine musical instrument, cost was not a concern to her.

When she reached the music stand, Hattie stopped short. Instead of a note with Jonathan's neatly printed list of hymns for the next morning, all she found was dust. It was apparent Jonathan had not told the new minister about the arrangement.

By the time she finished, mere annoyance turned to anger. How could Jonathan have forgotten to tell the new minister to leave her the list? She laughed at herself for being upset. One visit to the parsonage would straighten out the misunderstanding.

Her inner voice scolded her as a fussy old maid.

"I am," Hattie said aloud, as she closed the door to the church.

"Did you say something to me?"

The sound of a man's deep voice behind her startled Hattie. She turned, surprised to see someone who could only be Reverend David Long standing so close he cast a shadow over her entire body. She judged his height to be well over six foot three. His sandy brown hair curled around his shirt collar. For a woman, such beautiful hair would have been a blessing. For a man, especially a man built like this one, she assumed he considered it a curse. More enticing than his stature or his hair were his piercing blue eyes. She'd have to watch her step where this man was concerned.

"Were you talking to me?" he said for the second time.

"Ah … no. I was just muttering to myself. You must be the new minister."

"Then you have me at a disadvantage."

Hattie sensed a blush crept into her cheeks. "I … I'm Hattie Fairchild," she stammered, extending her hand. "I play the piano. I was on my way to meet you, because I didn't find a list of the hymns for tomorrow's service."

David took her hand. She became painfully aware of the feel of flesh against flesh. Any proper lady would have worn gloves if she were out for an afternoon stroll. Of course, Hattie wasn't strolling. She was cleaning, but no one knew she carried lemon oil and soft clothes in her

17

music bag on Saturday afternoon any more than they knew about the novels that occupied the same space on Sunday mornings.

David smiled at her comment. The action caused a pair of deep dimples to appear in his clean-shaven cheeks. A comment her mother often made popped into her head. 'Dimples in a child's cheeks are the touch of the angels; a dimple in its chin is the mark of the devil.'

Hattie didn't believe in either angels or devils, but this man, despite his size, looked angelic with those dimples. They were so deep she could get lost in them.

"I just found Reverend Hill's note about the hymns," David continued, bringing Hattie back to the present. "I was hoping to get here before you arrived. Unfortunately, I see I'm a bit late. I was having a little trouble with tomorrow's sermon."

* * * *

David cringed at the white lie he'd told. His sermon had been written for days. He'd purposely waited to come over from the parsonage until he knew she'd be done. Jonathan had left a note detailing Hattie's schedule, right down to how long she spent at the church on Saturday afternoon.

Everyone told him about the mysterious Miss Fairchild, from Jonathan to Ralph Mason. From what he'd heard, she came and went without people even seeing her. The general consensus, he concluded, was that Hattie Fairchild was an old maid and more than a bit strange.

David didn't care how strange she was, the lady intrigued him. He couldn't help but wonder if her flaming red hair and emerald green eyes hid a tempter or a passionate nature. Whichever, she certainly wasn't the woman everyone described. He couldn't be so cold as to call her old. If she'd seen her thirtieth birthday, he'd be surprised. He supposed by the rural standards of Mortonville she was old. In Philadelphia, he knew several women who opted to marry later in life. It certainly didn't make them old.

"I'm sorry if I've caused you any inconvenience," he said holding her hand a bit longer than necessary. He enjoyed the blush the gesture brought from her.

"That's ... that's perfectly all right, Reverend Long. I usually take the list of hymns home to practice them."

The woman certainly had a knack for stammering, he'd give her that. "I thought perhaps you practiced here on Saturday afternoons."

He didn't have to make the comment. He knew perfectly well what she did on Saturday afternoons. On Thursday, he had talked to the young girl who did the cleaning. When he asked her about cleaning in the balcony, she said no one ever went up there, so she never bothered.

One trip to the balcony told him someone bothered. The pews up there were covered with a layer of dust, but the piano carried a high gloss shine. The keys were as perfectly white as they had been on the day they were installed. From other pianos he'd seen, keys often yellowed with lack of proper care.

Only one person in the congregation would take such good care of the piano and she now stood in front of him. From the faint smell of lemon oil, he knew his assumptions were correct.

"In the late afternoon the light is much better at my home than in the balcony," she said, in an attempt to explain why she didn't practice at the church. "I could light a lamp, but it seems a waste of good lamp oil."

"Could I persuade you to play through them for me now?" David said. "Since I'm not familiar with your technique, I prefer not to be surprised tomorrow morning."

David wondered if he saw Hattie cringe at his suggestion. If she did, it was only momentary. She flashed him a brilliant smile before turning back to return to the church.

Once inside, he allowed her to lead the way up the broad staircase to the balcony. He enjoyed watching her climb the stairs.

"It smells fresh up here," he observed.

A sunbeam streaming in through the only window in the balcony accented the highlight in her hair and softened the expression on her face. He could tell by the look in her eyes she was trying hard to bite back a tart reply.

"I wondered who took such good care of the piano," David continued, "when the pews up here were dust covered and in dire need of a good cleaning."

"An instrument like this cries for attention. It takes little effort to keep it looking like new. I'm certain no one else cares as long as it produces music for the congregation to sing to on Sunday morning."

"I'm pleased to see you care, even if no one else knows what you do when you come on Saturday afternoon."

"I trust this won't be spoken of again," Hattie declared, her head held high, her expression suddenly stern.

"Not unless you want to speak of it. After today, there shouldn't be any reason for me to intrude on your Saturday afternoons again. Now, can we run through the hymns?"

He watched as Hattie pulled the piano bench out and seated herself. Without saying anything more, she found the first number David had written down and, after opening the case covering the keys, began to play the familiar notes. He could see his mother's delicate fingers playing the same songs on the piano in the parlor as well as the one at church.

"Was my playing to your liking?" she said, once she sounded the last note of the last hymn.

David almost jumped at the sound of her voice. "It was perfect. Some people tend to rush the tempo."

Hattie looked at him, her eyebrows raised. "Rush the tempo? You sound as though you know music."

David smiled. He hadn't meant to be so transparent, but somehow his background tended to shine through. "I guess I do. My mother plays at church and gives lessons through the week. I'm afraid I was her only failure. She always said these hands weren't made for piano playing." He held up his hands for emphasis and Hattie reached out to touch them.

"They are rather large, but I have a feeling it was the boy and not his hands that wasn't made for piano playing. Not everyone who appreciates music has the ability or the desire to play it."

"You are very perceptive, Miss Fairchild. I'll look forward to hearing you play at the service tomorrow morning."

She nodded and then hurried back down the stairs, leaving him alone in the balcony. Once he heard the outside door close, he sat down where Hattie had sat moments earlier. He could still feel her dainty fingers against his large ones. He wished she had stayed a bit longer, but George warned him about her being a bit strange.

Once assured he was completely alone, David began to play one of the few classical pieces he still remembered. He hadn't exactly lied when he told Hattie he never mastered the piano. Although he wasn't a failure, he wasn't his mother's prize student either.

* * * *

Hattie looked over her shoulder at the church. Reverend Long was indeed a handsome man. He could also prove to be a great temptation. Over the next few weeks, she would be careful. David Long, she was certain, would prove to be a worthy adversary.

The last thing she needed was to be exposed as a non-believer. If such a thing were to happen, she would have to admit the truth about not only her life, but also her family. She just couldn't have the secrets she'd worked so hard to bury coming to the forefront to haunt her.

Before returning home, Hattie made her way to the general store. With all her morning and early afternoon chores, she'd not been able to pick up her mail.

"Good afternoon, Hattie," George Ransom greeted her. "It looks like you've been over at the church. Did you meet the new minister?"

"Yes," Hattie replied, "but not by my choice."

"What is that supposed to mean?"

"I usually don't run into anyone on Saturday afternoons. Jonathan usually left me a note with the songs for Sunday written on it. Today it wasn't there. Reverend Long forgot to leave it for me. He was bringing it over just as I was leaving."

"You sound as though running into him was an imposition. You could do a lot worse, Hattie Fairchild."

The thought of anyone, let alone George Ransom, hinting someone like the new minister might be interested in her was almost too outlandish to be believed. She neither wanted, nor needed, a man in her life. The thought of any man, to say nothing of the new minister intruding on the life she'd built for herself, was almost more than she could stand.

"I have some mail for you," George said, changing the subject. "Mostly it's the usual ads for the shop, but there is a letter from Nebraska."

Hattie took the neat stack of letters. After shuffling through them, she selected the one from her sister, Laura.

"Thank you, George. Before I go, I need some white thread and a package of needles."

After George totaled her bill, she pulled out her coin purse and counted out the correct change. "When will you be getting in that new fabric you told me about last week?"

"I received a wire from the supplier in Chicago this morning. It said I could expect the shipment to be on Wednesday's train."

Hattie thanked him and hurried home. She was anxious to read the letter from Laura.

Once back in her kitchen, Hattie brewed a cup of tea before going to the parlor to read her letter.

> Dear Hattie,
>
> Spring has never been so late or so beautiful here before. It has been a peaceful year, since Caleb did not come home this winter. He sent money for the children and me, even though Gary insisted we shouldn't take it.
>
> Gary finished the eighth grade and has been very busy with the planting as well as working for one of the neighbors, helping with the milking and other chores. I am so proud of him and the way he cares for Jesse and me.
>
> How I wish you could know at least the youngest of my children. As for the older boys, I am afraid I've lost them to their father. Contrary to what anyone believes, I know who they are and what they have become. It saddens I have failed as a wife and mother.
>
> From the sound of your letters, you are happy with your life in the tailor shop. I also rejoice over the fact you are able to attend church on Sunday mornings. I only need to close my eyes to hear you playing the piano. You have no idea how very lucky you are. The children and I tried to attend church in Clarkston several years back, but we were turned away at the door. It seems as though Caleb Tyler's wife and children are not welcome among their

congregation.

As I write this letter, the light is beginning to fade. Soon evening will be upon me and I will need to close down the house for another day.

I pray for your continued prosperity and enjoyment of life.

Your loving sister,
Laura

Hattie set aside the letter and cried bitter tears. How could life have been so cruel to Laura? Hattie's beautiful older sister deserved better than an abusive husband who robbed banks, murdered innocent people, and corrupted their sons.

Even worse than a husband who was a monster, were the uncaring people in town that would not allow Laura and the children to worship in their church.

It was no wonder Hattie clung to her non-belief. Better to be a hypocrite by attending church and not believing, than to believe and not live that faith.

Chapter Three

David's hands were clammy as he paced the small room behind the altar area of the church. He had no idea why he was so nervous. The people were members of his congregation. They certainly weren't argumentative prosecutors or jurors who needed to be convinced of the innocence of his clients. These people were believers, hungry for the word of God as interpreted by the Reverend David Long.

The door to the room was slightly ajar so he could have a small area where he could see the congregation. Through the opening, he heard the buzz of conversation. He smiled to think of his father equating such overheard snatches to chickens in the hen house. They all clucked so one could not be distinguished above the others.

The first chords of the prelude wafted down from the balcony, instantly silencing the members. Some of them, he was sure were cut off in mid-sentence. David was pleased to recognize the tune and waited until he knew only a few bars remained before leaving the room to take his place in the pulpit.

Even with the heat of mid-July, the church was packed. Women in high-necked, fashionable dresses and bonnets, fanned themselves with stiff paper fans attached to highly polished wooden sticks. The men wore stiffly starched shirts with string ties and coats.

The church council occupied the front pews, as though their presence gave a silent blessing to the new minister.

"I've been told you always begin your services with Holy, Holy, Holy. For now, some things will remain the same."

David wondered if he heard a collective sigh of relief when Hattie played the first stanza of the familiar hymn. Feet shuffled and pages turned as the congregation stood to sing the words they all knew by heart.

After the singing ended, David gave the mandatory prayer and scripture readings. Just as the people in front of him were settling down for a long and powerful sermon, he invited the children to come forward.

One by one, children of all ages made their way to the front of the church and joined David in sitting on the floor. Once he had about twenty youngsters around him, he began talking to them.

"It's really hard coming to a new town. I don't know anyone here. It's a little like Jesus when he'd go around the countryside. During those times, he loved the children because they were so pure and honest. I want you to know you can always come to me and ask any question you want about the Bible or my sermons. I know you can ask your folks, but sometimes they get busy. That's when you can come to me. Now, I need to talk to your folks about a few things, but I hope you'll listen too. I want us all to become very good friends."

* * * *

Hattie sat at the piano, her novel in hand. Although she held her opened book in her lap, she couldn't take her eyes from the giant of a man surrounded by the children who usually fidgeted next to their parents.

Even after the children returned to their seats, Hattie found concentrating on her book next to impossible. While Jonathan's sermons had been easily blocked out, David's seemed to echo off the walls of the church.

She was enchanted as he told of growing up in a small town on the outskirts of Philadelphia, playing in his father's blacksmith shop. The sermon ended with the story of how David heard the voice of God in the middle of a legal proceeding and became a minister.

Whether or not the man actually heard the voice of God, Hattie knew the story did what it was intended to do. It impressed the self-righteous parishioners of the church.

"A-Men."

David's booming proclamation of the end of his sermon took Hattie by surprise. In an attempt to start the hymn of the day on time, she almost dropped her book to the floor.

After regaining her composure, she played the hymn. It was unfamiliar to her as well as the congregation, but apparently Reverend Long knew it well as his thundering bass belted out the words. By the second verse, everyone else had joined him. At least his choice had been singable.

With Reverend Long in the pulpit, Hattie knew ignoring sermons and scripture readings would be more difficult than in the past. Lost in her thoughts, she automatically played the mandatory final hymn and the postlude.

After sounding the final note, she carefully covered the keys, packed her music bag, and made her way to the side entrance of the balcony. She'd found it when the church council first asked her to play. It afforded her the privacy needed to leave the church unnoticed while the parishioners stood around gossiping about the events of the past week.

As warm as the day was becoming, Hattie was glad to be out of the sweltering balcony and on her way home. Other than changing to a cooler dress and sponging herself down with cool water there was little that could be done to beat the summer's unrelenting heat.

It's too hot to eat. Hattie made her way to her bedroom to lay down for a short nap. With all the windows open, she was certain to catch whatever breeze would be available.

It took only moments for her to fall into a peaceful sleep, one filled with dreams of the new minister at the church and what it would feel like to be enfolded in his strong arms.

* * * *

David shook hands with each parishioner. He sensed mixed emotions among the members of his congregation. If they'd been given the choice, would they have picked this untried son of a blacksmith, who left the law and Philadelphia to preach in Mortonville?

"That was a good sermon Reverend," George said, as he pumped David's hand.

"Thank you, George, but I do wish you'd call me David."

"I don't see why that can't be arranged. Since I'm the last in line, I'll help you close up the church. Ruth asked me to be sure and bring you over for Sunday dinner."

"I'd like that. If the truth be known, my cooking leaves a lot to be desired." He turned back toward the empty sanctuary and glanced toward every corner.

"Are you looking for anyone in particular?"

David turned to face George. "I must have missed Miss Fairchild. I wanted to tell her how much I enjoyed her music this morning."

"You didn't miss Hattie. She is quite adept at slipping out the side door. Unless I'm mistaken, she's already home relaxing. She's a very private person."

"Doesn't she have friends she'd stay and talk to?"

"Let's table this discussion about Hattie's personal life until after dinner. I'm getting hungry, and I'm sure you must be as well. Ruth will have my head if we're late and the chicken gets cold."

David could almost hear his father saying the same thing. All women were proud of their cooking and none of them liked to be kept waiting.

Ruth's Sunday dinner reminded him of home. The roast chicken complete with mashed potatoes and gravy, stuffing, and fresh peas was much better than anything he could have made for himself.

With dinner finished, Ruth cleared the table while the children went outside to play. When David moved to the Ransom's front porch, Ruth brought out cups of coffee.

Over the next hour, David listened as George described Hattie Fairchild, Mortonville's resident old maid. David could almost visualize the drunken father who finally ended his life at the bottom of a bottle. It was no wonder Hattie took in sewing to help with the expenses. The natural progression of things was for her to sell the family farm and buy into the tailor shop.

"Hattie's a hard woman to get to know. We've been friends most of our lives and yet I would never be so bold as to tell you I know her. She's a very private person. I'm sure she feels she has good reason. We all knew about her old man, but she never let on like it bothered her, so no one tried to help."

David shook his head in sympathy. "You mentioned a sister. Whatever happened to her?"

"Laura was much older than Hattie. She married and moved away when Hattie was just a little girl. I think she and her husband are farming out west somewhere. Hattie gets letters from Nebraska.

Later that evening, David decided to take a walk. It came as no surprise when his unplanned route took him past the tailor shop.

Although the shop was dark, a light burned in the attached house. From the open window, he could hear the classical strains of Bach. It was the music his mother taught her students. This was the music he loved listening to on evenings like this when his mother would play to ease the tensions of his father's day.

"Whom do you play for Miss Hattie Fairchild?" he whispered to the wind. "Is there anyone special who listens to your music?"

David continued to stand in the shadows until the piano was silent and the light extinguished. Only then did he return to the parsonage. As he did, he vowed to be the one person in town to get to know the lovely Miss Hattie Fairchild.

* * * *

Hattie played the last note of the new Bach piece she had recently sent money to Chicago to buy. She knew purchasing so much sheet music was foolish, especially when there was no one but herself to enjoy it.

Once she turned down the lamp, Hattie had an eerie feeling, as though someone was watching her from the street. She knew she must be mistaken because at this time of night people were home preparing for bed. It would do no good to look out the window. The darkness of the night would hide any prying eyes.

Before retiring for the night, Hattie went to the kitchen and took pen and paper to write a letter to Laura.

> Dear Laura,
>   How I wish you had the farm in your name. If that were the case, you could sell it and move home to Illinois.
> I have more than enough room for you, Gary, and Jesse in

my home, and there is far too much work in the shop for me to do alone. We could have a good life here and Caleb would not be able to find you.

If you decide to take me up on my offer, I would gladly send tickets for you and the children. Mortonville is more civilized than Clarkston and the authorities would be able to protect you from Caleb.

Please give my suggestion some thought. It would be wonderful to have my family with me again.

Hattie

She reviewed the hastily composed note. As she did, Hattie analyzed the reasons behind her offer to Laura. What Laura would consider generous, Hattie knew was completely selfish. Even surrounded by a town full of people she'd known all her life, Hattie was lonely. In a world where women were considered strange if they weren't married and the mother of several children by the time they reached her age, she didn't fit in the pattern.

Unwilling to give in to her dark thoughts, Hattie turned down the kitchen lamp and made her way to bed. If luck stayed with her, the unsettling dreams of the handsome new minister would be kept at bay.

Chapter Four

David hung up the last of his clothes from the trunk he'd brought from Philadelphia. As he did, he looked at the number of suits now hanging in the closet of the parsonage's bedroom.

He remembered the words of one of his favorite professors. "Use your size to your advantage, David. You are a large man, but don't hide behind dark drab colors."

David had found a tailor who enjoyed being not only creative, but also well compensated by the young lawyer who soon became known for his flamboyant style.

For summer, David owned a lightweight white suit, as well as ones in light blue and tan. Likewise, his winter wardrobe contained suits of dark blue, brown and black wool. To wear with these suits were fine linen shirts in several colors with matching ties.

After yesterday's service spent sweltering in the black wool suit, David knew he had to visit Mortonville's tailor. He definitely needed more than one black suit and the colored shirts would never do in his newly chosen life's work. He couldn't help but smile at the thought of visiting Hattie's shop and having her measure him for the much-needed clothing.

The clock in the parlor chimed twelve times. David wouldn't have needed it to tell him it was noon. His stomach had been rumbling for almost an hour.

After closing the trunk, he caught a glimpse of himself in the full length, freestanding mirror on the opposite side of the room. "No one would mistake me for a successful lawyer," he said aloud.

The reflection smiled back at him. Instead of the well pressed white suite with its dark colored linen shirt and white tie, he would have worn in public, the reflection was clothed in blue cotton pants with a comfortable work shirt, its sleeves rolled up to his elbows.

David smiled, thinking of Reverend Kanter. He could never remember seeing him dressed in anything but a black suit and white shirt. He couldn't help but wonder how the good people of Mortonville would view the new minister once the shock of getting to know him wore off.

A knock at the wooden screen door that allowed fresh air to enter the parsonage without giving the ever-present flies' free reign stopped David before he could enter his kitchen.

On the porch, he recognized Gertie Kellogg and two other ladies from the church. To his dismay, their names escaped him.

"Good day, ladies. Won't you come in?"

"Good day, Reverend," Gertie said. "I was over at the store this morning and Ruth mentioned how it might be a good idea if we ladies of the church saw to your needs for food until you're settled. I don't know why I didn't think of it myself, you being without a wife and all. We've never had an unmarried minister before."

"What Gertie is trying to say," one of the other women explained, "is that we haven't been very considerate of you since you arrived. We all seem to get caught up in our own lives and forget about the needs of others."

David began to grin. From the aromas coming from the baskets the trio carried, he anticipated a delicious dinner with enough left over for supper. "I guess I'm as new at this business of being a preacher as you are at having a bachelor as your minister. With luck, maybe you ladies will be able to teach me to cook."

His comment brought nervous laughter from his visitors. Within moments, David pulled enough dishes from the kitchen cupboard to set the table for four. As soon as he did, the ladies set out the bowls of food. His mouth began to water over the potato salad as well as the thick slices of ham and baked beans.

"There should be enough for your supper tonight. Tomorrow, I've arranged for Jennie Ames and Marge Simons to bring you your dinner. After that we'll worry about teaching you to cook," Gertie declared.

When the dishes were washed and put away, David prayed his

visitors would leave. Instead, they sat back down at his table and began to discuss the Ladies Aide Society, the Mission Society, and the Sunday School.

"I don't like to criticize, but I've never heard of anyone preaching to the children," Gertie began. "It's not like we don't have a Sunday School program here. Our children are given a Christian education. I just don't think that it should be something that is included in our worship service."

David was shocked by the comment. "Just where would you suggest the children learn about our Lord?"

"I think what Gertie means is we teach our children to be seen and not heard. It ain't right for young'uns to be standin' up in the front of the church that a way."

"If I may quote our Lord," David said, trying to remain calm. "'Suffer the children to come unto me.' I want these little ones to be as comfortable in the Lord's house as they are in their own homes. As a child, I never missed a Sunday of sitting at the feet of my pastor and listening to the words of my Savior being explained so even a child could understand. That is the kind of memory I want for the children of Mortonville.

"Well, I never," Gertie declared.

"Think about it," Judy Toller cautioned. "Maybe the preacher has a good idea. If we'd involved the children more, maybe my Jake would have had more respect for his pa and me. Maybe he would have stayed and helped us run the farm rather than runnin' away out west to be a gunslinger, then gettin' himself killed by the first man he went up against who was faster."

The women nodded their heads in agreement, and David breathed a sigh of relief. He'd won the first of many battles he would fight over the changes he planned for his congregation. Even with this one small victory, he knew it would take the winning of many battles and even then he could lose the war. Not everyone would be pleased with his new ideas and getting his point across wouldn't be easy.

By the time his guests left, David was mentally drained. It was nearly four, so he decided to postpone his trip to the tailor shop for another day. After spending an afternoon with these well-meaning ladies, he knew he had better be rested before his next meeting with Hattie.

Hattie's Preacher

* * * *

Precisely at four in the afternoon, Hattie pulled the shades covering her shop windows. Once the shop was officially closed for the night, she walked the short distance to the general store to get her mail and post the letter she'd written to Laura.

"Good afternoon, Hattie," George greeted her. "You look downright beat. Which is it, this hot spell or the work that's getting to you?"

"A little of both, I guess. I sure wish I could find an assistant. When it was Abe and me, we were able to keep up with the work and even catch our breath on occasion. Now, I work in the shop all day just to get the stitching done. There's no time to think about the books until I close up for the night. I hardly have any time for myself anymore. I'm to the point of putting an ad in the Gazette for someone to do piece work at home. There must be somebody who could use the extra money."

"If it wasn't for the store, I'd take you up on your offer," Ruth said, joining the conversation. "I'm certain there are lots of women who could use the money if their men folk would let them. Unfortunately, most of the men around here are so bullheaded they think the only thing their wives are good for is housekeeping and having babies."

Hattie laughed with Ruth over the foolishness of the male of the species, even though she caught the hidden meaning behind her friend's words.

The men of Mortonville weren't so much afraid of their wives independence as they were of them associating with Hattie Fairchild. It was a known fact she'd never had a suitor. Her drunken father ran off any young man who so much as set foot on the farm. More than once a shotgun blast had sent a prospective beau running. The only thing he'd accomplished was to give his youngest daughter a lonely life.

Years ago she'd longed for just one of the young men to defy her father and pay her court. Maybe even make her his wife. By the time her father died, anyone who would have considered marrying her had already found someone else.

"Good afternoon, David."

Hattie put aside her thoughts and turned to see the new minister. The sheer bulk of the man was overwhelming. Standing in the doorway to the store, he blocked out even the strong rays of the afternoon sunlight.

Once he stepped into the store and Hattie wasn't blinded by the sunlight at his back, she noticed the way he was dressed. If she didn't know better, she would have never guessed him to be a preacher. In his blue pants and work shirt, he reminded her of a farmer come into town for supplies.

"George, Ruth, Miss Fairchild," Reverend Long said, touching the brim of his hat. "Do you have any mail for me yet?"

"Got in a couple of letters from Philadelphia. I would have expected at least one to be from a young lady, but the handwriting ain't from no…"

"George Ramson," Ruth almost shouted. "You know as postmaster you ain't supposed to be prying into people's mail."

Hattie couldn't help but laugh. George was no different than his father had been. They both were the salt of the earth, and she numbered them among her closest friends, but they knew the business of every man, woman and child in town. They always had, and they always would.

"You won't find any letters from young ladies in my mail box," David replied. "The closest would be from my mama. Never had time for courting in Philadelphia. The law is a jealous mistress."

Hattie listened, as entranced by the new minister's voice now as she had been on Sunday morning in church. Even now, she couldn't picture him in a courtroom any more than she could honestly believe him to be a man of God.

"What time do you open your shop in the morning, Miss Fairchild?"

Reverend Long's question took her by surprise. "Ah, eight in the morning."

"Good. I'll be over to see you in the morning. I find I'm sorely in need of some new clothing."

Hattie felt her hands begin to become clammy. "N .. new clothing," she stammered.

"You do make clothing for people, don't you?"

"Yes, yes of course I do. I'll look forward to seeing you in the morning."

Without engaging in further conversation, Hattie retrieved her mail from Ruth. More than anything else, she wanted to get out of the general store and away from the man who made her heart do flip-flops.

Once outside, she took several deep breaths to calm her nerves and then hurried home, her heels beating a sharp rhythm against the wooden sidewalk.

She had no doubt about her abilities as either a seamstress or a tailor, but the thought of measuring this man for a suit made her heart race.

Abe's careful notes gave her a file on each and every man in town. She had only to find the card with the man's name printed on the top to know sleeve length, neck, chest, waist, and inseam measurements.

In the time since Abe's death, she had been called upon only once to measure a young man and then his mother had been with him to ease his embarrassment. If the truth were known, it had eased Hattie's as well.

Tomorrow, she would be totally and utterly alone in her shop with Reverend Long. Somehow she would have to find a way to focus her thoughts on things other than the handsome minister while she took his personal measurements and added them to Abe's meticulous files.

* * * *

David watched as Hattie hurried out of the store. He couldn't help but wonder if it were his imagination or if Hattie had noticeably paled when he mentioned stopping at her shop the next morning.

"What's eating at Hattie?" George said, shattering David's inner thoughts.

"You know what's wrong as well as I do," Ruth responded. "She's had more than she can handle ever since Abe died. If you ask me, she needs help and is too proud to admit it. Abe knew what he was doing when he took Hattie on. I've never seen anyone do finer work."

"Is there any reason why she can't get good help?" David said.

George and Ruth exchanged knowing glances. "You're new in town, David," George finally said. "Hattie is, well, don't get me wrong, but she's a bit strange. There's not another woman in Mortonville who is pushing thirty and still not married. I don't know of anyone who would want his wife or daughter working in her shop. I can't imagine any self-respecting young woman taking a man's personal measurements."

"Surely Hattie must know what she's doing. An assistant wouldn't be expected to take the measurements, would they?"

"That's exactly what Hattie thought when she took the job with Abe," Ruth said. "At the time, Abe's wife, Marta, died and Abe was in the same position as Hattie is now. He was a tailor, had been all his life. Marta had been the seamstress. Since Hattie did piece work for them, she was the logical choice. Once she started, Abe decided to teach her to help him with the tailoring as well. I agree it's not a job usually done by a woman, but it's one Hattie handles well."

David nodded. How sad a woman who did only what was required to survive was branded as strange, different from the other women in town. It was a shame that good Christian people had so little compassion for someone who chose a different path in life.

Chapter Five

Hattie was up and busy in her kitchen before the sun crested the eastern horizon. When she first came to work for Abe, he informed her Marta always had fresh baked goods and coffee for the customers. Every day since her arrival, Hattie rose early to bake pies, cakes, cookies, and coffee cakes.

The aroma of rhubarb coffee cake made her mouth water. It was a recipe she'd adapted to whatever fruit was in season.

Why she took the extra care this morning, Hattie had no idea. Just because Reverend Long was coming to order new clothes gave her no reason to fuss, only to be nervous.

Once the coffee cake was in the oven, Hattie prepared her own breakfast. It was definitely too hot for bacon and eggs. Instead, she opted for a slice of bread with currant jelly along with a glass of cold buttermilk from the springhouse.

Precisely at eight, the bell above the door of the shop jingled merrily. In response, Hattie carried the plate filled with slices of coffee cake along with a pot of coffee into the shop. For a moment, she wished she'd skipped breakfast. Her stomach was tied in knots over the prospect of having to measure the minister for a suit.

"Good morning, Hattie," Gertie greeted her.

Hattie breathed a sigh of relief. "Good morning to you too Gertie. What brings you here so early in the day?"

"I got a letter yesterday from my Susan. She's living in St. Louis with her husband, you know. Anyway, she's in a family way and I thought it would be nice to surprise her with a special christening gown. I decided I just didn't have the time and Susan would cherish one made by you."

Under other circumstances, Gertie's condescending tone would have upset Hattie, but she had always thought highly of Susan. When the girl first announced her upcoming wedding, she'd insisted on having her dress designed and made by Hattie. During the sessions for planning and fitting, she and Hattie became fast friends.

"I think I know exactly what you have in mind," Hattie said, going to the old file cabinet where Abe and Marta kept sketches of each garment they ever made. Under the letter 'C' she found several patterns for christening gowns. It took only moments for Hattie to find the one she was wanted. Hattie knew it would be expensive, but if anyone could afford something special, it was Gertie Kellogg.

When Hattie turned back, she saw Gertie take another piece of coffee cake. If Hattie's calculations were right, it wasn't the woman's first. There were at least three pieces missing from the plate.

"You amaze me," Gertie said, her mouth full of the sweet dessert. "How do you manage to always have something special for your customers?"

"You must know it was Marta's habit. I only continued what she started."

"It still makes this shop special. Oh, this is perfect. No matter what the cost, I must have it for my grandchild. With a project like this, I suppose you won't be able to help out the other ladies of the church."

"Help out?" Hattie seated herself across from Gertie.

"The new minister, Reverend Long, is a bachelor. From what Ruth Ransom told me, he's not much of a cook, so we're providing him with meals until he can master the art of cooking for himself."

"Maybe it's just as well I'm so busy here. My talents run more along the lines of baking. Cooking was never my strong suit. Mama and my sister, Laura, were the cooks in my family."

"I'm certain you underestimate yourself. I realize the weekdays are out of the question, but Sundays might work for you. If we get in a pinch, we'll keep you in mind. Of course, I have heard how busy you are. Have you found anyone to help you?"

Hattie pushed aside her cup of coffee. The strong brew that usually gave her day a good start did nothing for her today.

"Not yet. I don't know of anyone who is interested. It's hard work. If it were just a seamstress shop it would be different, but considering I do tailoring as well makes most women shy away. I can't say I blame them. Men's suits are not the easiest things to make."

"Well," Gertie said, looking around the cluttered shop, "you do need help. Maybe you should advertise in one of the papers back East. There must be a tailor who wants to start a new life. I know you think I'm just a fussy old busy body, but I am concerned about you. I've noticed how tired you look lately."

A lump formed in Hattie's throat. She had, indeed, considered Gertie to be one of the biggest gossips in town. This more compassionate side of the woman brought unbidden tears to her eyes.

"Is something wrong dear?" Gertie inquired.

Hattie shook her head, and took a gulp of coffee. "I must have a speck of dust in my eye."

"A speck of dust, my great Aunt Fannie. You're on the verge of tears. Mark my words, somehow we're going to get you some help. As a matter of fact, as soon as I leave here, I'm planning to write my sister in Ohio. Maybe she'll know someone who wants to relocate."

"Thank you Gertie," Hattie said, getting to her feet to hug the older woman. "You really are a good friend."

* * * *

David rinsed his breakfast dishes in the sink and hurried out the front door to go to Hattie's shop. He couldn't help the groan that passed his lips when he saw the church council making their way toward the parsonage.

"Good morning, gentlemen," David greeted them. He prayed his disappointment didn't carry through to his voice. "What brings you over here so early in the morning?"

"We wanted to talk to you about what your plans are for our congregation," Edmond said.

"Well then, why don't you come in? I have some cake left over from yesterday, and I do know how to brew a mean cup of coffee."

David listened as four of the six dining room chairs scraped across the hardwood floor while he prepared to brew a pot of coffee. If only he'd left the dishes sitting on the table, he could have left the house early enough to have missed the long and boring meeting that loomed ahead of him.

"Not bad coffee, Reverend," Ralph said, once David joined them at the table.

"It's not coffee we came to discuss," Herman Kellogg declared. "Until my Gertie came over here yesterday, I was ready to jump all over you for that business with the young'uns on Sunday morning. She explained it to me the way you did to her. I like the sound of your idea. Now I want to hear more. What else do you have planned?"

David glanced down at his clasped hands. How many of his plans should he reveal at this point? Was the council ready for his ideas to bring the church up to modern day standards?

David finished his cake before he answered Herman. "The first thing I plan to do is move the piano down to the main floor where it belongs. I noticed on Sunday the congregation is always a half a stanza behind piano when they're singing. No one is at fault. It's just that the sound doesn't carry well enough and that makes it hard for everything to be together. Besides the piano is much too beautiful an instrument to be hidden away in the balcony."

Across the table, Ralph Mason beamed. "I always knew that piano was special. I sent all the way to Chicago for the thing, and no one ever sees it. It's stuck in my craw ever since it arrived. I wanted it downstairs five years ago, but some of the old fogies on the council said it had always been in the balcony and it would stay there."

Inwardly, David wanted to cheer. He'd been successful in his second battle. This war might not be as hard to win as he first thought.

One by one he detailed his intended changes until a knock at the front door alerted him to the fact it was dinnertime.

By the amount of food the women prepared, it was evident they expected the council to still be there.

Even though dinner ended and the dishes were cleared, the meeting with the council continued. Each proposal David made met with mild opposition, followed by reluctant acceptance.

40

Before he knew it the afternoon slipped away as quickly as had the morning. It wasn't until the clock struck four that the council decided to call it a day.

"We've done a good day's work," Edmund declared.

"Don't you mean we monopolized David's entire day?" George corrected. "I just happened to remember you saying you had plans for today."

"Plans are made to be broken," David replied. "Whatever I had to do can be done tomorrow. Edmund is right. We did accomplish a lot. The next thing we have to do is find some good strong men to move the piano."

"Since it sounds like you'll be busy tomorrow, Reverend," Ralph said, with a wink, "we'll work on gettin' together a crew for Friday morning. I sure would like to see 'our' piano up in front where it belongs on Sunday."

David chuckled as the men who took up his entire day made their way back to their homes and families. He had plans for the next day. They were the plans that got sidetracked so easily with the arrival of the council this morning.

As he turned back to the parsonage, he realized how lonely his life was. Although his new vocation was rewarding, he missed sharing his day not only with his parents, but also the friends he'd known since childhood. He knew friends and family would be acquired in the near future, but for now, another lonely night awaited him when he went back into the house.

* * * *

Hattie pulled the shades and turned the sign from Open to Closed. Only two slices of coffee cake remained on the plate, but the person she'd baked it for hadn't even tasted it.

'You're a fool, Hattie Fairchild,' her inner voice scolded. 'You're not fit to be any man's wife. No man wants an old maid who is set in her ways. As for a handsome minister, what do you have to offer someone like him? He deserves a woman who believes. That certainly isn't you. Did you think you could win him over with a plate of coffee cake?'

"I don't know what I thought," she said aloud. "I certainly know who and what I am. I don't need the voice of conscience telling me I don't measure up. Pa certainly told me that enough times for me to remember."

Frustrations mingled with exhaustion as she prepared her supper. She'd been a fool to get her hopes up, even to be nervous about Reverend David Long coming to be measured for a new suit. Even if he came, it was because she was the only tailor in town. It would have been business and nothing more. She couldn't allow it to be more. The man needed a woman to be a helpmate. What he didn't need was a woman who didn't believe in God.

With supper finished, Hattie began to work on the christening gown for Gertie. She could easily purchase the required lace, but considering the gown was for Susan's baby, it had to be special.

From the sewing chest in the hall, she retrieved a fine pointed tatting shuttle as well as a ball of tatting cotton. Within a matter of minutes, the delicate lace pattern began to take shape. She would never be able to charge enough to pay for the time making the lace by hand would require, but at least it would take her mind off Reverend Long's missed appointment.

Unfortunately, the tedious work did little to stop the silent ramblings of her overactive mind. If her letter persuaded Laura to leave the farm, she would have her solution. Laura wasn't as talented with a needle as Hattie, but she could learn. If Laura were living here, her daughter, Jesse could also be trained with a needle. With the three of them working together there would be no need for an outsider, no need for a man.

Bitter tears stung Hattie's eyes until she could no longer see the work she held in front of her. From the mantel, the clock Abe so loving wound every Sunday morning, chimed ten times.

Although she knew she should be tired and ready for sleep, her body was still tense. She knew the only way she could relax was to vent her frustrations on the keys of the piano.

Setting aside her handwork, Hattie carried the lamp to the piano. Once seated, she selected several classical pieces and began to play with a passion.

* * * *

David found the silence of the empty parsonage almost deafening. To put his thoughts in order, he decided to go for a walk before retiring for the night.

He walked aimlessly, without purpose for several minutes. His mind was too cluttered with the events of the day to even notice in which direction he walked.

He prayed to God he was doing the right thing for these people. For that matter, was he doing the right thing for himself?

His answer came in the strains of classical piano music floating on the evening breeze. As soon as he heard it, he looked up to see he was standing in front of the tailor shop.

Had he disappointed Hattie Fairchild today?

From the beauty of the music she played, he knew she would never be satisfied with a big man like him. She was a delicate woman. One he could only admire from afar.

No matter what feelings she stirred in him, he would have to ignore them. Someone like Hattie deserved more than the life of a minister's wife, living in a parsonage with nothing but the clothes on her back to call her own.

Chapter Six

Hattie cursed herself for sleeping so late. Luckily, she had filled the cookie jar on Sunday afternoon.

After washing her face, she quickly pinned her hair into its neat bun and donned a cool cotton dress. She had too much work to do to oversleep. Her breakfast would have to be cookies and coffee.

By eight, she opened the shop. Hattie was busy with the finishing work on the trousers George ordered last week. Instead of sitting toward the front of the shop, she sought out the bright morning light streaming through the East window.

With the way the shop was situated she could use the bright sunlight throughout the day. In the morning, she enjoyed the large window to the East, by noon the sun would shift to the South, and in the late afternoon she would move to the West window.

She was so engrossed in the intricate stitches, the sound of the bell above the shop door did not penetrate the depth of her concentration.

"Miss Fairchild."

Reverend Long's deep voice startled Hattie so much she jabbed the needle into the fatty part of her hand at the base of her thumb. "Oh!" she exclaimed.

"I'm sorry," David said, crossing the length of the shop to join her in the Eastern most corner of the room. "I didn't mean to startle you. I thought you'd hear the bell."

Hattie looked down at her hand and suppressed the urge to put the injury to her lips to stop the flow of blood. Instead, she put aside her work and got to her feet.

"I should be the one apologizing to you. I was so intent on my work, I didn't hear you enter. I know it's hard to imagine, but it happens. I become immune to the sound of the bell. Can I offer you some coffee and cookies?"

She couldn't help but feel guilty about the cookies. They weren't fresh, not like yesterday's coffee cake. For the second time since getting up, she cursed oversleeping and not making fresh baked goods.

To her surprise, his hand went to his ample midsection. "I shouldn't indulge, but if the truth be known, I have trouble saying no to desserts. My greatest weakness is cookies."

Why couldn't he hate sweets? Hattie crossed the room to pick up the plate of three-day-old molasses cookies and pour a cup of coffee.

"Do you take cream or sugar?"

"I like it black. I tried it with cream and sugar once and decided I didn't like to cover up the taste of the coffee."

Hattie smiled. She liked her coffee black as well. Her father often ridiculed her for trying to be like a man. He said no civilized woman drank black coffee. For the first time in her life, she wasn't ashamed of her preference.

"Great cookies," David said, before Hattie could turn back with the brimming cups of coffee.

"Thank you. I'm sorry they aren't fresh. I'm afraid I overslept this morning."

David began to laugh. "Didn't anyone ever tell you the best molasses cookies aren't the fresh ones? I always liked the ones my mother made and let set a few days so I could dunk them in my milk or my coffee."

Hattie stiffened as David's description brought a long forgotten memory to the forefront.

'Don't dunk your cookies, Hattie,' she could hear her father say. 'It ain't ladylike. No self-respecting man wants a woman who acts like a child for his wife.'

"Haven't you ever dunked?" David studied her.

"It's been a long time," Hattie admitted. She broke a cookie in half and immersed it in the dark liquid in her cup. The taste of molasses and spice mingled with the strong coffee to produce a warm memory of childhood. "I'd forgotten how delicious this was. My pa said dunking cookies wasn't ladylike. I certainly don't know why not."

David's booming laughter put her at ease. "Neither do I. My mother is a very delicate lady, and she enjoys dunking her cookies."

Hattie knew such easy conversation should make her blush, but it was as though she'd known David Long all her life.

"I wanted to apologize to you for yesterday. I know I told you I wanted to be here, but the church council showed up before I could get out of the house."

"Apology accepted. Now what did you have in mind in the way of a suit?"

"Suits, Miss Fairchild. I have but one black suit and it's made of wool. I'd like at least four lightweight suits for summer as well as three more for winter. I also need several white shirts. I'd like to see what kind of fabric you have."

Hattie's mind raced. The amount of fabric needed for the suits and shirts Reverend Long requested would be very expensive. Somehow she would have to find a way to absorb at least part of the cost to ease the burden for the minister.

On the opposite wall of the shop stood a tall cupboard. In it, Hattie stored her stock of fabric. "I don't have much call for black in the summer, but Abe always kept a bolt of black linen on the shelf. I can get more within the week. The white won't be a problem, but I'm afraid I won't have any wool in until the first of September. I do have enough left over from last winter for one suit. That is, if you approve of the fabric."

* * * *

David ran his hand over the bolt of material Hattie held out for his approval. He'd never seen a finer piece of linen. Abe Levens had a good eye for quality.

David's mother taught him to appreciate quality. She'd come from a good family, hardly what one would expect of a blacksmith's wife. She'd always insisted on having the best and William Long fit the bill. He was a man, not unlike this linen. He was of the best quality.

From the look on Hattie's face, David knew she was concerned about the cost of the yardage needed to make the clothing he requested.

"This material will do nicely, especially if you think you can get more."

"Good," Hattie replied. "Before I can start, I'll need to get your measurements. The light is better by the East window, so if you don't mind, I'd appreciate it if you'd go over there and stand."

David did as she said. He couldn't help but smile when she picked up a small step stool and followed him to the window.

In addition to the stool, she carried a pad of paper and a tape measure, with a pencil stuck behind her ear. With the exception of the stool, she looked very professional. He wondered if it was his imagination or if her hands were trembling.

"Neck, eighteen," Hattie said, as she made a notation on her note pad.

She put the pad in the pocket of her skirt and ran the tape around his chest. Again she repeated the measurement before writing it down on the pad. With each measurement it was the same, until she dropped to her knees to take the last one, that of the inseam for his trousers.

As she reached tentatively toward his crotch, he took her hand in his. "It's thirty-six inches."

"What?" she questioned, her eyes widening with surprise.

"My inseam measurement is thirty-six inches. That particular measurement must be quite embarrassing for a woman to take."

He liked the way her face reddened to almost the same shade as her hair.

"I rarely have to do it. Abe kept very good records. While a man's chest, neck, and waist measurements are subject to change, his arm length and inseam stay the same. Abe has a file with the measurements for every man in town on his desk. It makes my job much easier."

"After spending yesterday with the church council, I'm surprised the men in town continue to patronize your shop. They certainly have set ideas about women."

His statement brought a smile to Hattie's lips. "They don't have much of a choice. Abe ran the only tailor shop in town. When he took me on as an assistant and then left the business to me, there were a few raised eyebrows, but they got over it. Unless they want to go to Springfield or Chicago, they have to accept me."

David nodded. He could see in what a precarious position Abe Levens left Hattie. Men were always slow to accept women in any role other than wife and mother.

"This being Wednesday, I doubt I can have the suit ready for next Sunday, but I'll do my best."

"I can make it through another week with the wool, but not much more."

"Why do you have to wear wool? You were a lawyer in Philadelphia. Didn't you have to wear suits to court?"

David couldn't help but laugh. "What I wore in court wouldn't be acceptable. I was known for my flamboyant style. My summer suits were white, light blue, and tan. How many ministers have you seen who don't wear black?"

"I'm afraid you're asking the wrong person. The only preacher I've known was Reverend Hill. He wore a lot of black, but until I get you outfitted properly, I doubt anyone will make much of a fuss. This is a farming community. Clothes aren't exactly the most important things to these folks."

David hadn't given the matter much thought until now. On Sunday, he'd seen the way his parishioners dressed. He'd noticed only a few of the men wore suits and they were from town. The farmers wore clean work clothes, their wives simple housedresses.

He saw none of the fancy clothes worn by the elite in Philadelphia. There, his parents had been well-respected members of the community, even though his father did common labor with his hands. Unlike the clergy in his home church, here he certainly wouldn't have to be so concerned about the proper attire for a man of the cloth.

* * * *

By the time David left the shop, Hattie was emotionally drained. Being close to the man, actually taking his measurements, told her she was playing with fire.

She'd never felt such an attraction for any of her customers in the past. Of all people, why did she have to be attracted to David Long? She could never keep up her pretense if she became close to the minister.

She doubted the man would ever understand if he learned she preferred novels to Sunday sermons and scriptures. Being exposed would mean giving up playing the beautiful piano at the church. She didn't know if she could stand the embarrassment of exposure and being shunned.

Rather than give in to the tears that threatened to fall, Hattie picked up the sewing she'd abandoned earlier. Any thoughts of closing the shop during the noon hour seemed absurd. The events of the morning took away any appetite she might have had.

As she sewed, she contemplated her options. The easiest would be to close the shop and move from Mortonville to some other small town in need of a seamstress. Surely there would be one who could use a church pianist who didn't believe in God. One that didn't have a handsome single minister who could easily see through her act.

Thinking of such a drastic action saddened Hattie. She'd lived in Mortonville all her life. Contemplating leaving made her sad. The town housed her memories of friends she'd made and the one man who trusted her enough to leave her his business. She couldn't let Abe down in order to avoid David. It wouldn't be fair to the man who treated her more like a beloved daughter than an employee.

The bell jingled merrily drawing Hattie's attention from her work.

"I thought I'd check on those trousers," George greeted her.

"I'm just putting the finishing touches on them. I would have been done sooner, but I had a surprise customer this morning."

"I know," George replied. "David said he wanted to come over yesterday, but I'm afraid the church council waylaid him. Is he really in such dire straits as far as his wardrobe is concerned?"

Hattie laughed. "To hear him talk he is. I think he has a rather warped idea of what you want in a minister. If you were to check his closet, I'm certain you would find several suits and shirts, but I'm afraid only one would be black with a white shirt. From what he said, he was rather a flamboyant dresser in Philadelphia."

"What do you mean?"

"He ordered four black linen suits and three black wool ones. He went on to say he has a white, tan, and light blue suit, but feels none of them are appropriate. I'm almost afraid to think of what he has for winter to say nothing of shirts."

"Do you have enough material to fill his order?"

"There's enough linen for one suit and the same is true for my black wool. Of course, I won't have a problem with the white for the shirts and the rest can be ordered. It's the cost that worries me. I've been trying to figure out how I can cut corners with my labor, but the material he selected is very expensive. Even at cost…"

"Don't fret about the cost, Hattie. Something can be worked out. You fill the order and the church council will see to it you're well compensated."

Hattie nodded. She understood exactly what George meant. The council would keep the new minister happy, no matter what the cost.

By midafternoon, she finished George's trousers and had Reverend Long's suit cut out of the linen. When he'd been in the shop she noticed he preferred a leather belt to the suspenders fancied by most of the larger men in Mortonville. She'd taken an eyeball measurement so she'd know what size to make the loops, which would act as a carrier for the belt he wore.

As she cut, she dwelled on the word flamboyant. To her mind it meant bright colors, like the parrot portrayed in the book on birds Abe kept in his extensive library. The thought brought a smile to her lips. She certainly wouldn't equate Reverend David Long to a parrot.

* * * *

David made himself a meal of cold roast beef and freshly sliced tomatoes. As he did, he drafted a letter to his parents.

> Dear Ma and Pa,
> Mortonville is very different from Philadelphia. The youngest man on the church council is older than me and the others are set in their ways. Change will be difficult here.
> The women of the church have taken me at my word and decided I cannot cook. Therefore, they bring me my dinner each day at noon and there is more than enough to

provide for my evening meal. Next week they plan to teach me to cook.

More interesting than the church council or the women is the town's tailor. Miss Hattie Fairchild is close to thirty and has never married. In addition to being the tailor, she is also the seamstress and plays the piano at church. I may be wrong, but I fear her faith is not as strong as one might think by her weekly participation in the service. Each parishioner I have asked has told me she did not attend church prior to the time when she went to work for the first tailor, Abe Levens, five years ago.

Please do not mistake me. Her music is inspired. It is as though God guides her fingers across the keys. Since the piano is in the balcony, I cannot tell if she listens to my sermons or sleeps through them. What I do know is she has a private entrance so she can come and go unnoticed. I didn't even get a chance to comment on her playing last Sunday.

Today I visited her shop to be measured for a suit, or should I say several suits. I never thought I would be content to wear only black, but my new vocation demands it. All went well until it was necessary for her to take my inseam measurement. Luckily, I remembered what my previous tailor said it was. It saved her the embarrassment of ... well, I'm certain you know.

I am not sure of my feelings for this woman. Were it not who and what I am, it would be different, but I cannot expect someone as delicate and beautiful as Hattie to ever have feeling for me.

Pray for me here in this new town. I want these people to become responsive to the changes needed to bring their church up to date.

My love to both of you,
David

With the letter finished, David fought the urge to go for a walk past

Hattie's shop. Getting into such a habit wouldn't be good for someone in his position. It was best to stay aloof, not become intimately involved with anyone in the community. It had been good advice for his law practice and even better for his position in the pulpit.

Chapter Seven

Hattie was glad no customers came to the shop on Saturday morning. It gave her time to finish not only the trousers for Reverend Long's suit, but also a fashionable vest. The coat would be finished next week, but at least the minister would not spend another Sunday sweltering in the July heat wearing his wool suit.

The final pressing took almost an hour, as she wanted all the seams to be properly flattened and the creases in the trousers to be sharp. Once she was happy with her work, she transferred the pieces to one of the wooden hangers Abe insisted she must special order from Chicago.

After a light lunch, she made her way to the church. When she finished with the cleaning of the piano, she would make a stop at the parsonage and deliver the clothing to Reverend Long.

In the heat of the day, she heard children at play, and nodded greetings to townspeople who were spending the lazy afternoon on their front porches in their rockers.

"Going to the church to practice, Hattie?" one woman called as she passed.

"Guess I'm as predictable as the sunrise. I need to pick up the songs for tomorrow morning."

"We're so lucky to have someone with your talent in our community. I learned how to play when I was a child, but I'd never do it for anyone but myself."

"It's nice to have something I enjoy appreciated by others. I'm glad it gives you pleasure."

The woman smiled broadly at Hattie's compliment. Amy Totter was someone Hattie knew by sight, but wouldn't number among her close friends. To be truthful, she rarely saw the woman smile. She guessed there was probably a reason, there usually was. One had only to listen to the gossip to know Amy's oldest son, Fred, had the same weakness for drink as Hattie's father. Even though the man and his wife rented a farm on the outskirts of town, it was common knowledge Amy and her husband, Rube, often paid Fred's outstanding debts. It made Hattie more sympathetic to the woman than most would be. She'd lived the horror of what strong drink could do to a man. She could only imagine the anguish of seeing it destroy one's own son.

As usual, the church appeared deserted when Hattie opened the side door and climbed the back stairs to the balcony. Her footsteps echoed in the empty building, giving her a sense of security.

Familiar dust mites floated on a sunbeam welcoming her, as one would an old friend.

She picked her way around the rows of seldom-used pews, while she waited for her eyes to adjust to the dimly lit balcony. When she reached the area where the piano always sat, she stood shocked. The instrument she'd so lovingly cared for was gone.

"Are you looking for something, Miss Fairchild?" Reverend Long's booming voice sounded from the sanctuary.

Cautiously, Hattie peered over the half way of the balcony. "My piano is missing."

"Not missing, just repositioned," David replied.

Hattie watched as he moved aside to give her a good view of the piano, which now stood off to one side of the altar.

Without comment, Hattie hurried down to the main floor of the sanctuary. The fact Reverend Long stood beside the piano, his arms crossed over his chest, a silly grin on his face did little to appease her anger.

"Whose idea was it to move the piano down here? Do you have any idea what damage could have been done to it? This is a precision instrument. It is probably out of tune!"

"One question at a time, my dear Miss Fairchild. Moving it down here was my idea, but Ralph and the rest of the council agreed with me. An instrument as beautiful as this deserves to be seen by the congregation to say nothing about being heard."

"Heard?" Hattie exclaimed. "It seems to me it can be heard quite

54

well."

"It certainly can, but there is a delay. I could hear it last Sunday. The congregation was always singing a half a stanza behind you. I'm positive we will hear a distinct difference tomorrow. As for the tuning of it, I have a friend who promised to come and visit once I get settled. He's been blind from birth, but was a neighbor of ours. We were always the best of friends. While I went to school in the neighborhood, Clarence attended a boarding school for the blind. There, he learned to tune pianos. Although I don't think this one needs his special talent, I plan to ask him to look at it while he's here. Why don't you try it for yourself?"

Hattie felt ill at ease with David so close at hand. Instead of making further conversation, she put down her music bag as well as the hanger with the vest and trousers on it.

Once unencumbered, she seated herself on the bench. In front of her the hymnal was already open to the first hymn. As she played the familiar notes, it was evident the piano was in perfect tune.

Hattie wondered how the move could have been achieved without causing damage to the delicate instrument. As she recalled, when it arrived from Chicago, it had been taken to the balcony still in its shipping case. With it came a representative of the company who manufactured it. The man had lovingly unpacked it and tuned it to perfection.

"There doesn't seem to be any damage," she declared. "What I don't understand is how you managed to move it?"

David still leaned against the piano disarming her with his boyish grin. "I could tell you it was done by magic, but I doubt you would believe me. In actuality, we found several young farmers who were able to carry it downstairs as though it was a baby sleeping in its mother's arms."

The mental picture David painted brought a smile to Hattie's lips. She would have laughed out loud if she hadn't thought of the novel she usually carried in her music bag. With the piano in such close proximity to the altar, she knew there would be no chance whatsoever to read the stories she so dearly loved during the lengthy sermons. It was true last Sunday she'd had no trouble in listening to Reverend Long's message, but his first sermon was written to make an impression on his new congregation.

* * * *

David knew he should have warned Hattie about his plans to move the piano from the balcony to the main floor of the church, but knowing and doing had been two different things. It was too much of a temptation to see the look on Hattie's face when she realized her beloved piano was no longer hidden away. With it in plain sight, she too would be open to the scrutiny of the townspeople each and every Sunday.

The expression on her face had been worth the deception. Listening to her play the familiar chords made David wish it was proper for him to continue to do so for the rest of his life.

The process of moving the piano from the balcony to the main floor had not been quite as easily accomplished as he described it to Hattie. He remembered shouting at the young men to be careful, to keep the instrument as level as they would a coffin at a funeral, as they carried it down the wide staircase.

When he at last drew his attention from Hattie, David noticed the rumpled black clothing on the front pew where it had been dropped. "Don't tell me this is my new suit? You can't have finished it already."

Hattie jerked her head up to meet his gaze. "Oh dear, I worked so hard to get this much done and pressed and now ... now..."

David enjoyed seeing the frustration in her eyes. The linen was indeed wrinkled, but it was nothing an iron couldn't fix. It was something else his mother insisted he learn when he first announced his move to Illinois.

Carefully, he picked up the hanger and examined the garments suspended from it. The trousers were the best quality he'd ever seen. Instead of a suit coat, the hanger held a fashionable vest. Had he still been practicing law, he was certain he would have ordered several in various colors. In his new profession, such high fashion seemed almost too vain.

"I wouldn't have thought of a vest," he said.

"Considering our current heat wave, I thought it would be a more practical option, especially since I won't have your coat finished until next week. There is one thing I would like to suggest, though."

"Suggest?"

"Yes, suggest. It is a shame to allow the moths to enjoy the suits you wore in Philadelphia. George and I have been talking about it. We can see no reason why you should invest in an entire new wardrobe, when you have a perfectly good one in your closet. I really don't think it's written anywhere that you have to wear black to be a preacher. George said it's about time someone shakes up the members of the church council."

David stared at Hattie in disbelief. "You certainly aren't suggesting…"

"I most certainly am suggesting exactly what you think. I've always thought black was a disgusting color. When my folks died, everyone insisted I should wear it for a year. I hated it then and I hate it now. I'll gladly make your suits, but I would much rather see you dressed—ah how did you put it—yes, a bit more flamboyantly."

David assessed Hattie's appearance. She wore a summer frock of a cool cotton fabric with short sleeves. Its white background sported bright orange flowers with green leaves in an outrageous pattern that most women would have shunned as improper.

"Something tells me I'm not the only person who is flamboyant in Mortonville." The blush creeping into Hattie's cheeks told him he'd struck a chord with the woman who stood beside him.

"I'm not what most folks call conventional, if that's what you mean, Reverend Long. You might as well know, I've never been one of the pillars of society. My pa was a drunk, and my ma worked herself to death trying to keep him in drinking money. I wanted a better life. Some consider me a bit strange, both in my actions and my dress, but I do what I do to please no one but myself. I understand why you want the congregation to see this beautiful piano, but they may want to find a new pianist when they see how I dress when I come to church. I refuse to wear drab colors which are neither flattering nor to my liking."

If David ever harbored a doubt about red heads having a temper, Hattie's outburst dispelled it from his mind. It flared so quickly he knew clothing had nothing to do with it. For that matter, neither did the moving of the piano. There was a reason she insisted on hiding herself away in the balcony on Sunday mornings, and he intended to find out what it was.

* * * *

On her way home, Hattie thought about her outburst. How had Reverend Long taken it? He probably considered her as strange as most of her neighbors. She knew it shouldn't bother her, but it did.

In her entire life she'd never expected anyone to like her. At least not the way a man did a woman he considered special. Now more than anything, she wished Reverend Long would make her feel wanted.

As soon as the thought crossed her mind, she dismissed it. Even if Reverend Long made her feel special whenever he looked at her, she knew she could never admit it to him or anyone else. To do so would mean she would have to admit her non-belief in the God he served not only by his faith but also by his calling. Once she admitted such a thing the special looks and feelings would disappear. It was better to enjoy silently his unintended attentions than to open herself to the ridicule and shunning of her friends and neighbors.

"Are you going to pass by without stopping for your mail?" George said as he stepped from his store to intercept her.

"I guess I was lost in thought. Do you have something for me?"

"Not much, but I always like to have you stop by for a chat. Speaking of which, how did you like where we put the piano?"

"I don't. Of course, since I wasn't consulted, my opinion doesn't count for much."

"What did David think of that temper of yours?"

Hattie laughed as she followed George into the store. "If you're referring to Reverend Long, he didn't say anything about it. Maybe he didn't notice."

"Didn't notice!" George exclaimed. "The man would have to be blind and deaf not to notice your temper. I doubt there is a person in town that hasn't been on the receiving end of your ire at one time or another. I don't mean it as a derogatory statement. It's just part of who you are."

"You know me too well, George Ransom. It's probably best I never married. No man would ever want to put up with me or my temper."

"If the man loved you the way you deserve, he would overlook your one fault."

"Only one? Really George, you tend to exaggerate."

"Exaggerate or not, I do believe we've gotten off the subject. We were talking about the new placement of the piano. David seems to think it will make a difference in the sound of the music. Do you agree with him?"

Hattie picked up one of the wicker baskets George kept by the door for his customers and began choosing some fresh vegetables for her evening meal. As she did, she recalled how different the music actually sounded. When the piano sat in the balcony, the sound was trapped by the close proximity of the instrument to the ceiling. With it on the main floor, the music resonated through the entire building, emitting a delightful sound.

"Perhaps he's right. It was just such a shock to go there and not find the piano where it has always been. I'm set in my ways. Change doesn't come easily for me."

"I'd argue with you on that count, Hattie," George remarked. "I've watched you change more than you think. We've been friends for too long for me not to have noticed. I've watched those changes take place. I remember how you wanted to become a teacher, but your pa made you take in sewing to help him buy his whiskey. I also remember how you sold the farm when he died and went into partnership with Abe. If the truth were known, Hattie Fairchild, I remember when you didn't attend church at all. Whatever it was that brought you to the Lord, I don't care, but don't tell me you can't change. I know you better than anyone in this town, and I know you can do it."

Before Hattie could answer, two more customers entered the store. She was relieved not to have to comment on George's statement. Of all the people in town, she hated deceiving him the most. Had things been different, she might have been his wife.

As though it was yesterday, she recalled the day George came out to the farm to take her fishing. He'd been the first young man to be met by her father with his shotgun before he ever got to the front door.

Grateful for George's other customers Hattie finished her shopping and made her way home. Walking the familiar route gave her time to think about Mortonville and the impact Reverend Long would have on the small farming community.

Hattie already knew the impact he had on her. With the moving of the piano, he was forcing her to be more attentive to his sermons than she had been to Reverend Hill's. To make matters worse, she felt an unnatural attraction for Reverend Long.

Before she arrived home, Hattie met two women from the church. One she hardly knew, but she'd been a friend of Maude Painter for years.

"There you are, Hattie," Maude said. "We've just come from your house. We were surprised to find you weren't home."

"You shouldn't have been so surprised, Maude," Hattie replied. "It's common knowledge I go to the church on Saturday afternoon to get the hymns for Sunday morning."

"It doesn't matter," Jenny Blake replied. "We've found you so everything is all right. We're setting up days when people can provide meals for the new minister. We were wondering what day we could put you down for?"

"Me?" Hattie said in disbelief. "Aren't there enough good cooks among the married women in the congregation?"

"That's not the point and you know it," Maude declared. "Everyone in the church has to take their turn. You must realize, it would be different if Reverend Long were married. I have an unmarried niece in Rockford. I've written my sister and invited Katie to come and visit. She would make a perfect preacher's wife."

"You're getting off the subject, Maude," Jenny scolded. "When can we put you on the list to cook, Hattie?"

Inwardly, Hattie seethed. She didn't want to sign up for anything, and she certainly didn't want to hear about Maude Painter's niece coming to throw herself at Reverend Long. "It's very hard with my business. The only day I would have free is Sunday and then I have to play at church, so you see…"

"Good," Maude declared, without giving Hattie a chance to finish. "We'll put you down for tomorrow."

"But .. but…"

"I realize it is short notice," Jenny interrupted, "But Reverend Long certainly isn't fussy about what he eats. You'll do just fine."

"Just fine," Hattie muttered as she walked away from Maude and

Jenny. Her mind spun with ideas of what she could possibly serve for tomorrow's noon meal. Unlike the other women in town, she wouldn't spoil her meal by dragging it over to the parsonage. If she had to feed the minister, it would be in her dining room.

By the time she reached home, she knew exactly what she would do. It was still early enough for her to change her clothes and go down to the creek to do some fishing before dark.

It wouldn't take her long to catch a good mess of fish, clean, and store them in the springhouse. Tomorrow after church, she could boil some new potatoes in their jackets, bake the fish, and make cabbage salad. If that wasn't good enough for Reverend Long, maybe the old busy bodies at the church would leave her alone.

Chapter Eight

Sunday, David smiled when he saw Hattie sitting at the piano. Only moments earlier Jenny Blank told him Hattie would be providing his noon meal. If he got lucky, she would insist on serving him that meal at her home.

He took a moment to check out the way she was attired. It didn't take long for him to understand what she meant about not dressing like the other women in the congregation. She wore a crisp white blouse with short sleeves with delicate pansies embroidered on the collar. Her skirt was a bright grass green and, from what he could tell, was of a lightweight material. He was certain it was much cooler than the dresses worn by the other women.

Although he knew her fashionable upsweep was undoubtedly much cooler as well, he wished her hair hung loosely around her shoulders instead. It was almost a sin for such luxurious, thick red tresses to be pinned up away from her face.

Once she finished playing the prelude, David got to his feet. "Good morning," he greeted the conversation. "The Lord has given us a beautiful day to praise Him."

A glance toward Hattie gave him the feeling she was a more than a little uncomfortable with the new placement of the piano.

"As you can see," he continued, "several of the younger members of our congregation have generously helped in moving the piano from the balcony to the main floor of the sanctuary. I am certain you will enjoy not only the beauty of this instrument, but also the difference in tone."

Hattie's Preacher

* * * *

Hattie cringed at David's greeting to the congregation. She could feel every head in the church turn in her direction as well as every eye stare at her.

She hated being the center of attention. She could almost hear her neighbors as they whispered behind her back about what a shame it was that poor Hattie Fairchild couldn't find a husband.

Hattie was so lost in her thoughts, she almost missed David's announcement of the first hymn. She certainly never had such a problem when Reverend Hill occupied the pulpit and she sat in the balcony.

For some unknown reason, her hands trembled as her fingers moved across the keys to accompany the congregation as they sang the words slightly off key.

Once David began his sermon, Hattie longed for her novel. Knowing she would never be able to read it while sitting in plain sight of the congregation, she turned her attention to the mind games she played when she first attended church.

Once by one she tried to review the projects she would need to finish in the coming week. To her dismay, David's booming voice broke her concentration.

"As the Gospel tells us, many of the disciples were professional fishermen. Now as much as I enjoy fishing for pleasure and eating what I catch, I am not good enough at it to consider doing it for a living."

The comment brought laughter from Hattie's friends and neighbors. It made the fish a good choice for her dinner menu.

"I can relate to these men, though," David continued. "What they did, they did well. They made a good living, and yet they gave it up to follow Jesus. How much would you give up?"

Hattie tried to draw her thoughts back to the calculations for her next week at work, but found she couldn't shut out David's words.

"I never thought I could give up everything, but when God called me, I couldn't say no. It doesn't matter what anyone thinks, when God calls it is not easy to ignore Him."

Hattie wanted to shake her head in disbelief. The God she'd always heard about didn't ask, he demanded. Her father's God had been vengeful. He demanded punishment for disobedience, to say nothing of disbelief. No matter what David said, she knew she could never believe in anything her father demanded she accept.

By the time David's sermon ended, Hattie was more than ready to play the hymn of the day. After that she would only need to play for the collection, then the closing hymn, and the postlude before she would be free to leave the church and go home.

When the last note of the postlude sounded, Hattie collected her music and prepared to leave by the side door.

"The piano has never sounded so beautiful," Ralph said from behind her.

"Your music is always special," Maude commented, "but today it was ever more so."

"I always knew the piano belonged down here," Ralph continued, not allowing anyone else a chance to speak. "It's a good thing Reverend Long spoke up. You really are a treasure, Hattie. We can be proud to have you playing for us every Sunday."

Hattie didn't know what to say. In all the years she'd played for services so many people had never approached her at one time. "Thank you," she replied. "I'm pleased to know you enjoy my playing. Now, if you will excuse me, I do have things to attend to at home."

"That's right," Maude said, loud enough so that everyone within earshot could hear her. "Today is your turn to make dinner for the minister. We mustn't keep you. It would be a shame to spoil whatever it is you are planning to make."

Instead of slipping unnoticed out the side door, Hattie found herself swept up in the sea of parishioners making their way to the front door of the church.

Not quite certain what to say to Reverend Long, she fidgeted in the slow moving line, listening to those ahead of her as they exchanged pleasantries with the giant of a man who stood just outside the door.

At last, Hattie stood in front of him, her hand outstretched as she'd seen her neighbors do before her.

"Good morning, Miss Fairchild," David greeted her. His voice seemed softer and less booming than it had minutes earlier from the pulpit. "I enjoyed the music this morning immensely. I'm certain you must agree that the tone is much better with the piano moved to the main floor of the sanctuary."

"Yes, yes, much better," Hattie mumbled.

"I'm told you will be preparing my midday meal. I do hope it's not too much of an imposition on you."

Hattie shook her head no, all the time wishing he'd let go of her hand so she could think straight. His very touch made her mind spin uncontrollably and turned her brain to mashed potatoes.

"I realize this past week the women have been bringing my meals to the house, but it seems to be such a bother. Would it be an inconvenience to you if I came to your home for dinner?"

Inconvenience. The word spun through her mind, clearing any muddled thought she might have harbored. How could he have read her mind? How could he have known she wanted no part of carrying dinner the six blocks separating her shop and the parsonage?

"It would be no inconvenience whatsoever," she replied. "As a matter of fact, I was planning to suggest the same thing to you. I should have everything ready within the hour."

David loosened the grasp on her hand, and somehow Hattie managed to get her legs to move her forward in line.

"I can't believe you're planning to have the minister to your home for dinner," Maude scolded. "Who would be there to chaperone?"

"Who would be there to chaperone at the parsonage?" Hattie replied, answering Maude's question with one of her own. "We are not unruly teenagers that need supervision."

"When we suggested you prepare him a meal, we never expected you would share it with him. We thought you would take it to the parsonage and then return home."

"Would you have me eat my Sunday meal in solitude, Mrs. Painter?" David said, coming to Hattie's rescue. "It seems to me when you and Mrs. Blake brought me dinner this week the two of you stayed to share it with me."

"But ... but that was different. Jennie and I are married and ... and..."

"At the time, I'm certain it seemed proper to you. I see no difference with Miss Fairchild and myself sharing a meal. I'm sure she does not enjoy eating alone any more than I do. Now, if you ladies will excuse us,

Miss Fairchild has preparations to make, and I do so enjoy watching a woman at work in her kitchen."

David took Hattie's arm and escorted her away from the church and down the street leading to the tailor shop and her home.

"Thank you for putting those busy bodies in their place," she said once they were a safe distance from the churchyard. "How did you know I was planning to invite you to my house?"

"I didn't, but for most of my meals the food has been cold by the time I get to eat it. I really wanted hot food for a change. Hopefully, once I prove to be a fast learner, the deal ladies of the church will stop their endless stream of food deliveries."

"You know how to cook, don't you?"

"Guilty as charged. My mother insisted I should learn to cook when I was a young boy. She said one never knows where life will take a person and it would be a shame to starve for lack of knowing something as simple as cooking. My father was horrified by her suggestion, but he rarely crosses her on anything. He even allowed her to teach him to cook. It came in right handy when she got sick with the influenza, and I was busy with a case in Philadelphia."

Hattie laughed at David's story and the brief glimpse of what his home life was like. She knew she would like his mother if they were ever to meet.

* * * *

The sheer size of Hattie's home surprised David. From the street, it looked quite small and compact. In actuality, all he really saw was the parlor and part of the dining area. Across a wide hall sat a large kitchen as well as two closed off rooms he assumed to be good-sized bedrooms.

The furnishings although tasteful, depicted a bygone era. More than likely they once belonged to Abe Levens and his wife. Since he'd heard the Levens came from New York, the quality of the furniture said it had been purchased there as well.

The piano in the parlor was as highly polished as the one at the church. Hattie's loving hand was as evident here as it was in the sanctuary.

"Is there anything I can do to help you?" he inquired, when she came from the kitchen. Although she hadn't changed her clothes, she now wore a crisp gingham apron tied around her trim waist.

"I have to go down to the springhouse and get the fish and cabbage salad for dinner. I could use some help bringing it up to the kitchen."

David nodded and followed her out the back door to the little building positioned on the shore of the creek to take advantage of the fast running water to cool the food Hattie stored there.

"I hope you like your fish baked. I've never mastered the art of frying it to perfection."

"I don't think I've ever eaten baked fish, but it sounds good. Did you catch it or did someone bring it to you?"

Hattie laughed, but it was one of sarcasm rather than merriment. "You'll find I'm very self-sufficient. No one brings me anything. Last night, when the good ladies of the church told me I would be preparing your meal today, I went fishing. I'm certain you'll find this creek has very tasty fish."

"Is there anything you can't do, Miss Fairchild?"

He enjoyed the way his question caused her to blush from the opening of her blouse at her neck to the roots of her red hair.

"I have no ability or desire to run a farm. That's why I sold my parents' farm and bought half interest in Abe's business. It proved to be a wise decision."

By the time Hattie finished her explanation, they were back in her spacious kitchen. David enjoyed watching her prepare the meal. While the new potatoes came to a boil on the stovetop, she melted butter in a shallow baking pan before adding the fish filets and seasoning them with paprika. He couldn't help but remember how his mother always considered the spice too extravagant to use.

Within minutes, the aroma of baking fish added to that of boiling potatoes and a simmering pan of fresh peas. David watched as she bustled between the kitchen and dining room setting the damask covered table with fine bone china and highly polished silverware. Crystal goblets were filled with water and set next to cut glass saltcellars at both places. Adding to the extravagance were linen napkins wrapped in ornately carved ivory napkin rings.

"You set a beautiful table," David observed.

"Thank you. All of this belonged to Abe's wife, Marta. He insisted we have at least one formal meal a week. When I first moved here, he taught me how to set a good table and serve a formal meal. I must say I miss it."

"I take it you do not entertain often."

Again Hattie's laughter was without mirth. "Just whom would I invite? If I were to entertain a married couple, the woman would be certain I was after her man. In case you haven't noticed, there aren't many unmarried men or women in this town. As a matter of fact, Maude is bringing her unmarried niece down from Rockford so you can have some suitable female companionship."

David couldn't help but feel sorry for Hattie. She was the woman everyone in town relied upon to play the piano for church services and to make their clothing, but no one considered her their social equal.

* * * *

Hattie regretted saying anything about Maude's niece as soon as the words passed her lips. It was none of her business who the mother hens of this town deemed a proper companion for the new minister.

She left him standing in the dining room pondering her words. At least it gave him something to do that didn't include following her around the kitchen like a puppy dog.

A check of her peas and potatoes told her everything would be done at the same time. It had been a long time since she'd had to have a meal ready all at once. At least she hadn't lost her touch.

From the top cupboard, she pulled a large silver tray and placed a covered, divided, serving dish that held the peas on one end and potatoes on the other. On the other tray she placed the bowl with the cabbage salad and finished with a basket of hot rolls and a platter of fish in the center.

Before she could heft the tray, David appeared in the kitchen doorway. "Don't tell me you plan to carry that tray of food all by yourself."

"All right, I won't tell you, but if you don't get out of my way our dinner will get cold."

David clucked his tongue at her disapprovingly, then picked up the tray and carried it effortlessly to the dining room. By the time she composed herself enough to follow him, David started unloading the tray.

"Everything looks delicious," he said, as he held her chair.

The gesture took her by surprise. No one had held her chair since Abe died. It was another thing she missed. Keeping her tears at bay, was a mammoth task, but one she accomplished with more self-control than she thought possible.

She was ready to reach for the platter of fish when David clasped his hands and bowed his head. Memories of her father insisting on a lengthy table grace flooded her mind. Abe's table grace had always been short and tolerable. With David, she had no idea what to expect.

"Dear Lord," he began, "bless this food and the hands that prepared it. A-Men."

That was painless. She picked up the fish and put a piece on her plate.

* * * *

David couldn't remember enjoying a fish dinner more than he did this one. As good a cook as his mother had always been, her fish was greasy and had a strong taste. In contrast, this had been light and flaky.

"Everything was delicious," he said when Hattie brought out sponge cake with fresh raspberry sauce for dessert. "I don't know if I can eat anymore."

The look of disappointment on Hattie's face made him think of a child that did something special to please an adult only to have the efforts rebuffed.

"Let me help you with the dishes. When we're finished, I'd like to take you for a carriage ride. By the time we get back, I'm certain I'll be ready for dessert."

"Oh, I couldn't ask you to help me with the dishes. It wouldn't be right."

"My dear Miss Fairchild, you didn't ask. Besides if you do the dishes alone, it will be far too late for that carriage ride. I was hoping you could give me a tour of the area. I need to get my bearings, but all anyone wants to talk about is church matters. No one seems to think I have an interest in anything else."

David watched as Hattie's pout turned to a bright smile. "Considering I've already made a big social mistake by inviting you to eat a meal in my home, my reputation can't be hurt much more by allowing you to dry my dishes and going with you on a carriage ride. Of course, if you're going to share my dishpan, I must insist you call me Hattie. I can't even remember anyone but you ever calling me Miss Fairchild. It makes me more than a little uncomfortable."

David laughed at her comment. "I know how you feel. When I practiced law in Philadelphia, I was the youngest member of the firm, so no one called me mister. With everyone calling me Reverend, I keep looking around to see whom they mean. I'd appreciate it if you would call me David."

"You mean like we were friends?"

"Something along those lines."

David wondered where that conversation came from. The look on Hattie's face told him friendship was the last thing she expected and the one thing she craved.

Instantly, the atmosphere in the room changed. The earlier tension disappeared. It didn't take long for Hattie to clear the table and pour hot water from the kettle simmering on the stove into two dishpans.

Piece by piece, Hattie washed the delicate crystal and china while David pulled it from the pan of clear steaming water so he could dry it with the dishtowel she provided. By the time the last dish was returned to the china closet, the grandfather clock in the parlor chimed three times.

"Is it too late for our carriage ride?" Hattie inquired.

With the sun still high in the heavens, David assured her they would have plenty of time.

It took only a matter of minutes for them to cover the short distance from the shop to the parsonage. As they walked the quiet streets of Mortonville, David was aware of the strange looks they were receiving from the curious residents who nodded at them from their front porches.

Thor seemed happy to be hitched to the carriage and allowed to stretch his legs on the road leading out of town.

"How much exploring have you done?" Hattie said, once fields of corn that were taller than a man surrounded them.

"Absolutely none. Like I said earlier, my time has been spent between the church and the parsonage."

"If we stay on this road, we'll drive past Ralph's farm. The place my parents owned is next. After that it is just fields, I'm afraid."

David nodded. As much as Hattie swore she wanted nothing to do with the farm where she grew up, he could hear a hint of sadness in her voice at the mention of it. He didn't blame her. The thought of his parents and the home he'd left behind brought on pangs of homesickness, especially when he was alone at night.

Ralph's farm loomed ahead of them. It was as though it sprang from nowhere once they left the cornfields behind. Neatly painted red outbuildings were trimmed in white, while the white house sported black shutters.

If David thought this was a leisurely drive, he as mistaken. Ralph and his wife, Edna, sat on the porch. It would be impossible to pass by unnoticed.

"Afternoon Reverend," Ralph called, as soon as they were in sight of the house. "Edna just made a pitcher of lemonade. Will you join us?"

David looked at Hattie and saw her shake her head no.

"We'll have to take a rain check on it, Mr. Mason." David called back. "Miss Fairchild is giving me a tour, and I don't want to keep her out past dark. Thank you for the invitation, though."

"Watch your P's and Q's with the new minister, Hattie," Ralph called back. "We don't want his reputation to be ruined before the first month is out."

David knew Ralph meant the comment as one of jest, but the expression on Hattie's face told David the words hurt now as they must have hurt many times in the past.

"Thank you," she said. "I certainly didn't want to have to be civil to Ralph Mason today."

"I take it you and Ralph aren't the best of friends. Do you want to talk about it?"

Hattie smiled. "There's not much to tell. Ralph and my father were good friends. They grew up together on these two farms. Even though Ralph hated my father's drinking, he would never confront him about it. Ralph was one of Pa's pallbearers. I'm certain he thought I would sell him the farm. When I declined his ridiculously low offer, he was outraged. Since then, we avoid each other whenever possible. The only area where we are in complete agreement is the church piano."

By the time Hattie fell silent, the next farm came into view. Unlike the Mason place, the buildings were not in as good repair. Although someone was working on making the place presentable, they still had a long way to go.

"Pa preferred to spend his money on whiskey. The farm gave him enough to put food on the table and drink in his belly, but little else. It's a shame, since this is good land. Had Pa been a good a farmer as he was a drinker, he could have been quite prosperous."

"I'm afraid this wasn't such a good idea. Being here has upset you."

Hattie's mood changed instantly. "It's not this farm that upsets me. There is nothing here to hurt me any longer. I'm afraid I allowed Ralph to vex me. If you turn at the next crossroad, we can get back to town by another road."

David knew he shouldn't pursue the subject that obviously upset Hattie. He also knew he wanted more answers. "Other than his low offer was there a reason why you didn't sell the farm to Ralph?"

"More reasons than I can count. My father wanted a son. Ralph agreed with him. He never let me forget I'd let his friend down by being born a girl. When Pa died, Ralph was the first person to come to the farm. He didn't come to console me. He came to tell me how I let my father down. I'd let him die. In the same breath, he offered to buy the farm."

David's first impression of Ralph Mason hadn't missed the mark by much. It was no wonder Hattie kept to herself.

At the crossroads, David turned to the right and took the next road back toward town. He wondered if it was a coincidence the road ran parallel to the creek.

As they neared town, the sun dipped lower on the western horizon, casting long shadows across the fast rushing water running beside them.

"Does the creek ever overflow?" he said, breaking the silence between them.

"Every spring. Luckily, my place is high enough on the hill that I haven't been flooded out. Can't say the same for the springhouse though.

I've learned to watch the weather and get everything out of there before I lose it."

The road continued uphill until they were on the street that ran in front of Hattie's shop.

"I'm ready for some of that cake now," David said, once he stopped Thor. "If there's any of the fish left, could I persuade you to heat it up as well?"

Hattie's gentle laughter told him he'd paid her a high compliment.

"It shouldn't take me long to reheat things. It will be good not to have leftovers to contend with."

Once Hattie sat supper on the table, David was careful not to eat too much. The memory of her sponge cake and raspberry sauce inspired him to save enough room for the sweet treat.

The lightness of the cake rivaled any his mother ever made. He had no doubt any mention of this one aspect of Hattie's culinary talents to his mother would be a mistake.

Chapter Nine

Monday morning, Hattie pulled a pan of cinnamon rolls from the oven, just as the parlor clock struck eight. It took only a moment to transfer the rolls to a plate and set the pan to soak before she opened the shop for the day.

As she expected, Maude was her first customer. Hattie knew what was coming and wished she could turn the sign from Open to Closed.

"I didn't expect to find the shop open today," Maude greeted her. "I mean, I saw you and the new minister walk past my house yesterday afternoon and you didn't come back. I thought, well, you must know what I thought."

Tears Hattie promised herself many years ago not to shed rolled down her cheeks. "I know what you thought, Maude. You must have a very low opinion of me. I'm good enough to prepare a meal for Da ... ah Reverend Long, but not good enough to share it with him. As for going for a walk together, that's all we did. He wanted to go for a carriage ride and have me show him some of the countryside. If you don't believe me, ask Ralph Mason. You didn't see us leave because we drove out of town by the other road. Ralph didn't see us come back, because we returned by the creek road."

"I ... didn't know. You must admit..."

"I don't admit anything. I don't want to talk to you or anyone else right now. Tomorrow, maybe, we can be friends again, but for today, I want to be alone. I'm not feeling well, and I think I'll close the shop."

Maude stood for a moment, her mouth hanging open. "Well, I

never."

"I never either. We've been friends for a long time, but..." Sobs cut off Hattie's words. To her surprise, Maude enfolded her in a loving embrace of friendship.

"I'm sorry. I jumped to the wrong conclusions. It's just..."

"I know. Tomorrow things will be different. I promise."

Once Maude left the shop, Hattie pulled the shades and put the Closed sign in the window. She'd expected whispers behind her back, but not accusations to her face.

The smell of the cinnamon rolls mocked her. No customers would eat any of her fresh baked goods today. Out of frustration, she threw the untouched dessert into the wastebasket and returned to the kitchen.

When she finished the dishes, Hattie went out the back door and down to the creek. After stripping off her stockings, she sat with her back to the gentle slope of the shoreline and dangled her feet in the cool water.

Yesterday, having David share her table made her feel like a real woman. She wasn't the old maid that women didn't trust around their husbands. She was a desirable woman in her own right, who finally found a friend. The delightful feeling of belonging had been extinguished by Maude's biting accusations.

Why couldn't she be like everyone else?

When no answer came, she lay back against the bank to enjoy the warmth of the mid-morning sun. It didn't take long for the perfect summer day to lull her into a peaceful, if not uncharacteristic, sleep.

* * * *

David put on work clothes. He had some things he wanted to do around the church. With the piano out of the balcony, the extra space would make for a perfect storage area.

After finding some lumber stored in the shed behind the parsonage, he decided to build some cabinets for that area. It would be a good place to store the Christmas decorations that were now in his attic, as well as the extra hymnals he found piled in the small room behind the altar.

"Morning, Reverend," Ed Harmon greeted him as he left the house.

"Good morning, Ed. I didn't expect to see you here so early. Aren't you worried about your customers?"

"My boy is handling the shop. This morning, I'm more concerned about our decision to bring you to Mortonville, than I am about the shop. Several people came to me yesterday. I've called an emergency meeting of the church council. We'd like you to join us at the church."

The expression on Ed's face told David the meeting was serious. What could he have done to anger the council enough to warrant a Monday morning meeting? He certainly didn't think yesterday's sermon was anything that would cause such an uproar.

At the front of the church, Ralph, Herman, and George sat waiting for them to arrive.

"All right, Ed, what is this all about?" George demanded. "I have a store to run."

"You know I wouldn't call this meeting if it wasn't important," Ed declared. "I've had several of the ladies of the church over at my place both yesterday and today. It seems our new minister has been taking liberties with our church pianist."

"I've been what?" David demanded, getting to his feet to face his accusers.

"It seems," Ed began through clinched teeth, "that Maude saw you and Hattie walk past her house and never return. It is only logical to assume the two of you spent the night together."

It was Ralph who broke the tension by beginning to laugh. "Maude couldn't see a fly it if walked up the bridge of her nose. Besides, since the Reverend and Hattie drove past my place in his buggy they wouldn't have gone anywhere near Maude's place. So where did you take Hattie after you passed me?"

"We drove by the farm where she grew up and then came back to town by way of the creek road. After we had a bite of supper, I brought my buggy home. When I drove past Maude's place, she wasn't out on her porch. It's no wonder she didn't see me."

"You brought us over here on the word of the town gossip," George snapped. "I left Ruth in charge of the store, which should have been my responsibility, to come here and listen to this hogwash."

"Well, we can't have—" Ed began.

"We can't have what?" Herman said before Ed could finish.

"You know perfectly well what," Ed replied. "Hattie is a proper lady. It isn't right for her to be entertaining men in her home."

For the first time David realized what brought about this meeting. He'd almost forgotten Maude's comment about Hattie bringing his noon meal to the parsonage and leaving it there.

"Why do you people have a problem with me eating a meal with Miss Fairchild?"

"No one said anything about … about," Ed stammered.

"Of course you did," David interrupted. "You said it wasn't proper for Hattie to be entertaining in her home. What makes it improper?"

"She's not married and…"

"And what? How do women in this town get married? What if she were widowed?"

"Well," Herman said, "that would be different. A widow would have children to consider. It would be in her best interests to entertain gentlemen who might be interested in marriage so that her children could have a father."

David nodded, trying to understand the reasoning of these people. "In other words, an unmarried woman, with no family to find her a husband, is sentenced to a lonely existence. She must spend her nights as well as her days alone, without being able to entertain guests in her home. I am pleased to think I am a bachelor and not an unmarried woman."

"It's Hattie's fault for not marrying while she was still young enough to get a husband," Ralph said. "She's in the position she's in now by choice."

"By Choice?" George shouted getting to his feet. "As I recall, her pa ran off any young man who got within a hundred yards of their farm. I ought to know. He unloaded that twelve-gauge of his in my direction one Saturday when I went out there to go fishing with Hattie. At the time I would have liked to court her, but the memory of that buckshot kept me from going back."

"I can't believe Hank would do anything like that," Ralph declared.

"That's because Hank was your friend," Herman replied. "I knew him for what he was, a drunk who kept every eligible young man away from Hattie. I asked him about it one day before he got too drunk to make sense. His reply was he wouldn't have any no good running after Hattie like the scum who married Laura.

Among the members of the council, the men nodded their heads as though they all agreed with Herman's statement. As much as David wanted to ask about Hattie's mysterious sister and her husband, he didn't. He knew George had little or no knowledge of the woman. The men meeting with him this morning would not answer whatever secrets surrounded her.

"So, where does this leave us?" David finally said. "Are you planning to fire me because I had dinner with Miss Fairchild yesterday and took her for a carriage ride? If you are, I should remind you the woman who is the most concerned about this is the same one who told Miss Fairchild to prepare Sunday dinner for me. Should I start packing and get tickets back to Philadelphia?"

"Calm down, David," George said. "There has been a misunderstanding. I think we can all forget this meeting ever happened."

David decided not to let the church council off the hook so easily. "What if I want to see Miss Fairchild again, socially? Will I be subject to another meeting like this one? Will Miss Fairchild be confronted with accusations?"

"We'll take care of our womenfolk," Herman declared. "If you want to see Hattie, socially, it's no one's concern but yours."

One by one the men left the church until David sat alone in the front pew. With his hands clasped, he prayed for guidance. He enjoyed yesterday's outing with Hattie. For that matter, he enjoyed Hattie's company. Of all the women his mother insisted he keep company with in Philadelphia, none of them piqued his interest in the same way as Hattie Fairchild. After an hour alone with his thoughts and prayers, David abandoned his plans for the day. More than anything else he wanted to see Hattie and make certain the town's dirty accusations hadn't reached her ears.

* * * *

Several people were gathered in front of Hattie's shop. As soon as David arrived, they turned to face him, as though he could answer their questions.

78

"Is something wrong?" he said.

"The tailor shop is closed," one of the women replied. "The shades are drawn, and the door is locked. I would have sworn I saw it open this morning."

David passed the woman and went up to the shop. The sign read *Closed*, the door was securely locked and the shades were tightly drawn. Where was Hattie?

Leaving the crowd of women to their speculations, David went around to the back of the house. The kitchen door was open, leading David to believe Hattie had gone to the one place where she could be alone with her thoughts.

The silence of the summer morning made him winder if his hunch was right. Would he find her down by the creek?

As soon as he crested the top of the knoll leading to the creek, he saw her. For a moment, his heart pounded in terror. The way she laid against the bank, she could be asleep, unconscious, or dead. He almost lost his footing on the steep bank, waking her in the process.

"David?" she said, her voice sounding sleepy. "What are you doing here?"

"I'm looking for you, the same as half the people in town. Everyone is concerned about the shop being closed."

"They can be concerned all they want. I'm not opening until tomorrow and maybe not even then."

David sat down beside her and started untying his shoes. Once he took them off, he removed his socks. "Is this a private creek or can anyone join you?"

Hattie looked up at him as though she hadn't understood his meaning. It took only a glance downward for her to see his bare feet dangling in the water next to hers.

"It's a free country."

Her girlish giggle told him he'd said the right thing. "Do you want to tell my why you're here and not in the shop?"

The smile generated by his earlier commented faded. "You don't want to know."

"Something tells me I already do."

"How could you? Maude was my first and only customer this

morning. She said some terrible things. I'll never be able to face the people in town again."

Tears rolled down Hattie's cheeks, making David wish he was forward enough to take her in his arms to comfort her.

"You had Maude, I had the church council. I'm sure the topic of conversation was the same."

"The church council came to see you? Why?" Hattie's eyes were wide with surprise.

"They were defending your honor. You're well thought of by these gentlemen. Even Ralph stood up for you against Maude's accusations."

* * * *

Hattie stared at David. The pain of Maude's biting words was fresh in her mind, too fresh. It was one thing for a friend to make the accusations Maude did. It was quite another or a room full of strangers to say the same things to a man of the cloth.

"I'm sorry," she said, her voice little more than a whisper over the sob she was trying to choke back.

"What are you sorry for?" David put his finger under her chin to raise her face to meet his gaze.

"For getting you in trouble with the church council. I should have brought the meal over to the parsonage like all the other women. I was being selfish." By now, her tears flowed freely.

To her surprise, David reached in his back pocket and pulled out a blue work handkerchief. Once he had it in hand, he used it to wipe away the tears from her cheeks. "If you were being selfish, the same can be said for me. I certainly don't like to have my meals dropped off, like someone was feeding a stray dog. Your offer was made out of generosity and perhaps a bit of loneliness. I know how lonely I've been since I moved here. I can only imagine what your life has been like."

Hattie could hardly believe David's words. In all her life, no one ever told her they knew how she felt. If Hattie hadn't known it was improper, she would have thrown her arms around David's neck and kissed him. Instead, she cried even harder.

"How ... how can you know? How can anyone know?"

"I saw it in your eyes the first time I met you. I confirmed my suspicions when you left by the side door the first Sunday I was here. George said you were hard to get to know. That's not the case, is it?"

Hattie shook her head no. "I leave by the side door so I don't have to talk to the good people of Mortonville. They're all so condescending around me. If I hear one more person gush about how poor Hattie can't get a husband, I may not be so nice to them anymore."

"You have to meet them in the shop. How do you handle it there?"

Hattie looked into David's eyes. She had no idea when her tears ceased. She only knew David made the sun shine a bit brighter every time he smiled.

"The shop is different. When they come there, it's because they need me. It's my livelihood and has nothing to do with my marital status. My expertise with a needle and thread has nothing to do with anything, but the dexterity of my fingers."

"I think that's more information than I needed to know," David declared, making Hattie feel as though she was rambling.

In a way she was. Unlike the woman who had a brood of children, she had no human accomplishments. Each stitch was done with love, each seam an object of pride, each finished garment as precious as any child she could have had.

"By the position of the sun and the growling of my stomach, I would say its dinnertime," David said, dissolving Hattie's thoughts. "Since we depleted your leftovers last evening, allow me to take you to the café for dinner."

The invitation came as a shock. "Oh, David, do you think we should?"

"I know we should. I have the blessing of the church council to see you socially. As long as I don't tarnish your honor, it is perfectly acceptable for us to share a meal at the café."

Hattie got to her feet and dusted the dry grass from the back of her dress. To her surprise, David plucked several pieces of dry grass from her hair as well.

"If I were to allow you to go with me without getting rid of the evidence of your nap, we could be the topic of even more gossip."

* * * *

Once David and Hattie climbed the hill leading back to her home, David went around to the front of the shop while Hattie freshened up.

"Did you find her, Reverend?" One of the women who still stood outside of the shop spoke.

"Yes, I found her."

"Why is the shop closed?"

"Miss Fairchild decided it was too nice a day to be cooped up inside. She was down by the creek enjoying the early morning weather."

"But she's never done such a thing before."

David laughed heartily. "People do things they've never done before every day. Just recently I preached a sermon for the first time. As I see it, there is a first time for everything in life. God gives us these firsts so we can appreciate them and get a new outlook on our everyday activities."

The woman rolled her eyes and turned her attention to the man standing on the other side of her. The fact the woman lost interest in interrogating him so quickly was comforting. It meant he was no longer an oddity. He was becoming a member of the community.

Chapter Ten

Hattie smiled to see the sun shining brightly on Thursday morning. After spending a delightful afternoon with David on Monday, she'd been forced indoors on Tuesday and Wednesday by a pounding rain.

Although she knew the farms welcomed the moisture for the crops, Hattie cursed the forced solitude it dictated. She spent the long hours the shop was open sewing by lamp light rather than the bright sunlight to which she was accustomed. She got a lot of work done, but by the time she was ready to close for the day, she had a miserable headache.

Each evening after eating a light supper, she went directly to bed without playing the music she usually found relaxing.

With the sun finally breaking through the clouds, her spirits lightened. For the first time in two days the nagging headache was gone.

The coffee cake she set last night filled her kitchen with the delicious aroma of its cinnamon and sugar filling. Once it was out of the oven and glazed with a thin icing, she prepared to open the shop.

To her surprise, David waited outside the door for her to raise the shades and turn the key to open for the day.

"Am I late in opening?" She was unable to mask her pleasure at seeing him.

"I doubt it," he replied. "I was up early and thought about those baked goods I'm told you always make for the shop. Since the eggs I fried for my breakfast were a bit burnt, I thought I'd take a chance on you having my coat ready for a fitting."

"As a matter of fact, the coat is ready, and I just took a coffee cake out of the oven."

Hattie turned back toward the shop so she could compose herself. If she hadn't, she would have been unable to conceal the smile finding David on her doorstep prompted.

* * * *

Although David anticipated Hattie's baked goods, it was the woman he came to see. With the rain, he'd spent needed hours at the parsonage as well as the church. In doing so, he realized how much he missed seeing Hattie.

It amazed him how she'd became so important to him in such a short period of time. He hadn't expected to find a woman his own age, without the attachment of a husband and children.

"I've got your coat right here if you'd like to try it on," Hattie remarked as she crossed the room carrying the coat on a heavy wooden hanger.

David took it and smiled when he saw the lining. Instead of the silver gray silk with which she'd lined the vest, he saw a hint of red flash from inside the coat.

"I'm sorry about the lining," Hattie said, a hint of laughter in her voice. "I planned to use the gray, like the vest, but I didn't have enough. What I had was this red with the gold fleur de lis pattern. If you don't like it…"

"Of course I like it," David interrupted, running his hand over the fine silk. "As I recall, I told you most of my wardrobe was on the flamboyant side. I must admit I was dreading wearing black for the majority of the time. This should spice things up."

Hattie's laughter reminded David of the trill of the wrens that nested outside his mother's kitchen window. "Do you find something funny?"

"I never expected a minister to want to spice anything up. As I recall Jonathan was a good man, but he was dry as dust. Black suited him very well. I only used the red on your coat as an emergency measure."

"Emergency?"

"I wanted you to have the coat and not have to wait for my next shipment of gray to come in."

David took a minute to study the red silk lining. "As far as I'm concerned," he replied, "it never needs to get here. The red suits me just fine."

Hattie raised her eyebrows at his statement and then watched as he tried on the coat. He enjoyed the feel of her fingers as she traced the shoulder seams and assessed the fit.

"It's a real shame," she said, once she took a step back.

"What do you mean?"

"The fit is perfect. I'm afraid this will need no further alterations. That means there will be no reason for you to visit the shop."

"What about all the other suits I ordered?"

"Oh David, you must realize you don't need so many black suits. One for summer and one for winter are plenty. I've given your wardrobe a lot of thought, and your tailor in Philadelphia was right. Just by looking at you it's easy to see you wear colors well. It would be a shame to let such expensive garments become food for the moths. I think you should wear them."

"Are you trying to save me money or are you telling me the truth?"

"I've been accused of a lot of things in my life, David Long," Hattie declared. "As far as I can remember though, no one has ever called me a liar before today."

David was taken aback by her outburst. "I didn't mean it that way. I could tell by the look on your face the other day you were concerned about my extravagant taste. I assure you, I do have the ability to pay for the things I ordered."

A look of shock reflected in Hattie's eyes. "Money was the last thing on my mind. I may not be one of your most pious parishioners, but I do not lie. I do agree with your tailor in Philadelphia. You are a big man, so why hide behind drab colors? I have an eye for style and color. That and playing the piano are my only talents."

Color rose in Hattie's cheeks making David wonder if it were from anger or something else. Even the expression in her eyes suddenly changed. What had caused such a metamorphosis?

"Aren't you going to say something?" Hattie spoke, silencing his thoughts.

"About what?" David said.

"About your wardrobe," she replied.

He knew it wasn't what she meant, but since he had no idea of what else she could mean, he said nothing about his suspicions.

"I've been giving it some thought as well," he finally said. "I agree, it's a shame to let such expensive clothing get moth eaten. I even broached the subject to a couple members of the church council. Starting on Sunday, I will be wearing a more colorful wardrobe."

The smile returned to Hattie's eyes. Whatever it was that concerned her earlier, apparently disappeared as quickly as it came.

"Well, now that our business is concluded," she said with a wink, "could I interest you in a piece of coffee cake and a cup of coffee?"

David's mouth literally watered at the suggestion. "It seems to me that was part of the reason for my visit this morning. I would very much like to sample some of your fresh baked goods."

* * * *

Hattie's hands shook as she went about the rest of her day's work. David's early morning visit left her shaken in more ways than one.

How could she have let it slip that she was a non-believer? Thank goodness he hadn't picked up on her mistake. Or had he? At the time, he'd been bewildered, but would her words become clear to him later in the day or even in the week?

As much as she didn't want to admit it, David Long was becoming very important to her. Just seeing him at her door this morning made her smile uncontrollably.

She couldn't let David become important to her. She remembered what it was like growing up with Pa. Did she want the rest of her life to be like that?

Hattie couldn't even formulate a silent answer. The memory of her father was too painful. Whenever he came home drunk, he would beat her for some imagined wrongdoing while he'd been gone. "Vengeance is mine, sayeth the Lord," he would declare.

Those words always accompanied the severe beating she endured and were followed by a recitation of Bible verses all degrading women. In her father's eyes, women were a necessary evil, a blight on the face of the earth. It was sinful she'd been born a weak girl child and not a boy who could help with the farm work and carry on the glorious Fairchild name.

If David's God in any way resembled the God of her father, she wanted no part of religion. Even though she found David's sermons hard to ignore, she was reluctant to believe fully. She didn't want to become like the people who turned away when Pa made her life a living hell on earth. The good people of Mortonville went to church on Sunday morning and condoned Hank Fairchild's drinking as well as the way he treated his family for the rest of the week.

* * * *

Throughout the week, the churchwomen continued to come at noon, but now they were teaching him to cook. Day by day he'd shown them what a quick learner he was.

Today, he arrived home just in time to be greeted by Maude and her recipe for fried chicken. He'd amazed her by adding a few of his mother's special touches.

By the time she left, David knew his lessons would soon come to an end. It wouldn't take long for word to spread that the new minister knew more about cooking than he let on.

David was just preparing his supper when he recalled the strange conversation he'd engaged in with Hattie. What had he said that changed her mind so quickly?

As soon as the thought crossed his mind, he realized it was nothing he'd said or even done. Hattie's own words were what caused her such distress. As he recalled she said something about not being the most pious of his parishioners.

When he first arrived, he'd questioned Hattie's faith. Even as he did, he'd wondered about his assumptions. From all accounts, Hattie was a proper lady. How could she play the piano so beautifully on Sunday morning and not believe?

* * * *

The next morning David paid a visit to George's store. Of all the people in his congregation, the one he knew he could trust was George.

"Can we talk?" David said, once he and George were alone.

"Of course, David. Let's go over to the church. Ruth can take care of things here."

David waited while George took off his shopkeeper's apron and told Ruth where he was going.

"This conversation wouldn't have anything to do with Hattie, would it?" George inquired, once they were seated in one of the pews.

"It would. I've made no secret of the fact I'm interested in her, socially."

"So, what do you want to know?"

"Does she believe?"

George looked at him as though he didn't understand the question. "I've known Hattie all my life, but I don't know how to answer your question. Her Pa was a real Bible thumper. He was a self-proclaimed preacher. When I was a kid, he'd spout scripture in the tavern to anyone who would listen. For that reason alone, I'd say she was a believer. Of course, if I'd have had to endure the beatings that girl took from Hank Fairchild, I don't know if I'd put much store in God."

"Yet she comes to church. She even plays for services."

"Abe went to church every Sunday. He even donated large sums of money. All it meant was he did what was expected of him. Anyone who knew him, understood that in his home he practiced the Jewish faith. Until Hattie took over the shop it was never open on Saturday. That was Abe's Sabbath."

"Do you think it's an act with Hattie?"

"Your guess is as good as mine. I think it's something you should ask her."

David remained at the church long after George left. Hattie's lack of faith, if indeed it was lacking, should bother him. Instead it intrigued him. He wanted to know more about the self-proclaimed preacher who raised her and perhaps turned her from the love of God. Then and only then could he help her find the love she needed.

* * * *

For a Friday, the shop was uncharacteristically quiet. One or two customers had been in to pass the time of day and discuss the cost of new dresses, but no one was serious about buying.

Hattie was just getting ready to put the Closed sign in the window so she could enjoy her noon meal when a large shadow fell across her work area. When she looked up she saw David enter the shop, a wicker basket clasped in one of his big hands.

"Do you have plans for dinner?"

The heat generated by her blush surprised her. At her age blushing was usually a thing of the past. Since David Long came to town, she seemed to do it more and more often.

"I was just closing up so I could fix something."

"Good. I brought us a picnic."

Hattie looked from the basket, to David's rain splattered shoulders, to the steady downpour outside her window.

"Don't you think we'll get wet?"

"It wasn't raining when I started over here. Could we eat in your kitchen?"

Hattie giggled. "Why not?"

In all her life, no young man ever suggested she accompany him on a picnic. She had nothing to fear. Yesterday's comment certainly went unnoticed by David.

Once in her spacious kitchen, David unpacked cold friend chicken, a jar of baked beans, and a jar of watermelon pickles. Hattie's contribution was a half pan of brownies from this morning's baking.

"Which of the ladies of the church do I have to thank for this delicious looking meal?" she said, after setting the table with her everyday dishes and silverware.

"The good ladies are teaching me to cook. The beans are courtesy of Ruth. Yesterday, Maude decided to teach me how to fry chicken. I think she discovered my secret of already knowing how to cook. I guess it was a day for disclosing secrets."

For a moment, Hattie's heart froze in her chest, and her stomach roiled uncontrollably. David knew. Since that was the case, why was he here? For that matter, why was he smiling?

Without saying more, David seated himself at the table. After saying grace, he began filling his plate. Half-heartedly, she followed suit. One taste of the chicken told her Maude hadn't fried it.

"This isn't Maude's chicken," she observed.

"I added a few of my mother's special touches. I'm afraid they ended my lessons."

"You didn't come here to exchange recipes, did you?"

David reached across the table and clasped her hand. "I could say I came to see you."

"But you won't, because it's not the truth."

"I wouldn't go that far. I did come to see you, but I also think we need to talk. I'm concerned about you. Help me understand why you don't believe."

Hattie pulled her hand from David's grip and then pushed her chair from the table. She took her plate of half-eaten food to the sink and stood staring out the window at the now steadily falling rain.

"Do you have someone else in mind to play for Sunday services?" she finally said.

To her surprise, she felt David's hands resting on her shoulders before he turned her to face him. "Is that why you think I came?"

"Are you going to tell me you aren't concerned about my non-belief?"

"No. It concerns me greatly, but it's no reason to replace you at the piano. It is also no concern of anyone, but you and me. I want to help you find God."

"How do you want to help? Do you want to use a willow switch or will your bare fists do the job for you? I can tell you, I've been beaten by the best, and I know every Bible verse about how women should be fed to the dogs."

Defiantly, she turned her face upward to look into David's eyes. To her amazement, he was crying. She'd never seen a man shed tears before.

"My poor dear Hattie," David said, taking her in his strong arms. "What did your father do to you? How could anyone claim to love the Lord and at the same time beat a child?"

The warmth of David's embrace fought against the chill of her father's bitter words within her mind.

'Spare the rod and spoil the child,' her father's voice echoed trying to defeat David's love. For once, Hattie wasn't listening.

"Parents beat their children, that's how they learn right from wrong," Hattie replied, repeating the logic her father taught her from infancy.

"No, Hattie, parents spank their children as punishment. A swat on the behind never endangered a child's life. A beating on the other hand, is never acceptable. Our Lord loved the little children and rebuked his disciples when they sent them away."

"But God says vengeance is his."

"Only if his words are taken out of context. Give God a chance, Hattie. Let me help you find the way."

David's words frightened her. She couldn't control the tremors that took over her body. "I ... I don't know, David. Maybe God doesn't want me. My own pa told me I wasn't his choice in a child often enough. What if God feels the same way?"

"God loves you unconditionally. All He asks is for you to open your heart and listen to His word. Are you willing to open your heart, Hattie?"

David's question should have troubled her. Instead, the trembling ceased. In its place, a soothing warmth captured the coldness of her heart.

'You're only a woman, Hattie,' her father's voice echoed in memory, as though trying to drown out David's logic. 'Women ain't nothing more than the Lord's leavings. Their only purpose in life is to pleasure a man. Married or single, they're all the same whores and sluts. The married ones just ply their trade legally.'

The tremors started anew.

"What's wrong, Hattie?" David held her more protectively against his chest.

"It's Pa's words. No matter what you say, they won't go away."

"Tell me about them."

She allowed him to guide her away from the kitchen and take her across the hall to the parlor. Once seated on the divan, he took her trembling hands between his. Although she was suddenly chilled, David's touch was warm and comforting.

"Let me into your world. Tell me about the demons that torment you."

"Oh, David, you can't...You don't want me in your church. I'm only a woman. Pa said women are the Lord's leavings. The only thing they know is to be whores and sluts. I've tried so hard, but even though he's been gone all these years, he won't leave me alone or let me forget it."

As soon as she spoke the words, they seemed to lose their hold over her.

"Did he take you to church when you were a child?"

David's voice sounded far away, making Hattie open her eyes to assure herself he still sat at her side. Once convinced he hadn't left her, she shook her head no.

"Church and God are for men folk," she replied, again repeating the words she'd heard her father say so often.

"But you've seen women in church."

Unable to think for herself, she continued giving voice to her father's opinions. "Their men are too weak to make them stay in the house where they belong."

"Why do you go to church?"

"At first it was because Abe said it was good for business. When George's father asked me to play the piano, I seized the opportunity. Where else in town could I do something I so loved and have others hear my music. I certainly would never set foot in the tavern. That was Pa's favorite place. I wanted no reminders of him."

"I still don't understand," David said when she stopped to take a breath. "How could you attend church every Sunday for five years and not get something out of the sermons?"

Hattie thought for a moment. A complete stranger was uncovering her innermost secrets. It was something no one had ever done in the past.

Before she could answer David's question, a flash of lightening illuminated the entire room. It took less time than a heartbeat for the clap of thunder to rattle the dishes in the china closet. The sheer force of the storm made her jump.

No sooner had Mother Nature unleashed her fury than the mantle clock struck one.

"I should reopen the shop," Hattie said, pleased for an excuse to end the conversation with David.

"No one will be out in this weather. If you feel you must reopen, we can continue our conversation in your shop."

Hattie signed deeply. It was as though even nature was on David's side. No one in their right mind would brave this storm to stop at the shop today. On this Friday afternoon, her friends and neighbors would be content to stay indoors and watch the magnitude of the storm from their windows.

"We might as well get comfortable. I have a feeling this is going to be a long afternoon. Would you like some coffee and brownies?"

Hattie was about to get to her feet when David stopped her. "The dessert can wait. You haven't answered my question."

"I'll answer you, but you might not want to hear what I have to say."

"That sounds mysterious. Since I enjoy a good mystery, do you plan to tell me now or make me wait?"

"Perhaps it's best if I show you," she replied, getting to her feet. This time David didn't stop her. She crossed the room to the bookcase built into the wall of the parlor.

In front of her, the floor to ceiling shelves were filled with books. Classical novels from generations past mingled with modern works. Some of the books belonged to her, others to Abe. She'd read dozens of them over the past five years, but still had more to read before she was finished.

"You know I carry lemon oil in my bag on Saturday. On Sunday mornings my music bag contains a book. When Jonathan was our preacher, I had no trouble reading during his sermons, especially when my piano was in the balcony."

To her surprise, David began to laugh. "Maybe I should check out some of these titles. I do hope they're appropriate reading for a proper lady like you. As for your piano being moved from the balcony, you must admit, it sounds better in its current location."

The storm outside raged with a fury while inside the tension seemed to drain. Hattie's worst nightmares. Her worst fears had come to life and for some unknown reason the world hadn't come to an end.

* * * *

David looked over the titles on Hattie's bookshelves. Homer's Odyssey shared shelf space with Uncle Tom's Cabin.

"If these books helped you ignore Reverend Hill's sermons," he said. "What do you do to ignore mine, since you're no longer hidden away in the balcony?"

"You're not an easy man to block out. Believe me, I've tried. The first Sunday, I opened my book, but never read a word. Of course, you know what happened last Sunday. Since I couldn't read, I tried the mind games I used when Abe first suggested I go to church, only they didn't work."

Before David could say more, another flash of light illuminated the storm-darkened sky. This time there was no time lag between the lightening and the accompanying thunder. He knew the strike had to be close.

With the wind and driving rain, a branch broke off from the maple tree across the street and shattered the front parlor window. To David's horror, it had been driven with such force it hit Hattie on the temple, knocking her unconscious.

Uncertain exactly what to do, he prayed for help. As though God guided his hand, David scooped Hattie into his arms and carried her away from the destruction of the storm to the security of her bedroom.

The cut on her forehead bled profusely, mingling its bright red life flow with her neatly piled red hair.

From the pitcher beside the bed, he poured water into the basin. On the side of the washstand he saw a linen towel and dipped it in the water so he could bathe the cut.

"Hattie! Hattie where are you?"

David recognized George's voice as well as those of several other members of his congregation.

"We're in the bedroom," David called back, without thinking of how damning the words sounded. "Hattie's been hurt."

From nowhere the room filled with people, all concerned for Hattie's wellbeing as well as his presence at her bedside.

"What happened?" George said.

"I think that last bolt of lightning hit the maple tree across the street. One of the branches came through the parlor window and hit Hattie. She's lost a lot of blood."

"It's the Lord's doing you were here," Ed declared. "I've already sent someone for the doctor. The storm has passed. We'll start repairing the damage immediately."

For the first time, David realized the rain had stopped. Dear Lord, he prayed. Did you send the storm to bring Hattie closer to you? If so, why did you allow her to be injured? Keep her safe and give me the strength to bring her into your loving embrace.

Chapter Eleven

Hattie awoke to a pounding headache and the sound of hammering coming from somewhere close enough to be in her house, mingled with the buzz of conversation.

Unwilling to open her eyes because of the throbbing pain, she forced herself to finish the process of waking. To her surprise, her bedroom was semi-darkened and the hammering sounded even closer than it had during the milky period between sleep and full consciousness.

As her eyes adjusted to the dim light, she recognized Maude sitting on one of the dining room chairs. She couldn't help but wonder who would have brought it into the bedroom.

"Maude?" Hattie whispered. The hoarseness of her voice came as a shock, as did the extremely dry mouth she was experiencing.

"Oh, Hattie, you've been asleep for so long. I didn't think you'd ever wake up."

"What's going on?" Hattie's voice grew stronger with each word. "Did I hear voices?"

Hattie looked past Maude to see David enter the room. She wondered why he looked so tired. For that matter, what were Maude and David doing in her house?

As she watched, Maude got up from the chair and left the room. Once she was gone, David took her place.

"What's going on?" Hattie repeated the question she'd asked Maude moments earlier.

"How much do you remember?"

Hattie closed her eyes and tried to concentrate. As she did, the horror of David uncovering her darkest secret brought on fear, followed by the peaceful memory of David's quiet understanding. Instead of terror, she experienced a warm feeling she had never expected.

"You brought over a picnic and then asked about my disbelief. What I don't understand is why I'm in bed and who is making all that noise?"

"There was a bad storm. It wasn't a twister, but close enough for me," David said, filling in the gap in her memory. "The maple tree across the street was struck by lightning. A limb came through the parlor window and hit you in the head. That was yesterday afternoon."

"Yesterday?" Hattie blinked.

David nodded. "Your friends and neighbors have been repairing the damage ever since. The doctor said you'd probably sleep through the night, but I didn't believe him. The ladies of the church took turns sitting with you so you wouldn't wake up alone."

"If it's morning, why is it so dark?"

"The storm moved past yesterday, but another one formed and has been pelting us with rain since just before dawn. That's why everyone was in such a rush to get your roof repaired to say nothing of the front window."

Although Hattie had dozens of questions, she fought the urge to go back to sleep.

"That's right, Hattie," David urged. "Sleep is the best thing for you. I'll be here when you wake up and will answer all your questions."

With each word, David's voice sounded farther and farther away. Before he finished speaking, she drifted off to sleep.

* * * *

David waited until Hattie's breathing became even as she slipped into a deep sleep. Once he was assured she slept peacefully, he returned to the parlor where the men were working on the repairs.

"You look tired, Reverend," Ralph observed. "I know you've been up all night. Now that she's awake, why don't you go in the spare bedroom and get some sleep."

David shook his head no. Somehow this tragic accident had been his fault. If he hadn't confronted Hattie, she would have been in the shop,

97

away from the danger of the falling limb.

Was God testing him? He only wanted to bring Hattie into God's loving arms. Instead, he almost lost her.

"I agree with Ralph," George declared. "You look beat. Maude told me about Hattie waking up and knowing who you were. It's a good sign. It would be a better sign if you were to get some rest now. It won't do anyone any good if you were to get sick too. There's no sense in sending you out in this storm, though. I doubt Hattie will care if you catch some sleep here."

David knew protesting would do no good. In the short time he'd been in town, these people had become his close friends. They cared about him as much as the people in Philadelphia. Perhaps even more. Philadelphia was a big town. This was a close-knit community.

Reluctantly, he left the parlor and made his way to the spare bedroom. A glance toward the room where Hattie slept told him Maude had returned to the chair next to the bed.

From the kitchen, he could smell the food the other women were preparing. Even though he'd eaten nothing since the chicken yesterday at noon, the smell of soup simmering on Hattie's stove turned his stomach.

Once he closed the door and lay down on the bed, his body relaxed against the softness of the mattress. Sleep came quickly and with it dreams.

Instead of Hattie's unconscious form in his arms, she was standing in front of him, willing to allow him to hold her, the way a man holds a woman. As he did, he realized how perfectly her petite form fit against his larger frame.

You were sent to Mortonville to save Hattie, a strange voice sounded above the visual picture his dream painted. *You must do this for two reasons. The first is for Me. I want her to know My love. The second is for you. I created man and gave him woman as his helpmate. Hattie is the woman I made for you. The road to winning her love for both of us will not be an easy one, but it will be worth the journey.*

When the voice became silent, the dream faded as well. Once it was gone, David drifted into a deep and peaceful sleep.

* * * *

"You are one very lucky lady, Hattie," Dr. Connors said, as he changed the bandage on her head.

She winced in pain when he touched the injured area. "You have a strange conception of lucky, Doc. My definition of the word doesn't include this pain."

"Sarcasm doesn't become you. When I said you were lucky I meant it. If you'd been alone it's hard telling what would have happened to you. It's a good thing Reverend Long was here when that limb came through the window."

Hattie nodded. There was no reason to say anything about why David was here. The last thing she needed was for her friends and neighbors even to guess she didn't believe the same way they did.

"Now," Dr. Connors continued, "I want you to stay in bed for at least the next three to four days."

"Three to four days?" Hattie echoed, sitting up as though she planned to get out of bed right then and there.

As she did, she regretted the action. Not only did it make her head throb as though some wild Indian was using it as his drum, but she immediately became dizzy. Before she continued, she sank back against the pillows.

"Who will play for services tomorrow? As I recall, when Harriett Baumgartner died there was no one other than myself who could or would do it."

"Not to worry," David said, stepping from behind Dr. Connors. "I'll be playing tomorrow morning."

"You?" Hattie struggled to get to a sitting position. Once she was almost there, a wave of dizziness overcame her forcing her back against the pillow. "I thought you said you couldn't play."

David's smile was unnerving. "You misunderstood what I said. I told you I wasn't my mother's prize student. I never said I didn't learn. Playing the piano isn't something at which I'm perfect, but I can fill in when needed."

"Like your ability to cook?" she said.

"Something like that," David replied.

Hattie closed her eyes. She could tell it would do no good to argue with either Dr. Connors or David. For the first time in five years, she would not be going to church on Sunday morning. In five years, no one else played for the congregation. The negative thoughts running through her mind brought stinging tears to her eyes.

"Don't cry, Hattie," David said, as though he thought the words would in any way soothe her torment.

She felt his weight on the mattress moments before he took her hand in his.

"If you're worried about missing my sermon, I'll be pleased to come over and repeat it for your tomorrow afternoon."

Hattie almost choked on her tears at his suggestion. "You're going to do what?"

"It doesn't matter what anyone is planning to do," Dr. Connors said. "Hattie, you need to rest. I've talked to the ladies and they've already set up a schedule so you won't be alone for the next few days."

"Is that necessary?" Hattie protested. "In my entire life no one has ever taken care of me."

"Then this will be a new experience. You will do as I say. Never fool with a head wound,"

"I agree with the doctor," David said. "From what I've heard, you're a very independent woman. I've decided to spend as much time as possible here making certain you don't give the ladies too much trouble. Now, close your eyes and get some rest. I'll be going home soon. Since I'm convinced you're going to be all right, I can use some sleep. I'll be back tomorrow after church."

"When you do," Hattie remarked, "don't bring over your sermon. I don't think I'm up to listening to it." Her comment met with hearty laughter from both David and Dr. Connors.

"I think your patient is on the mend," David said. "Her tongue is just as sharp as her wit."

Hattie fell asleep listening to David's deep voice, as he continued talking to Dr. Connors. As soon as sleep overtook her, dreams followed. In them, David held her hand and whispered comforting words in her ear. His touch combined with his words to make her feel like a beautiful young girl.

'You're not good enough for a preacher, Hattie,' her father's drunken voice drowned out David's words. 'No man in his right mind would want an old maid.'

"Don't listen to him, Hattie," David shouted to be heard over her father's ranting.

* * * *

"Who is staying here tonight?" David spoke, once he was assured Hattie slept peacefully.

"I think it's best if it's my wife and me," Dr. Connors replied. "I also think you should spend the night here as well."

"Me? Why?"

"Because I've been watching you these last two days. I can count the number of hours of rest you've had on one hand. I won't even go into what you've had to eat. You won't eat or rest if you go home. If you stay here I can keep my eye on you and give you something for sleep."

Dr. Connors' statement shocked David. He didn't think anyone noticed how he picked at the food the women served to the workers. As for his lack of sleep, he'd thought that had been concealed as well.

"Are you talking about a sedative?"

Dr. Connors nodded. "It's evident you're concerned about Hattie. We all are, but it's only natural for you to be more so, considering you were here when it happened."

David breathed a sigh of relief. It was one thing for Dr. Connors to equate his concern with being at Hattie's side when the accident occurred. It was quite another for him to guess at the feelings growing within him for her.

Before David could consider a relationship with Hattie, he would have to help her find the faith she so stubbornly ignored. God said it in David's dream earlier. The journey would not be an easy one.

As the brightness of day became the darkness of a starless, moonless night, the people who worked so diligently all day made their way home. When at last David was alone with Tom and Phyllis Connors, he ate enough to satisfy them before going to the room where Hattie lay in her bed.

"I'm surprised to see you here," Hattie said, when he entered the room. "It's gotten so quiet, I thought everyone went home."

"Doc and Phyllis are still here, and they asked me to spend the night as well."

"I don't see why. Everyone is blowing this out of proportion. I took a little knock on the head. I'll have a headache and a scar where Doc stitched me up, but I certainly don't need to be fussed over. For that matter, I can't understand why you're here."

"It seems Doc decided I'm his patient the same as you."

"But why?"

"That's what I asked. He tells me I'm not getting enough sleep."

"I only told you the truth," Dr. Connors said from behind him. "I came to tell you I have a sedative mixed up for you, so tell Hattie good night."

* * * *

"Why is David here?" Hattie questioned Phyllis.

"You really don't know, do you," Phyllis replied.

Hattie wished Phyllis wouldn't talk in riddles.

"By the look on your face, I guess I'll have to explain it to you. No one has been able to get Reverend Long to eat or sleep since the accident happened. He's very concerned about you. If you ask me, he's falling in love with you."

"He's what?" Hattie was completely shocked by Phyllis' statement.

"It's as plain as day to everyone but the two of you. He's very taken with you. The way I heard it, he even told the church council he planned to see you socially. If that doesn't tell you he's taken with you, what does?"

Tom returned to the room and indicated Phyllis should leave them alone. Once she left, Hattie looked up at her lifelong friend. "Is David sick?"

"I wouldn't say he's sick, in the usual sense of the word. He's worried sick. It's the reason he hasn't been eating or sleeping."

"I don't understand. What does he have to be worried about?"

"The same thing everyone in town is worried about. You could have been killed when that limb came through the window. You were unconscious longer than you should have been and it took seventeen stitches to close up the gash in your forehead. If that's not reason enough for people to worry, consider the fact David cares for you."

Hattie didn't reply. Instead, she accepted the beaker of medicine Tom held out to her. After drinking the sweet tasting liquid, she drifted off to sleep. For the first time in her life, she fell asleep with a smile on her lips. The thought of David caring about her was more than enough reason to smile.

Chapter Twelve

By Monday, Hattie was able to sit up in bed without feeling dizzy. To her disappointment, although she'd persuaded David to bring her the tatting shuttle and length of lace she was working on for the christening gown, she found herself unable to concentrate for more than a few minutes at a time.

"I wish you'd listen to the doctor," David said, when she put down her handwork in disgust. "He told you to stay in bed and rest for three to four days."

"I am in bed," Hattie protested. "I don't have much choice with you and half the town crammed into my house. I can only guess what kind of mess they are making out there."

"Fussing won't do you a bit of good. The doctor says you need rest, and it's my job to see you get it."

"You'd do better supervising the work in the parlor," she replied tartly.

Instead of the look of disgust she'd expected her comment to bring, David began to laugh. "I think you must be feeling better. You certainly are cranky. My mother always said it was a surefire sign of someone getting well."

Before Hattie could reply, Gertie hurried into the room. "The Lord does answer prayers!" she exclaimed, waving a sheet of paper in her hand.

"Just what are you prattling about?" David said.

"The other day, Hattie and I were talking about all the work she has

104

piled up," Gertie began. "I suggested writing to my sister in Ohio. Well, here's the reply. It seems there's a young widower named Thaddeus Newlin in her town who has been doing piecework for the local tailor. Hattie knows how it is with piecework. It seems the young man has a three-year-old daughter to care for and support. He needs something more permanent."

"Is he willing to move here?" Hattie was unable to hide her excitement.

"Minnie says this is just the opportunity he's been looking for. I talked to Herman and he said as long as the men are working on your repairs, they could easily build on an addition so the little girl could have her own room."

"You can't mean to move him in here?" David interrupted.

"Where else would they stay?" Hattie was unable to hide her amazement at David's sudden burst of jealousy.

"Certainly not here," David protested. "It wouldn't be proper."

"It would be just as proper as when I moved in here with Abe. At the time, he needed a housekeeper and a partner. It's the same now. I need help and this Thaddeus is in need, too. As I see it, I'm repaying the debt I owe to Abe."

"Repaying a debt, indeed," David muttered, as he got to his feet and left the room.

* * * *

David went into the kitchen, only to find several women busy preparing diner. The last thing he needed was to have to make polite conversation. For now, he wanted to be alone.

After exchanging the necessary pleasantries, he went out the back door and down to the creek. He needed the solitude to set his thoughts straight.

Ever since he arrived in Mortonville, everyone told him how Hattie needed help. Why, now that Gertie found a solution to Hattie's problem, did it upset him?

He knew the answer. It wasn't because Hattie was getting help. It was the fact the help came from a young man who would be sharing Hattie's home. It wasn't right.

Thaddeus Newlin wasn't a man old enough to be her father, like Abe Levens. If he had a three-year-old child and Gertie's sister called him a young widower, he could prove to be someone who could win Hattie's heart.

He was only thinking of Hattie's reputation.

Was he? Was he thinking of Hattie's reputation or his feelings? Did this man intimidate him? Was he afraid Hattie would choose him instead?

David shook his head to rid himself of his negative thoughts. Hattie deserved the help. It only made sense that she would feel obligated to open her home to this young man and his daughter, the way Abe did for her.

Yes, David, the voice he'd come to equate with God seemed to say. *Hattie is doing her Christian duty. It's your job to show her that is what's she'd doing. You must help her to understand I've been with her even though she considers herself a non-believer.*

The sound of someone calling his name jerked David back to reality. To his surprise, he was seated on the creek bank. He had no idea when he had sat down. From the position of the sun, David realized he'd been asleep for at least an hour or more.

"Where are you, Reverend?" Herman Kellogg called for a second time.

"I'm down by the creek," David replied. "I guess I fell asleep."

"Gertie sent me out here to get you for dinner. No one knew where you went, but one of the women in the kitchen said she saw you head out this way over an hour ago.

"I wanted to be alone for a while."

"To think on that young man Gertie's sister, Minnie, wrote to her about, I'll bet. I read the letter. He sounds like a nice young man and I do mean young. Minnie says he's only twenty-one. If you ask me that's too young to be raising a baby alone."

Thaddeus' age came as a shock to David. At twenty-one, he would have had no idea how to be a husband to say nothing of a father. No matter what his feelings about the man who might be sharing Hattie's home, he had to give the boy credit. Without a wife, raising a child must not be an easy task.

* * * *

Hattie read the letter from Gertie's sister over for the third time. Thaddeus was a young man who needed as much help as he could get.

As terrible as her childhood had been, she couldn't begin to imagine being orphaned at the age of five and forced into an apprenticeship he probably didn't want.

The letter said Thaddeus fell in love with his employer's daughter. When the girl died in childbirth, his father-in-law not only fired Thaddeus, but refused to see the little girl who lived when her mother died.

"You must have that memorized by now," Gertie declared.

"I'm just trying to decide what to do. I think I've finally come to a decision. I have enough money put aside to cover the cost of the train tickets for them to get here. Will you take care of it for me?"

"Are you certain, Hattie? Herman and I were planning to loan him the money for his fare."

"That's very nice of you, but it's not necessary. I planned to pay for my sister and her family if she would have taken me up on my offer to move here. Since she didn't, the money is still there to be used for Thaddeus."

* * * *

Even though Hattie was able to get up and around by Thursday, there was no way she could go to the station to meet Thaddeus' train.

As David drove his carriage toward the station, he wondered how Hattie managed to talk him into doing this. He'd just tied Thor to the hitching rail when the train whistle broke the silence of the morning. The sound of it brought to mind the memory of his own arrival, only weeks earlier.

At that time, he'd known what his future held and what was expected of him. For this young man the prospect of coming to a new town, to meet people who would hold his future in their hands must be frightening.

If David had any qualms about recognizing Thaddeus, they were dissolved as soon as the young man got off the train. He was very tall and painfully thin. The little girl who held his hand looked as though she would cry at any moment.

"Mr. Newlin?" David said as he crossed the platform to close the gap between himself and the newcomers.

"Yes," the young man replied. "I expected to be met by Miss Fairchild."

"That's a long story. I'm David Long, the minister here in Mortonville. Hattie asked me to meet you. As soon as your bags are unloaded, I'm to take you over to the shop."

"We have our bag," Thaddeus said, indicating the small valise he carried in the hand that wasn't holding his daughter.

"Just one bag for the two of you?"

"It's all we need. We don't have much. Minnie's sister made this offer sound too good to be true."

"It's true," David assured him. "You'll find Hattie to be a very fair woman. She's opening her home to you and your daughter. In return, she will expect you to assist her in the shop. She has a good business, but she needs help."

Thaddeus nodded and followed David across the platform to the waiting carriage. David thought about asking to carry the valise, but decided against the idea. It was apparent Thaddeus was a proud young man.

The cut of the young man's suit had not escaped David's scrutiny either. If it were any indication of the quality of the man's work, Hattie made the right decision in sending for him to help her.

* * * *

Hattie paced the newly repaired parlor. The steady stream of townspeople who helped in restoring her home as well as adding on the third bedroom and fencing in the backyard dwindled to a mere trickle. Today, only a few people came to help in the placement of the new furniture in the room they'd built for the little girl who would soon arrive.

The smell of the new paint, that at first nauseated Hattie, now made the house smell fresh. Everything from bedding to curtains had been either quickly made or donated. It was the type of room any little girl would enjoy having. It certainly didn't resemble the loft where Hattie slept throughout her entire childhood.

The bell above the shop door jingled merrily, signaling David's arrival with Thaddeus and his daughter, Samantha.

"Is this our new house, Papa?"

The sound of a child's voice thrilled Hattie. At her age, she knew the only children she'd be allowed to enjoy would belong to others.

"Yes, Sammy, this is our new home."

"You should withhold judgment on it until you see more than the shop," David said.

Hattie wondered if she heard tension in David's voice. When she first asked him to meet the train, she hadn't considered his strange behavior when the letter from Minnie first arrived. Could the women who insisted he was jealous possibly be right?

The trio who entered the parlor portrayed a picture in adversity. David's sheer bulk overshadowed the young man at his side. Thaddeus was almost as tall as David, but he was so thin it made Hattie almost cry. In contrast, the child was as near to perfect as a child could be. Her hair had been as carefully combed as anyone could, considering the mass of unruly brown curls covering her head. Her dress was a miniature replica of a high fashion gown. Her blue eyes were wide with amazement at the size of the house behind the shop.

"Welcome," Hattie said, extending her hand to Thaddeus. "I'm so pleased you could see your way clear to accept my offer."

"It is me who should be saying such things to you. I owe you a great debt. In time, I will be able to explain everything to you. For now, I will find a way to repay you for the money you spent for our train tickets."

Hattie smiled. "Repayment is something that will never be spoken of again. When I needed a job, the man who built this business took a chance on me. When I, like you, suggested repaying him, he told me someday I'd be able to do the same for someone else. Today I've finally paid him back. In the future, I'm certain you'll do the same for someone else."

Thaddeus seemed to be at a loss for words as he pumped her hand vigorously. It didn't surprise her to see tears in his eyes. He was a young man who knew little of life but the bad. Hopefully, she could introduce him to the good side of things the way Abe did for her five years earlier.

"My name is Sammy," the little girl tugging at Hattie's skirt for attention declared.

Hattie stooped in front of the child so she could get down to her level. "It's nice to know you, Sammy. I'm certain I'll enjoy having another woman in my house. You can call me Aunt Hattie. Would you like to see your room?"

Sammy nodded.

"Good," Hattie said, getting to her feet. She held out her hand to the little girl. "If you come with me, I'll take you to see it. You're very lucky. When the people in town heard your daddy was coming to help me, they built you a beautiful new room."

Sammy looked up at her father as if waiting for his nod of approval before taking Hattie's hand.

* * * *

David watched as Hattie and Sammy left the parlor. Hattie looked so natural with the child in tow. David knew it wouldn't take long for her to become so attached to Sammy the age difference between Hattie and Thaddeus would no longer be an obstacle.

When Thaddeus started to follow Hattie, David stopped him. "Let Hattie have a few minutes alone with your daughter. I think we need to talk."

Thaddeus looked past David to follow Hattie and Sammy out of the room with his eyes. Once they were out of sight Thaddeus turned back toward the parlor and one of the overstuffed chairs placed on either side of the fireplace. After he seated himself, he clasped his hands in front of his as if waiting for a reprimand.

"Relax, Thaddeus," David began. "I only want to talk to you."

Thaddeus exhaled as though he'd been holding his breath. "I'd appreciate it if you called me Thad, Sir."

"Then Thad it is, but only if you call me David."

A smile crossed Thad's lips. As it did, David realized it was the first time he'd seen the young man smile at anything other than his daughter.

"If you want to tell me what a wonderful opportunity Miss Fairchild has offered me, you can save your breath. I know what she's giving me and I also know I don't deserve it. My father-in-law can tell you how little I deserve, since in his mind I killed his daughter.

Thad became so agitated David was sorry he'd suggested their talk. "I'm certain you misunderstood my intentions. I merely wanted to get to know you better."

"I'm sorry, sir … David. I'm not used to polite conversation."

"I gathered as much from the letter from Minnie Trapp. It can't be easy raising a child alone. Have you had anyone to help you?"

Thad shook his head. "When I got to Ohio, I knew piecework would be too little to support us, so I took a job cleaning a bank after they closed. It did grow into more work since several other businesses asked me to do the same for them. At first, Sammy was little enough for me to take her with me in a basket. Once she started walking, my landlady at the boarding house watched over her while I was gone."

David marveled at the young man. Although Thad looked as though he rarely ate enough, Sammy was the picture of health. It was evident Thad's efforts went toward his daughter rather than himself.

"Are there many children in your congregation, David?" Thad said when his previous statement met with silence. "I would certainly like it if Sammy had some playmates her own age. I'm afraid the boarding house was populated by older gentlemen who doted on her, but there were no children."

David ached for Sammy. His own childhood had been filled with games of tag, red rover, and hide and seek with his friends. He wouldn't have changed any part of those glorious days. It would be a shame if Sammy didn't have the same memories when she became a woman.

"You asked about church," David finally said. "Are you a religious man?"

"When my wife first died, I cursed God. I'm not proud of it, but I won't deny it. I grieved for three days and wouldn't even see my daughter. When I finally held her for the first time, I realized God entrusted me with my own personal miracle. From that day on, she's been my life, and I've thanked God for her."

"You'll be most welcome at church," David declared. "I'm certain Sammy will find several suitable playmates. There are even children her own age who live just a few houses away."

* * * *

111

Hattie picked up the valise Thad brought in with them and carried it into the pink and white room her neighbors had built and decorated for Sammy.

While the little girl excitedly explored her new bedroom, Hattie opened the case and began to unpack the clothes. It was hard to believe this child didn't have a mother. Each piece of clothing was neatly folded and packed in such a manner as to decrease wrinkling.

At the bottom of the case, Hattie found Thad's meager belongings. Besides two pair of pants and two shirts, she found a nightshirt and a pair of winter underwear. The thought of a tailor with such a limited wardrobe told her he'd spent every penny he earned to give his child the best life in his power.

By the time she finished hanging up the last tiny dress, Sammy had curled up on the bed, her thumb in her mouth. Her even breathing told Hattie the child was sleeping soundly. Since a light breeze ruffled the curtains, Hattie pulled a light blanket from the closet and put it over Sammy's sleeping form.

As quietly as possible, Hattie left the room and pulled the door shut behind her. After crossing the hall, she saw David and Thad engaged in conversation.

"The poor little lamb was completely exhausted. Before I knew it, she crawled up on the bed and fell asleep."

Thad looked up, an expression of relief in his eyes. "She was so excited she hardly slept on the trip here. If she took a nap without putting up a fuss she had to be tired."

"Speaking of tired, Hattie," David said. "You look beat, I'm afraid you've been trying to do too much. Why don't you relax, while I take the dinner the ladies left out of the oven?"

Hattie didn't argue. As excited as she was over the arrival of Thad and his daughter, the nagging headache screamed for her to rest.

Once she seated herself on the sofa, Thad got up from his chair and walked over to the piano. The way he lovingly ran his hands over the keys brought a smile to Hattie's lips.

"Do you play?"

"Not so anyone would want to listen. One of the only memories I have of my mother is her helping me play the notes. Before I could play well, she died. What I do know, I've picked up on my own. I guess you could say I play by ear."

Thad sat down on the piano bench and then looked at Hattie as if asked for her approval to play the piano. When she nodded, he began to play what many would consider a simple tune. To Hattie, it showed the young man had a talent, which hadn't been nurtured. She'd never considered giving anyone piano lessons, but as the notes swirled around her head, she knew she would enjoy tutoring not only Thad, but Sammy too.

* * * *

David picked up a pair of hot pads from Hattie's kitchen table before he retrieved the casserole dish one of the women put in the oven earlier in the morning.

The music coming from the parlor didn't carry Hattie's style, leaving him to believe it was Thad who played. The thought knotted his stomach with pangs of jealousy. He'd found yet another thing Hattie and Thad had in common.

"Something smells good," Thad said as he entered the kitchen.

Thad's comment startled David. He'd hardly realized the music stopped. "The ladies of the church have been very kind to Hattie since the accident. Is she coming out for dinner?"

Thad laughed. "I think she is as tired as Sammy. She's sound asleep in the parlor. You mentioned the accident on the way over here. How badly was she injured?"

"Dr. Connors said she should still be in bed, but keeping her down isn't an easy task. Of course, once you're living here and working with her every day, you'll see what I mean."

Thad looked at him strangely before pulling out a chair to sit down at the table. The gesture prompted David to do likewise. Before David could bow his head, Thad began the table grace.

"Dear Lord, we thank you for this, your bounty. I also thank you for sending Miss Hattie into my life. When the darkness of despair was threatening to destroy us, you provided. A-Men."

David raised his head, confused by the words of Thad's prayer. He waited until both he and the younger man had filled their plates and started eating to make comment.

"What did you mean?"

Thad looked up, his fork held in mid-air. "If I'm not mistaken you're talking about my prayer. I didn't say the words lightly. Until I got the wire saying Miss Hattie wanted me to come here to work with her, I was ready to give up. No matter how hard I tried, I knew I would never be able to provide the kind of life Sammy deserved. As hard as it was, I'd decided to try and find a family to take her. I knew she was young enough she wouldn't remember me. I figured it was best, since I prayed she'd have a loving mama and papa to raise her."

The tears running down Thad's cheeks touched David's heart. "Why would you give away your daughter, your flesh and blood?"

"I don't expect anyone to understand, but my most cherished memories are of the hours I spent sewing with her by my side. Unfortunately, to make enough money to support Sammy I had to leave her in the care of strangers. It wasn't right, but it was what I had to do. Just prior to receiving word of this position, my father-in-law found us. He said he would make certain Sammy was taken from me, because I couldn't be mama and papa to her. He was prepared to take legal action against me. I decided rather than put her through such a thing I'd give her away willingly. It was then I received Miss Hattie's offer and..."

"And you thought Hattie would be her mother as well as your wife," David said, interrupting Thad's narrative.

The look on Thad's face told David he'd said the wrong thing. Thad's eyes radiated disbelief at the accusation. "I ... I never considered such a thing. Miss Hattie's offer was a Godsend for me. It gave me the ability to give my daughter a good life and still be able to be with her. Over the past three years I've thought of marriage, but..."

"It's all right, Thad. You don't have to explain. I jumped to the wrong conclusion. I'm sorry. It's just..."

This time it was Thad who interrupted David. "It's just that you are fond of Miss Hattie. Do you love her?"

David began to smile. "I must be very transparent. I doubt if you'd call my feelings love, as I don't know her well enough to declare such a thing. I do care for her, though."

"Pardon my forwardness, David, but it's evident you do more than care for Miss Hattie. I assure you the last thing I would ever do is take advantage of my benefactor."

David's jealousy shamed him. "I guess you're right. Hattie is special to me. I shouldn't have jumped to the wrong conclusions."

Before Thad could reply, Hattie came into the kitchen. "I must have fallen asleep," she said as she entered the room. "Have I missed dinner?"

"We were just starting," David said, getting to his feet to hold Hattie's chair. "As soon as we eat, I think you should lay down for a proper nap, though."

To his surprise, Hattie didn't argue. Instead she nodded meekly and allowed him to fill her plate. David wondered if the feisty pianist had mellowed at the thought of having Thad and his young daughter to care for.

Chapter Thirteen

July's stormy weather gave way to August's hot dry days and sultry nights. For Hattie, the heat of late summer meant listening to Sammy as she played in the back yard.

Having Thad helping in the shop made her days go faster. At times, it seemed as though Abe's spirit was smiling down on her. He'd never meant for her to have to shoulder the load alone.

As for Thad's work, it was as good as either she or Abe ever did. Her customers were equally impressed and displayed their pleasure with more orders than Hattie ever saw in the past years.

In the evenings, she enjoyed playing the piano as she always had in the past, only now she tutored Thad and Sammy first.

The only thing to mar Hattie's new life was Thad's insistence on evening devotions. It all started innocently, with Thad sitting at the piano holding Sammy on his lap. He read to her from the worn Bible Hattie had found packed with his clothes, as though he was reading her a bedtime story. Not only did he read the passages, he explained them to Sammy so she could easily understand their meaning. As he told Hattie, he always read ahead after Sammy was asleep so he would have time to consider how to bring the story to life for his little girl the next evening.

At first Hattie tried to tune out Thad's voice by concentrating on her novel. She soon found Thad's explanation of the ancient words intriguing and started listening. Against everything she'd ever told herself, Hattie began to enjoy Thad's reading of the text her father often used to belittle her.

When David learned of Thad's evening devotions, he started dropping by to join them at least three times a week. His presence thrilled Thad and made Hattie uneasy.

She knew David would love nothing more than to see her embrace the God he preached about on Sunday morning.

"It's time for bed," Thad said once he finished the evening's reading.

"Do I have to?" Sammy protested.

Hattie smiled at the familiar exchange between father and daughter. The night would begin with Sammy going to bed in the pink and white room where she willingly took her naps. Sometime in the night, Sammy would make her way to the bed where her father slept.

Hattie knew why the little girl preferred her father's bed to her own. Memories of the nights she cried herself to sleep after Laura married and Hattie spent her nights alone in the loft were renewed by Sammy's night fears.

"She's in bed," Thad announced when he returned to the parlor. "It's anyone's guess as to how long she'll stay put."

"I can understand her not wanting to sleep alone," David said.

His statement took Hattie by surprise. In the weeks she'd known David, he'd spoken only of his parents, leading her to believe he was an only child.

"What do you mean?" Thad said, while Hattie still contemplated David's strange comment.

"I had an older brother He was twelve and I was eight when he died. If he'd lived, we would have been considered twins since we so closely resembled each other. Papa was thrilled with our size and decided Joe would follow in his footsteps. Joe liked working at the forge and, even though he was young, he learned to shoe horses. Unfortunately, it was his passion that killed him. He was shoeing a horse and got kicked in the head."

"How terrible," Hattie sympathized, as she dabbed at her eyes with the hankie from her apron pocket.

"It was. I remember being so lonely at night that every little sound frightened me. Being a boy, I didn't say anything to my folks about it, but I'm sure they knew."

"So is that why you became a lawyer?" Hattie replaced her hankie.

David nodded. "My father was insistent about me not being a blacksmith. Until God started talking to me, I thought it was what I wanted as well."

"In other words," Thad commented, "I shouldn't worry about Sammy crawling into my bed at night."

Hattie smiled. In trying to explain Sammy's strange behavior to Thad, they'd certainly gotten off the subject, she was glad they did. From the things David said, she knew much more about him than when the evening began.

"What we were getting at," Hattie finally remarked, "is that Sammy has slept with you all her life. Adapting to sleeping alone will take longer than a few weeks."

* * * *

By the time August ended and September began, the weather turned unseasonably cold. As Sammy's birthday came closer, Hattie spent her evenings making a sleepy doll for the child.

Ever since the conversation about Sammy not spending her nights in her bed, Hattie remembered the sleepy doll she'd had as a child. Even though she'd been certain her parents knew nothing of her night terrors, her mother gave her the doll. From that day forward, the loft hadn't seemed so lonely.

Finally the day of Sammy's birthday arrived. With it came three little girls from the church to help celebrate the event. Hattie finished frosting the cake she'd promised Sammy she would make and listened as the girls squealed at being caught during a game of blind man's bluff.

"Thank you," Thad said when he entered the kitchen.

"For what?" Hattie said.

"For bringing me here and treating Sammy the way a child deserves to be treated. This party is something I never would have thought of giving her."

Hattie beamed at the compliment. As a child she'd envied her friends in town when their parents fussed over birthdays and holidays. It always hurt to think no one ever fussed over her. The one time she'd asked to have friends over ended in a severe beating at the hands of her father.

"It was nothing. I hope she likes the doll."

"I just hope it works to keep her in bed at night."

Hattie laughed at Thad's comment. Since coming to Mortonville, he'd learned to appreciate the privacy of Sammy having a room of her own.

Before Hattie could respond, the little girls traipsed into the warm kitchen, their cheeks pink from playing in the crisp autumn air.

"Who wants cake?" Hattie said.

Four young voiced chimed, "I do," in unison.

Hattie put a slice of chocolate cake with boiled icing on each of four dessert places from her set of fine china. Earlier, she'd polished her silver and put a tiny dessert fork next to each plate. To go with the sweet treat, she poured hot apple cider into elegant teacups. After serving the children, Hattie cut slices of cake and poured cups of cider for herself and Thad.

When at last the little guests departed, Hattie went into her bedroom and brought out the sleepy doll she'd so lovingly crafted. Sammy's eyes went wide with surprise when she saw the doll wore a nightdress and cap.

"She's beautiful," Sammy declared. "What's her name?"

Hattie remembered calling her doll Laura, but it was not her place to name the doll. "What do you think she should be called?"

Sammy knotted her brows as if in deep thought. "I think I will call her Diana. My daddy says that was my mommy's name and she was very pretty."

* * * *

To everyone's surprise and delight, once Diana began sharing Sammy's bed, the child's late night trips to her father's bedroom ended.

"I don't know how to thank you," Thad said one night after Sammy went to bed "As much as I love my daughter, I do enjoy my uninterrupted sleep."

David began to laugh. "I can't say I blame you. It seems as though our dear Hattie has a solution for everyone's problems."

Hattie looked at David puzzled by his statement. "Just what problem did I solve for you?"

"By inviting me into your home to share devotions with you and Thad you saved me many lonely nights."

Hattie's stomach churched at his comment. Although she listened when Thad read each night, she still had doubts as to how the words applied to her.

"You know you're always welcome in my home. It even satisfies the good ladies of the church to think we aren't here alone since Thad and Sammy live with me."

Hattie found David's smile to be contagious. "I told you before, I got the approval of the council to see you socially."

"What do you mean the approval of the church council?" Thad said.

Hattie sat back and listened as David explained about the flap his first visit to her home caused. Even though David made light of the situation, it still made Hattie uneasy.

Before the Sunday when David came to dinner, her life had been very lonely. Hattie remembered the accusations Maude had made. How things changed in a matter of a few weeks. Thankfully, David stood up to the gossip and insisted the two of them keeping company wasn't anything sinful.

If the truth were known, if David hadn't been with her during the storm, she could have lain unconscious for hours before anyone found her. As much as Hattie insisted she needed to go back to the shop, she knew with the storm she would have stayed in the parlor. The day had been so dark, she couldn't have worked. The limb would have still come through the window, and she would have been injured.

"Isn't that right, Hattie?" David said, drawing her attention from her innermost thoughts.

"What? What did you say?" Hattie stared at him.

To her amazement, both David and Thad were laughing. "I couldn't resist," David admitted. "You were so lost in thought I knew you didn't hear a word of what we were saying."

Hattie didn't see what was so funny until she realized David and Thad weren't making fun of her, but were enjoying a good laugh shared between friends.

"I guess I must have portrayed quite a picture. I was thinking about all the changes in my life." To her surprise, David got up from the chair he usually occupied and came over to sit next to her on the sofa.

"Is there anything you want to talk to me about? We never did get a chance to finish our conversation on the day of the storm."

Hattie thought back to the day when she admitted to David she didn't really and truly believe in his God. Since then, little by little, she'd allowed the words of the Bible readings to slip through the small crack in her protective shell.

As though Thad thought his presence might make Hattie uncomfortable, he closed his Bible and got up from his chair by the fireplace. "It's been a long day," he declared. "I think I'll go to bed. Morning comes early."

Hattie waited until Thad left the room before she spoke. "When I was lost in thought, did you and Thad plan this?"

"Not really. He knows I've wanted to talk to you alone for quite some time. He also knows you've avoided being alone with me since he and Sammy arrived."

"I've avoided it because I know what you want to talk to me about. You're concerned about my faith or should I say my lack of it?"

She watched David's expression and knew she came very close to the truth behind his desire to talk.

"Guilty as charged," David replied. "We only scratched the surface before the accident. As much as I'd like to see your faith grow, I know it's something I can't push. I know you aren't reading your novels during my sermons, but are you listening to what God is telling you?"

Hattie sat back and collected her thoughts before answering. She knew changes were taking place in her life, but did the hand of God bring them about? Only David knew of her lack of faith. Only David could ask her these questions and expect honest answers.

"I don't know how to say this," she began. "I don't even know if you'll understand what I'm going to tell you."

"Try me," David replied. "I'm as new at this as you are, but we'll never know how much I understand if you don't confide in me."

David clasped Hattie's hand. To her surprise, the gesture put her immediately at ease.

"When I'm in church or Thad is reading at night I have a warm feeling. The only way to describe it is like when we're having a snowstorm and I'm sitting in front of the fireplace drinking hot cocoa. It's warm and soft and comforting." She paused to allow the impact of her words to penetrate fully.

"It sounds like the Holy Spirit is starting to work within you. By the tone of your voice, I'm willing to bet there's more."

Hattie lowered her eyes so they didn't meet his. "There's more. I have those feeling when I'm in church or with Thad and Sammy, but when I'm alone it's different. The verses I heard during the day are repeated in my dreams, only its Pa's voice saying them. No matter what the verses say. Pa uses them against me. When I wake up I know Pa is right. I'm not good enough to..." She left the last words unspoken. It was too painful to continue.

"God is working to help you, Hattie. Turning your life around isn't easy, especially when the past has such a tight grip on your mind, Eventually, God will ease the hurts but it will take time and patience. Your faith wasn't destroyed overnight. It won't be restored quickly."

Slowly, Hattie raised her head, until she met David's gaze. Instead of judgment, she saw understanding within the depths of his deep blue eyes.

Chapter Fourteen

The usually cold temperatures of September gave way to one of the most beautiful Indian Summers Hattie could ever remember. Cool nights became crisp autumn days with blue, cloud-free skies.

For Hattie, the attentions of David, the enthusiasm of Thad, and the sheer excitement of having a child in the house enhanced the beauty of the season. Instead of weekly trips to the church to pick up hymns, David often appeared at the shop just prior to closing and stayed for Saturday dinner. Once the dishes were washed, he usually suggested they take a walk along the creek or a carriage ride into the country.

It was just after dinner on a late October Wednesday when Maude bustled into the shop. By her manner, Hattie knew Maude had some gossip she could hardly wait to share.

"Can I get you a cup of coffee, Maude?" Hattie said, as she got up from her seat by the window.

"That would be nice," Maude replied, eyeing a plate full of brownies sitting on the table beside the stove.

"Here you go." Hattie handed Maude a full mug. Once she accepted the steaming cup of coffee, Hattie offered her a brownie.

"It certainly is nice you can take a few minutes to relax," Maude observed. "Everyone in town is raving about the quality of Thad's work."

"I doubt you came here to talk about Thad."

"Oh Hattie, you are so perceptive. I just heard Edna Mason's cousin's daughter is arriving from Philadelphia tomorrow."

"Isn't that nice," Hattie replied "I know how lonely Edna gets out at the farm. It's a shame she and Ralph never had children."

"Well, from what I hear, she's going to have her hands full with this girl. The word is she's in a 'family' way and there's no father. Of course the story Edna tells is that the girl's husband was killed in some sort of an accident, but I don't believe a word of it."

"Why not?"

"If she were a grieving widow, wouldn't you think she'd want to be close to her parents and in-laws when the baby is born? If you ask me, she's a girl in trouble, and her folks don't want anything to do with her."

Hattie ached for the young woman whose family considered her an embarrassment. She'd lived the life of an outcast in her own home for far too many years not to remember the feeling of loneliness.

"If that's the case, then it's good of Edna to give her a place to stay."

"Honestly, Hattie, I can't believe you'd say such a thing. If what I've heard is true, the girl sinned."

Hattie bit back the comment sitting on the tip of her tongue. As she recalled, Maude's first child was born less than six months after the wedding.

"Just what would you have the poor child do? Hattie said.

"That poor child as you call her was woman enough to get herself in a 'family' way. She should have insisted the man marry her."

"What if he refused? What should she have done then?"

Maude's expression told Hattie she had no answer.

"That was an interesting visit," Thad observed once the door slammed behind Maude.

"Her visits usually are," Hattie replied, as she picked up the dirty cup from the table.

"I didn't mean to overhear," Thad began, "but I do feel sorry for the girl, the same way you do. I know what it's like to be an outcast. Believe me, it wasn't easy for me being alone with Sammy. After my father-in-law fired me and refused even to see Sammy, everyone looked down on me for not having a wife to care for my daughter. Some people even said I murdered her by getting her pregnant."

Hattie shook her head. How could these people call themselves

Christians and behave in such a manner? Even though she'd never practiced any semblance of faith, she couldn't be so cruel to another person.

* * * *

By Sunday, Hattie heard more than one version of the story about Edna's cousin's daughter. Without turning around from her position at the piano, Hattie knew the exact moment when Edna and Ralph entered the sanctuary with their houseguest. The usual buzz of conversation that preceded the beginning of the service ceased abruptly.

Wanting to break the tension caused by the silence, Hattie began to play the prelude earlier than usual. As soon a she played the last note, David took his place in the pulpit.

As usual, Hattie's mind remained overactive. She and David had talked about the girl several times since Maude's Wednesday visit. David made it clear he would address the subject in this morning's sermon. Now she wondered how he could interpret such a sordid state of affairs into the message he hoped to impart.

"My sermon for today is based on the eighth chapter of John beginning with the first verse," David began.

As he read the words of the text, Hattie understood. She never thought David could find a passage in the Bible that would fit this situation. For the first time, she listened intently to what David had to say. She never heard the scriptures used as an excuse for sin before.

"In the story I just read," David continued, "the woman had committed adultery. We don't know if she was married or single, young or old. All we know is the neighbors were accusing her. She isn't shouting her innocence, so we must believe she was guilty. The Pharisees used this woman and her unlawful behavior to trap Jesus. Instead of being trapped, he turned their accusations against them.

"So how does this affect us in the nineteenth century? Well, the last time I looked, there was no one without sin. My biggest sin is overindulgence. Eating is not a sin, but I like to eat to excess."

Hattie laughed with the rest of the congregation when David patted his midsection for emphasis.

"My sin may not seem as great as that of the woman in the story, but

125

in God's eye it is still a sin. So, when our lord told the people that he who is without sin should cast the first stone, he knew no one in the crowd was sinless.

"Often we are quick to judge others without knowing all the facts. When we judge them, we tend to forget about our own faults.

"If nothing else sticks with you from today's sermon, let it be this, no one is without sin. Before you jump to conclusions about others, explore your own lives. In such circumstances, let God be the judge and jury, I don't mean that criminals should be allowed to roam free, only that we should be more tolerant of our neighbors when their lives are less than perfect."

When David concluded his sermon with the words A-men, a strange silence prevailed throughout the congregation. Hattie wondered how many of the people were contemplating David's words and searching their hearts to see if they were guilty of the charges he had just leveled against them.

Hattie respected the silence for a few moments longer than usual before she began to pay the hymn of the day. As she struck the first note, she became aware of the shuffling of feet and the flipping of the pages in the hymnals. She wondered if it was her imagination or if the friends and neighbors who stood behind her sang with more gusto than they ever had in the past.

Finally the service ended, and Hattie began to pack her music into her bag. She almost jumped when someone touched her shoulder.

Hattie turned to see a girl who looked no older than eighteen standing in front of her, If this girl was a widow, it was evident she wasn't grieving. By the same token. If Alisha was in a 'family' way, she couldn't be very far along and definitely not embarrassed by her condition. Alisha wore a red wool suit with a crisp white blouse open way too far at the neckline. It showed much more of the girl's chest than any decent woman in Mortonville would be comfortable showing. Hattie knew something wasn't right, but she couldn't put her finger on what it could be.

"You have my sympathy," Hattie said, extending her hand in greeting.

"Thank you," Alisha replied, looking down toward her feet to avoid

Hattie's eyes. The gesture was so forced, Hattie wanted to shake her in disgust.

Edna and Alisha made polite conversation while Hattie finished putting her music into the bag. Once she finished, they started toward the line of parishioners who were greeting David.

To Hattie's horror, when Alisha made her way to the front of the line, threw her arms around David's neck and kissed him passionately on the mouth. It was immediately evident they were more than just casual acquaintances.

Hattie could feel her stomach begin to knot. She knew Alisha came from Philadelphia, but never in her wildest dreams did she think the girl would know David.

Unable to stand the thought of facing David, she turned away. Being the last in line she found it easy to make her way to the balcony. From there, she could slip out the side entrance she used so often in the past.

How could she have been so gullible? She silently seethed. Those two weren't just friends. If she was in a 'family' way, maybe she came here because David is the father. All this talk about God and Christian duty was a ploy to get people to trust him. It's best to know before becoming too involved.

The bite of the November air dried the tears forming in her eyes before they could stream down her cheeks. Refusing to look back, she hurried across the snow-covered path to her home.

"Hattie?" Thad said as she entered the kitchen. "I thought you were fixing dinner for David at the parsonage today."

"You thought wrong," she snapped.

"I'm fixing something for Sammy and me. Can I get something for you?"

Thad's expression told Hattie he was as confused by her return to the house as she was by the greeting Alisha gave David. "No thank you, Thad. I just want to be alone."

She left Thad in the kitchen and went to her room. Once the door was securely closed, Hattie lay down on the bed and allowed the bitter tears she'd refused to let Thad see fall freely.

* * * *

David shook hands with each parishioner in turn. At the end of the line, he saw Hattie behind Ralph and Edna Mason. Inwardly, he smiled at the thought of the meal Hattie was planning to prepare for him once the mandatory reception line ended and the church was closed up.

"That was a good sermon, Reverend," Ralph said, as he pumped David's hand.

"Thank you, Ralph." Once Ralph's sheer bulk stepped aside, David was shocked to see Alisha Palmer standing behind her cousin.

"Oh, David," Alisha gushed before she stood on tiptoe to put her arms around his neck and plant a kiss squarely on his lips. "I never dreamed I would find you out here in the middle of nowhere. As you can see, I've been banished from Philadelphia."

"Do you know each other?" Ralph looked surprised.

David nodded, remembering Alisha as the persistent younger sister of his last client. As he recalled, she'd flirted with him shamelessly all through the trial.

"I think it's best if you come to the farm for Sunday dinner," Ralph continued.

"But … but I have plans," David protested.

"Plans can be broken. If yours include Hattie Fairchild, I think she's already changed them for you."

David looked past Edna Mason to where Hattie stood moments earlier. It wasn't surprising to see she'd disappeared.

"From the way Alisha greeted you, it's evident we have a lot to talk over. We'll expect you as soon as you close up the church." Ralph started out the door and then turned back. "You have no choice in this matter Reverend. You will come out to the farm for dinner."

David watched as Ralph, Edna, and Alisha left the building. Once he was alone, he searched the sanctuary. Hattie had to be somewhere. After checking downstairs, David made his way to the balcony, He found it empty, but felt a draft coming up the back stairs. Hurrying down the steps, he found the door leading outside ajar. Outside, he saw a woman's footprints in the light dusting of snow covering the church lawn. The tracks made it evident this was Hattie's means of escape.

After closing the door, David climbed back up to the balcony and returned to the sanctuary. It took him a few minutes to turn down the lamps necessary for this morning's service considering the weak light the overcast November day provided. With that done, he put on his overcoat, left the church, and walked the distance between there and the barn behind the parsonage.

Thor raised his head in greeting, as though surprised at being hitched to the closed carriage David acquired just over a week ago. The brisk wind combined with the light snow that had been falling all morning made David doubly glad for the warmth it provided.

Before heading out of town, he drove over to Hattie's home Thad answered his knock at the kitchen door promptly.

"Is Hattie here?"

The look on Thad's face told David more than any answer he could have given.

"You don't have to answer. Can I talk to her?"

"I don't know what's going on, David. Maybe I don't want to know. Hattie came back here after church. She was very upset. She went right to her bedroom and slammed the door. I can't say for sure, but I think I heard her crying. It's best if you leave her alone for a while,"

David made no response, Hattie had to have seen the greeting he'd received from Alisha and jumped to the same conclusion as Ralph. Until he cleared the air with the Masons, there was no sense in trying to profess his innocence to Hattie.

"Does this have anything to do with that girl who is staying with the Mason's?" Thad said before David could turn to leave.

"What if it does?"

"You must know the gossip that's been spreading about her. I feel sorry for her. If she is in the kind of trouble they say she is, maybe I can help."

"Help?" David questioned. "How?"

"I'd be willing to marry her and give her child my name."

"You don't know this girl. Why would you do such a thing?"

"Hattie helped me. Let me just say it might repay the debt."

"You're very generous, Thad, but you don't even know Alisha. It could be she's not worth the effort."

"Maybe she is. My offer stands. Just think about it."

David appreciated what Thad was trying to do, but he didn't know

Alisha the way David did.

On the drive out to the Mason farm, David thought about Alisha Palmer She was a beautiful girl. If he'd been younger, he might have succumbed to her flirting during her brother's trial. Instead, he gave her a wide berth.

Her brother, Willard, had a knack for getting into trouble. If their father hadn't bailed the boy out the first time perhaps things would have been different. Instead, Willard and Alisha grew up without the morals David learned at home. What puzzled David most was the way Mr. Palmer was handling his daughter's current situation.

By the time David arrived at Ralph's farm, the snow could no longer be called flurries. The chill of the day was bringing on a winter storm of major proportions, It made David wish he were at home enjoying the warmth of the parsonage while sharing one of Hattie's delicious meals.

"It certainly took you long enough to get here, Reverend," Ralph greeted him. The tome of the man's voice told David the next couple of hours were going to be rough.

"I had things to finish."

"Like Hattie Fairchild?"

"Like closing up the church and getting my horse and carriage," David replied. He certainly didn't like how close to the truth Ralph came.

"We were just about to start without you. I hope you like escalloped potatoes and ham. It's Edna's specialty."

David made some comment about looking forward to dinner before he took off his coat. When Ralph made no move to take it from David, he draped it over a convenient chair,

"It's a pleasure to have you here for dinner, Reverend," Edna said, when he entered her dining room.

David bit back a nasty response about how this was a command visit. "The pleasure is mine, Edna. I've heard what a good cook you are."

Ralph took his seat at the head of the table with Edna at the foot, leaving David to seat himself across from Alisha.

"Would you say grace, Reverend?" Ralph said.

To David it was more of a demand than a request. Obediently, David bowed his head. "Dear Father, bless this food and the fellowship we will share this afternoon. In the name of our Lord and Savior, A-men."

"You might want to rethink the fellowship part, Reverend," Ralph growled once David raised his head. "I doubt you'll find this a pleasant visit."

Edna passed David a large bowl. Before answering Ralph, David dipped a serving spoon into the potatoes and put a small portion on his plate. Under other circumstances, he would have enjoyed a larger helping, but his usual hearty appetite seemed to have disappeared.

"I'm not going to beat around the bush here. We all know why Alisha's parents sent her to stay with us. I know how badly Edna has always wanted a baby, so I agreed. Until today we had no idea who the father was and it didn't matter. Now everything is different. There is no way I'm going to raise your bastard."

"Did Alisha tell you her child belongs to me?" Although David's question was directed to Ralph, he never took his eyes from Alisha.

"She didn't have to, and you know it. That display at church today said it all. I've tried to get the truth out of her ever since."

"When is your child going to be born, Alisha?" David ignored Ralph's outburst.

Alisha lowered her gaze. "In June," she replied. "Oh, David, I didn't mean to get you in trouble. Of course, it would solve everything if you'd marry me. I mean it would make Cousin Ralph happy, and I'd be the respected wife of a minister. By the time the baby is born, most people will have stopped counting the months. You'll see, I'll be the sweetest little wife to you."

Alisha's words made David sick to his stomach. "You know I'm not the child's father and yet you'd agree to marry someone who doesn't want you?"

To his surprise, tears formed in Alisha's blue eyes.

"Is he right?" Ralph demanded. "Did you let me believe Reverend Long did you wrong? Do you even know him?"

David could tell Alisha was ready to break down. "I represented her brother, Willard, when he was in trouble last spring. His was my last case before the Lord called me to do His work."

"Tell me, Alisha, who is the father?" Ralph shouted, pounding his fist on the table.

"Calm down, Ralph," David said, suddenly sympathetic to Alisha's plight. "If Alisha hasn't told you by now, shouting won't change anything."

David ached to see Alisha's tears. If he expected either Ralph or Edna to comfort the girl, he was mistaken. After a few awkward moments, he pushed back his chair and went to her side to comfort her.

"Do you want to tell me who fathered your child?" he said, his voice low enough only she could hear him.

At first Alisha hesitated. Then she silently nodded.

"What happened?"

"It was right after you left practice as well as Philadelphia that Willard got into trouble again. Daddy went to your old firm to ask them to represent Willard, but they said no. I thought if I went and talked to them they would change their minds. Daddy said if anyone could get them to help Willard, it was me. I gave up a lot to get Mr. Avery to agree to help Willard."

An image of Jack Avery filled David's mind. The man was older than Alisha's own father. It was no wonder he didn't want to acknowledge her child. His daughter had three children of her own and his wife wasn't well. Something like this would probably kill her.

"I ... I don't know what to say, Reverend," Ralph stammered. "I'm afraid I didn't listen to your sermon closely enough this morning, I jumped to the wrong conclusion, I shouldn't have accused you without all the facts. How can we make it up to you?"

David returned to his chair, suddenly hungry for the first time since arriving at the Mason farm. "Alisha is going to need your help in the next few months. This isn't going to be an easy time for her. There will be a lot of hard decisions to be made. The child she is carrying deserves a loving family with a father as well as a mother. We all need to pray for guidance."

"Perhaps you will lead us in these prayers once we've finished eating," Edna said, as she passed the large serving bowl back to David.

The rest of the meal was spent in an uneasy silence. David concluded each person was lost in his or her own thoughts. Ralph, more than likely contemplated the ramifications of his accusations. Edna was, most certainly, thinking about having a baby to love. As for Alisha, her arrogant attitude was fading quickly. The flamboyant young lady he'd seen at church slowly disappeared in front of his eyes. David now realized her earlier actions came from desperation. All she really wanted was to find a father for her child. She hadn't thought of the consequences of her actions.

Unbidden, Thad's words entered David's mind. The young man offered a solution to the problem. Would his offer of marriage be acceptable to Alisha?

Over the past few weeks, David fought his personal demons over Thad. The jealousy he felt almost ate him alive. When he confessed his worst sin to be overindulgence, he'd omitted jealousy. He was as guilty as everyone else who heard his words.

Once he put the jealousy issue behind him, David saw Thad for the decent young man he was. David knew Alisha could find no better father for her child than Thad. After seeing how he cared for Sammy, David knew the young man's love would one day grow to encompass several more children. The question looming largest in his mind was if Alisha could accept the love Thad had to give.

"Help us Reverend," Edna begged, once dinner was finished and they were sitting in the parlor.

David took a deep breath before proposing Thad's suggestion. "When I first got here, you asked if I was late because of going to see Hattie. I wasn't truthful with you. I did go to her home, but I didn't see her, I doubt if she's very receptive to me right now. I did talk to Thad while I was there. I've gotten to know him quite well since he arrived. He's a good man, and he made a very generous offer. He said he was willing to marry Alisha and give her child his name."

"He doesn't even know me," Alisha gasped. "Why would he do such a thing for me?"

David explained about Thad's struggles in raising his daughter alone. As he elaborated about Thad's attributes, David realized he was arguing the young man's case. For the first time in months, he'd easily slipped from preacher to lawyer.

"How old is the little girl?" Alisha asked.

"She just turned four. Considering she has never had a mother, she is well behaved and ladylike. She's even learning how to play the piano. What she needs most is a mother."

David watched as Alisha closed her eyes. He could only guess as to what she was thinking. "I always thought I'd marry for love," she finally sighed.

"Reverend Long didn't say you had to marry this young man," Edna advised Alisha. "It's a very generous offer, but you don't have to take it."

"What other option do I have? If this man is willing to give my child his name, I can, at least, meet him."

"I don't think Thad is expecting you to fall in love with him instantly," David said. "You don't have to make a decision today. Take your time and get to know him. No one wants to force you into a loveless marriage."

Ralph and Edna, as well as Alisha stared at David for a moment, then nodded in agreement with his statement.

"I think I'd like you to lead us in prayer, Reverend," Ralph finally said, breaking the awkward silence.

David bowed his head and clasped his hands. Without looking up, he was certain the others did the same. "Dear Lord," he began. "Help Alisha to make the decision that is right for her unborn child. No matter what choice she makes, give her family the strength to support her decision."

He paused for a moment to compose his thoughts. To his surprise, Edna began to speak.

"Give us the wisdom to give Alisha the best advice. If this young man is serious, and Alisha agrees to become not only his wife, but also the mother to his child, help us to welcome him into our family."

Ralph picked up where Edna left off. "You know I've been none too happy about this situation, Lord. I did agree to raise the child, if that was what needed to be done. Whatever the outcome, give me the strength to do the right thing for this child."

David was ready to bring the prayer to an end when Alisha spoke up. "I know what I did was wrong, but I want my baby to have a good home. Help me make the right decision."

"You've heard the concerns of these good people," David said.

"Help them, as well as the people in this town, to be accepting of Alisha and her child. Allow them to open their hearts so they can help this child grow up in a loving family and community. A-men."

When David raised his head, it came as no surprise to see tears on the cheeks of both women, he prayed the girl sitting across the room from him learned from her mistakes. If Thad was, indeed, willing to take her as his wife, he deserved only the best she had to offer.

He remembered Alisha as a wild teenager who flirted outrageously with every man who crossed her path. It was no wonder she was in her current predicament. Seeing her now, he wouldn't have guessed at her past.

"I have to go out and start chores," Ralph declared, getting to his feet. As he did, the clock struck four.

"I shouldn't have stayed so long," David said, getting to his feet as well. "I'd best be getting back to town before it gets dark."

"You'd better rethink going back to town tonight, Reverend," Ralph announced when he turned away from the window. "We're having one devil of a storm."

David hurried to Ralph's side. He was shocked to see snow swirling past the window. Unlike the summer storm that so badly injured Hattie, the snow made no noise as it fell and drifted around the house.

His thoughts turned to Thor. He needed to care for his horse, to get him in out of the cold. "If I could borrow some overalls, I'll help you with chores after I put my horse in your barn."

"I'll see to your horse," Ralph replied. "If you want to stay in here where it's warm I won't fault you none."

"I wouldn't have offered if I didn't mean it. Your overalls might be a bit on the short side, but they should do. I know my way around a barn."

"Have it your way. Edna will get you something to wear. Once you're changed, meet me out at the barn."

David followed Edna to the spare bedroom and waited while she went to get him something to wear. He changed out of his suit and put on the overalls and flannel shirt she brought him. As he'd predicted they were about three inches too short, but at least he wouldn't be wrecking his suit.

Outside, the snow was falling harder than David ever remembered seeing it fall before. He'd planned to get back to town tonight, but knew it wouldn't happen until at least morning. When he did, he was going to try and talk to Hattie.

With the magnitude of the storm, he changed his mind, knowing it could be a couple of days before he'd be able to return home.

Beside the barn, he noticed his closed carriage. Thor had been unhitched and, by now was more than likely, enjoying a bucket of oats.

The warmth of the barn stood in direct contrast to the blustery cold of the storm "Do you usually get storms like this in November?" David said, once he closed the door.

"Depends," Ralph replied. "It's pretty early, but I've seen snow in October. The way it's snowing, it might be a couple of days before you'll be able to get back to town. Hope you don't have anything important to do."

Not important as far as anyone but he was concerned. David knew it would be hard enough facing Hattie without having to wait until this storm blew itself out.

Chapter Fifteen

Hattie awoke to the howl of the wind and a chill penetrating the lightweight quilt she was certain Thad placed over her sleeping body. She could hardly believe sleep came so quickly.

The clock in the parlor chimed five times, making her realize she'd slept the day away. Her stomach growled, attesting to the fact breakfast had been several hours earlier. She went to the parlor.

"I was beginning to get worried about you," Thad greeted her.

"Did you cover me?"

"Yes. When the storm started, I was chilly. I figured since you hadn't come out of your room you must be asleep. I knew you needed your rest, so I didn't want to wake you. I wouldn't have needed to be concerned about that as I don't think you even knew I came into your room."

Hattie smiled. "It's a shame your wife died. She missed out on what a good father you are. I'm certain you were a good husband as well."

Her comment met with silence. Hattie knew she shouldn't have mentioned Thad's wife. Such conversations always ended the same way. Even four years after her passing he got choked up when Hattie even said the word 'wife'.

She wished she would find a love as great as the one Thad and Diana had shared. For a few weeks she'd thought David was starting to care for her. After today, Hattie realized she'd only been a convenience, someone to pass the time with until he could be reunited with Alisha.

Now that David's past came to town, Hattie harbored no doubt that a wedding would be happening soon. Alisha's arrival from Philadelphia could only mean she'd come to town to find the man who did her wrong.

"What happened after I left church this morning, Hattie?"

Thad's question startled her. She hadn't heard him follow her from the parlor. Before she could turn to face him, he stood by her side.

"Why do you think something happened?"

"You came home like the devil himself was after you. You'd already gone to your room when David came here. I told him to give you a chance to calm down, He said he was going out to Ralph Mason's place for dinner and would stop when he got back to town."

"Considering it's after dark, I doubt we'll be seeing the good reverend anymore tonight. We may not be seeing much of him after the wedding."

"Wedding?" Thad echoed.

"From the greeting Alisha Palmer gave David this morning, I wouldn't be surprised if he was the father of her child. If he is, he should do the right thing by her."

"Hattie Fairchild!" Thad exclaimed. "I can't believe you just said that. You're as bad as Maude."

Thad's accusation shocked Hattie. Was she guilty of spreading vicious gossip?

"How could you think such a thing about David?" Thad pressed.

"You have no right to question me," Hattie retorted. "You weren't there. You didn't see the way she greeted him, I've never seen such behavior in church."

"Did you listen to David's sermon this morning? I doubt it. You're jumping to the same conclusion as David did when I first arrived. All it shows is that we are human. Petty jealousies are only normal. They work to…"

"To what, Thad? Are you saying this is God's way of testing me?"

Thad threw up his hands and sighed deeply. "You're missing my point. I don't believe God tests us. If anyone is testing anything, we are doing it to ourselves. God is there for us, Hattie. We just seem to get sidetracked by things like jealousy. Pray on this. Let God help you keep from being eaten alive by it."

"Papa, I'm hungry," Sammy said, before Hattie could comment on

Thad's statement.

Thad turned his attention to his daughter, leaving Hattie to contemplate their conversation. She wondered what Thad meant when he said David jumped to conclusions when Thad first came to town. She soon decided not to dwell on something she could find out later. Instead, Hattie considered Thad's suggestion about her praying.

I've been trying to get you to pray, Hattie, but you wouldn't listen to me.

Hattie shook her head. She couldn't have heard that. She must be imagining things. It must be because she missed dinner.

"I'm heating up the soup from last night," Thad said, breaking Hattie's concentration. "Would you like to join us?"

"That sounds good. I'll slice some bread."

As Hattie pulled the bread knife from the drawer, the aroma of the simmering soup made her mouth water. Yesterday she'd spent several hours preparing it. Last spring she bought the meat from Ralph when he butchered several pigs and steers. It was something he did every year. Most of the people in town looked forward to that particular event. It was good for the townspeople to get the cuts of prime meat to last them through the winter.

"Hattie thought of the beef and pork she'd worked so hard to cook and can. Like yesterday, she often added her canned meat to soups and stews, it made for easily prepared meals.

"You had a strange expression on your face a few moments ago," Thad commented, once they were seated around the kitchen table.

"My mind was playing tricks on me. I thought I heard…"

"You thought you heard what?" Thad pressed when Hattie paused.

"Nothing," she conveniently lied. "I was imagining things."

The look on Thad's face told Hattie he no more believed her explanation than she believed God actually spoke to her. Whatever she heard, it persuaded her at least to try to pray. What harm could it do?

By the time supper was finished and the dishes washed and put away, Hattie returned to her bedroom Even though she'd slept away the afternoon, she still felt exhausted.

Once she was ready to retire, she knelt beside her double bed. The hardwood floor was cold against her knees. The feeling brought back memories of her father forcing her to kneel for hours at a time repenting for sins she never committed.

"Dear God." to Hattie's surprise the words formed easily. "Dear God, help me to be objective where David is concerned. Help me to close my ears to the gossip spread by others and to seal my lips against the hurtful words I'm tempted to speak."

She waited for what seemed like an eternity, but no answer sounded in her mind. Instead, a feeling of peace encompassed her entire being.

By the time she crawled between the warmth of the flannel sheets, Hattie came to a decision concerning David. If he was the father of Alisha's child, Hattie would accept it. If he wasn't, she would step back a bit. For the first time she realized she had been too dependent on the attention David so lavishly bestowed on her. She'd begun to believe the feeling she harbored for David was love. It was time for her to face the fact she was too old for such foolishness.

* * * *

After Ralph finished the milking, David accompanied him back to the house for supper. Being with the Masons made David extremely uncomfortable, especially with Alisha watching his every move.

Once they washed up, Edna announced supper was ready. As he had at dinner, David seated himself across from Alisha, He was ready to begin saying grace when Ralph started speaking. As the older man droned on and on thanking God for everything from the food on the table to the blizzard that still raged outside, David found his mind wandering to the warmth of Hattie's kitchen.

What she must be thinking?

Before his mind could formulate an answer, Ralph's booming A-men brought David back to the reality of the supper table. Relieved to have the prayer ended, David filled his plate with slabs of roast beef as well as reheated mashed potatoes and gravy from a previous meal.

"David," Alisha said, her voice hardly more than a whisper. "I am so sorry for the way I behaved in church this morning. Can you ever forgive me?"

"You're asking the wrong person for forgiveness. You need to search your heart and talk to God."

He knew his request sounded strange, but he'd meant it to help Alisha. Her lifestyle had been less than desirable in Philadelphia, but now she had a child to consider. God's forgiveness was hers for the asking. David prayed she would turn her life around for the good of her unborn baby.

"Is it that easy?"

The spark of hope in her eyes surprised him. Could she have made such a drastic turn around in the few short hours since her outburst in church?

"God will forgive you if you ask Him. That's the easy part. You need to turn your life around, if not for yourself, for your baby. Here you are a stranger. No one knows what your life has been like so far. Make a fresh start. Make today your new beginning. In this room you have two good people who have opened their hearts to you. Give them reason to be proud of you. Allow them to be surrogate grandparents to your child."

David held his breath, he half expected either Ralph or Edna to protest his solution to the problem. Instead they both agreed with everything he said.

Once supper was finished and the women cleaned up the kitchen, Ralph suggested they play carom. As much as David wanted to go to bed and enjoy the warmth of the blankets, he welcomed the diversion of the game.

One game turned into two and then three before the clock struck ten, "Morning comes mighty early," Ralph said as he got to his feet and stretched.

David followed the lead of his host and retreated to the room where he'd changed clothes earlier. On the bed, he found a flannel nightshirt. He smiled to think how different this was compared to the one he wore at home. Although his was freshly laundered like this one, David never took the time to iron it. At first he found sleeping in the wrinkled garment uncomfortable, but in time he got used to it. Now even slipping the neatly pressed garment over his head brought back pleasant memories of living in Philadelphia with his parents.

The crisp sheets were cold against his bare feet, causing him to lie still until his body warmed up the muslin caressing his body.

Outside the storm became fierce. David listened to the howling of the wind. Inside, the silence of the sleeping house was shattered by Ralph's loud snoring,

For what seemed like hours, David lay awake listening to the sounds of the night. His mind spun with thoughts of how much he missed sleeping in his own bed and not having to listen to someone else in the house snoring.

Mingled with those thoughts were ones of Hattie. If it hadn't been for the storm, he would have been able to stop and talk to her on the way home. Instead, he was forced to spend an undetermined length of time snowbound with the woman who tried to force him into a marriage designed only to give her child his name.

As thoughts of Alisha crossed his mind, David wondered if by mentioning Thad's generous offer of marriage he was forcing her into a loveless union.

He had no idea how long he lay awake. When sleep finally came, his dreams were filled with Hattie. In them she condemned him for the accusations Alisha made against him, If Hattie, as well as the Masons believed such nonsense, what would the other members of his congregation think?

* * * *

Hattie tossed and turned throughout the night. As she did so, she blamed her afternoon nap. Once sleep finally came, her dreams revealed a deeper meaning for her restlessness.

The flamboyant young woman she'd met earlier proclaimed her love for David, insisting he had, indeed fathered her unborn child.

"Aunt Hattie, Aunt Hattie," Sammy's early morning greeting shattered the dreams Hattie had experienced through the night. "There's so much snow outside, Papa says I can make a snowman."

Hattie shivered at the thought of the storm that dropped so much snow on Mortonville.

"Are you bothering Hattie?" Thad said to his daughter.

"She's not bothering me, Thad," Hattie replied as she tentative stuck her left foot out from under the covers. The chill of the bedroom made her wonder if getting up to start the day was such a good idea.

Once Thad and Sammy left the doorway, she put aside her

indecisions and hurried to wash up and dress for the day. The heavy woolen skirt and warm sweater she chose from her closet chased away the chill of the bedroom.

To her surprise, the parlor clock struck eight at the exact moment she stepped from her bedroom into the hallway.

"Why did you let me sleep so late?" Hattie said when she joined Thad in the kitchen. The aroma of molasses cookies filled the cozy room.

"I thought you needed the rest. With the storm we had last night, no one will be in today."

Hattie glanced out the kitchen window. She certainly understood what Thad meant. Snow driven by the powerful wind clung to the glass. Beyond her transparent opening to the outside, drifts covered the backyard. There was no doubt the street in front of her shop looked much the same.

"Then why did you make cookies?"

"Sammy wanted them. She's been pestering me to bake them since she got up at six. I didn't think you'd mind.

"Of course I don't mind, but I still should have gotten up earlier. I suppose you've already had your breakfast."

Thad's laughter combined with the dirty dishes sitting on the drain board next to the sink confirmed that.

"I made oatmeal and kept a bowl of it in the warming oven for you. While you eat, I'll start shoveling a path to the street. I don't know how much good it will do, but eventually someone will need to get either in or out of the shop."

Hattie watched Thad put on a heavy coat, woolen mittens, a warm hat and galoshes.

"I want to go out with Papa," Sammy whined once Thad went out to begin work.

"You can go out later and play in the snow. It will be warmer then. While I have my breakfast, why don't you have a cookie and some milk?"

Sammy lost interest in going outside as soon as she seated herself across the table from Hattie. With the child concentrating on her sweet treat, Hattie turned her thoughts to the dreams that robbed her of the rest she needed. It surprised her to be able to remember them because usually her dreams faded with the coming of day.

If she were right about when Alisha's baby would be born, she wondered why the girl put on such a display. Even Hattie knew how long it took for a baby to grow and David had been in town for the past four months.

* * * *

"I'm going out to milk, Reverend," Ralph's booming voice sounded from beyond David's bedroom door. "I could use some help shoveling out to the barn."

Although he'd been awake for several minutes, David found himself procrastinating over getting out of bed. Without poking more than his nose out from under the pile of blankets and quilts that kept him warm all night, he knew the house was chilled.

"I'll be right out, Ralph," David replied half-heartedly. Unable to put off the inevitable, he threw off the covers and reached for the overalls and flannel shirt he'd worn the night before.

The silence of the house attested to the earliness of the hour. To David's surprise, he found Alisha in the kitchen building up the fire in the stove to start breakfast.

"I didn't expect you to be up so early," he greeted her.

"Mama said I would be sick in the morning. Instead, I'm sick at night. In the morning, I have lots of energy."

"I know next to nothing about these things," David confessed.

"But you know about women. I've only been here for a few days and I've already heard about you and the lady who plays the piano at church. Do you care for her?"

David seated himself across the table from Alisha. In the four months he'd been in town, no one asked him that particular question, "I do care for her."

"How do you think she'll feel about you when you got back to town?"

David relived the sinking feeling he'd had when he realized Hattie left the church by the side door. She'd witnessed the entire exchange between Alisha and him. Surely she must be thinking the worst.

"You didn't answer me. I made a terrible scene, I thought if the people here considered you the father of my child, you would have to marry me."

"I don't love you Alisha. I hardly know you. How could you have ever thought you could trick me into marriage?"

"Now it seems foolish. I've made a terrible mess of things."

Rather than say something David knew he would regret, he finished his coffee and got up from the table. I'm going out to help Ralph with the chores. We'll talk again after breakfast."

After putting on a warm coat and hat, David went out to help Ralph. The amount of snow between the house and barn surprised him, Sometime through the night the storm had quit, leaving a clear sky and bright moon to light the countryside.

"It looks like we got a good foot of snow," Ralph greeted him.

"At least there's no wind now," David replied. "If you give me your shovel, I'll see how much of this I can move while you're milking,"

Ralph handed him the shovel. "Don't get carried away. For now, we only need a path out to the barn, I doubt if anyone will be out from the dairy much before tomorrow. We'll have all day to clean this mess up."

Once he started to work, David tried to ignore the cold. After getting into the rhythm of shoveling, he allowed his mind to wander to the subject of Hattie.

Earlier Alisha mentioned Hattie's reaction to what happened after church yesterday morning, Thad's comment about Hattie being upset confirmed it. How could David expect to minister to Alisha's needs if he lost Hattie because of the outburst?

* * * *

"Good morning, Hattie," Maude chirped as she stomped the snow from her shoes.

"Why Maude, what a surprise. With the weather the way it is, I didn't expect to see you this morning."

"A little snow is nothing to worry about, especially when a dear friend like you must be hurting so badly about someone she cares for."

Hattie knew exactly where Maude was heading, but decided to play dumb. "Whatever do you mean?"

"Well, my dear, you must have seen that display in church

yesterday. I expected Reverend Long to, well I don't know what I expected, but it wasn't going out to the Mason farm for dinner. To make matters worse, I walked past the parsonage this morning and no one is there. I'm certain he spent the night with that girl."

Hattie's heart seemed to stop. Her breath came in ragged gasps. If David indeed spent the night with Alisha was it the first time?

"I've never heard anything so ridiculous in my life," Thad said, coming in from the living quarters.

"Whatever do you mean?" Maude said. "It's as plain as the nose on your face what's going on. Our new minister isn't as righteous as he makes out."

"Isn't he?" Thad responded. "I doubt there's a bit of truth to your gossip."

"But there's no one at the parsonage."

"Did it ever occur to you he might have gotten stranded out in the storm? David stopped by here yesterday. He told me Ralph insisted he come out to dinner."

"Well, doesn't that tell you something?" Maude insisted. "It's evident Ralph and Edna asked him to come to dinner so they could plan the wedding."

Maude's words hurt worse than Hattie thought mere words could. Even though common sense told her there was no way David could be the father, he was such an honorable man he might want to take Alisha as his wife to save her honor. No matter what Thad said, Maude made perfect sense. Considering Alisha's condition, a quick wedding would be the best solution for everyone involved.

Chapter Sixteen

"Are you ready to go back to town, Reverend?" Ralph spoke, once they finished eating their dinner and were enjoying pie and coffee.

"I'm ready, but I'm afraid my carriage would get stuck before I got out of your dooryard."

"You driving into town wasn't quite what I had in mind. I know you can't make it in that rig of yours, I was going to suggest you leave your horse and carriage here and let me take you there in the sleigh. When the weather clears up, I can bring your rig to you and Edna can bring in our buggy."

David didn't like the thought of leaving Thor at the farm, but he wanted to talk to Hattie. Too much time had passed. He could only imagine what she must think.

"It sounds like a good idea to me, I'm certain my being here is an imposition on Edna."

Around the table everyone agreed there had been no inconvenience, but David knew better. Even if no one admitted it, he realized the Mason house would be less tense without him.

"Can I go into town with you, Cousin Ralph?" Alisha said.

David looked up from his dessert. Alisha's question confused him. Why would she want to go into town when the weather was so unseasonable? Although the snow stopped overnight, the temperature dropped noticeably while he was shoveling.

"I don't think you should be out in this cold," Edna protested. "You must be concerned with the child."

"The cold won't hurt me, Cousin Edna, I'm not used to being stuck so far away from town."

David watched as Alisha began to pout like the spoiled child he so vividly remembered from their first meeting in Philadelphia. He'd seen her use that look to get her way several times during her brother's trial. "I tend to agree with Edna. You must think of your child. What could possibly be so important that you have to go out in this weather?"

"I want to talk to Miss Fairchild. I'm afraid my actions have caused her unnecessary worries."

While David considered Alisha's change of heart to be strange, Edna seemed to take it to heart.

"The sleigh is large enough to accommodate all four of us," she said, "With enough blankets, we'll be quite cozy. A little fresh air might do us all a lot of good."

The last thing David wanted was to have Alisha confront Hattie before he had a chance to talk to her and explain this bizarre situation.

* * * *

Hattie finished washing the last of the diner dishes. She smiled to see Sammy standing on a small stool to reach the sink so she could dry them.

"We do good together, don't we, Aunt Hattie?" Sammy said.

"We certainly do. You're doing a very good job with these dishes."

Sammy beamed at the compliment. "Papa says Reverend David likes you. Do you like him?"

"Reverend Long and I are good friends," Hattie managed to say. She knew any further explanation would be impossible.

The thought of David brought a lump to her throat. After what Maude said earlier, how could she face him?

Sammy stifled a yawn, giving Hattie something to think about other than the situation between David and Alisha. "It looks like someone could use a nap."

"Do I have to?" Sammy protested, before yet another yawn cut off any further words.

"You don't have to go to sleep," Hattie reasoned. "Just lie down and rest for a little while."

"I can do that," Sammy agreed, as she handed Hattie the wet dishtowel and got down from the stool.

Hattie smiled as she watched Sammy leave the kitchen and go to her bedroom. "You do have a knack with her," Thad observed when she returned to the shop. "How do you manage to get Sammy to take a nap without putting up a fuss?"

"It wasn't hard. I just told her she didn't have to go to sleep and could rest for a while. She was so tired, I'm certain she'll be asleep in no time."

Hattie picked up the garment she'd been working on all morning and began to make the necessary stitches. With all her heart, she wished for the innocence of childhood, which allowed Sammy to nap without the concerns of a grown-up.

The bell above her door jingled, alerting Hattie to the entry of a customer. Since she was working with her back to the door, she allowed Thad to greet the person.

"Good afternoon, David," she heard Thad say.

The mention of David's name made Hattie's hands tremble. He was the last person she wanted to see today, even if her heart said differently.

"I was hoping to have a moment to talk to Hattie," David replied.

Hattie got to her feet and turned to face him. She couldn't help the audible gasp that passed her lips as she saw Alisha standing next to David her arm linked in his. "I don't think you have anything to say to me, Reverend Long," Hattie snapped. "If you need someone to make clothes for your future wife, I'm certain Thad can accommodate you."

Without waiting for David to reply, Hattie stormed from the shop to her living quarters. Before she could slam the door between the two areas, David stopped her.

"We need to talk."

Her voice was low, almost a whisper. "Like I said, there's nothing to talk about."

"And I say there is. Get your coat."

"Why?"

"Because I want to go over to the church, where we can talk privately."

"We can talk privately here."

"With Sammy somewhere in the house and Thad in the shop? I don't think so."

Hattie turned to face David. The look on his face made her knees feel weak. He looked like a little boy who was trying to make amends for something he'd done.

"Sammy's taking a nap. She'll sleep for at least an hour. We can talk in the kitchen. No one will hear us."

David's expression turned from one of concern to a genuine smile. "At least you're willing to talk. You wouldn't have any cookies or cake in the kitchen, would you?"

Hattie tried to hold onto her anger, but his question brought a smile to her lips. "I don't think cookies have anything to do with what you want to talk about," she said, trying to regain her anger.

Once in the kitchen, David pulled out a chair and held it while Hattie sat down. Before he started to talk, he reached for one of the molasses cookies on the plate sitting on the table.

"What did you mean when you called Alisha my future wife?"

"What do you think I meant?"

"I think you're jumping to the wrong conclusions."

"Are you going to tell me you didn't know Alisha in Philadelphia?"

"I can't tell you that because it would be a lie. Alisha's brother was the last man I defended. She's a spoiled little girl, and she's in trouble."

"Are you the child's father?"

"No, but she told me who it was. You have to have faith in me, Hattie."

Faith, the word resonated in Hattie's mind. It seemed as though David was asking her to have faith every time she turned around. Faith in God, faith in David, what else would he eventually ask of her? If he did ask for more, would she be able to give it?

"David's right," Alisha said.

Hattie turned toward the doorway to see Alisha and Thad standing there together.

"I came here with a well-rehearsed lie about how my baby's father took sick and died. When I saw David in church yesterday, I was certain my prayers had been answered. I thought he would want to marry me

150

and give my child his name. I now know how foolish I was. I tried to get him to notice me when he was defending my brother and it didn't work. He didn't want me then any more than he does now."

"There will be a wedding, though," Thad declared. "I've asked Alisha to marry me."

Hattie could hardly believe her ears. "Why? You don't know this girl."

"Maybe not, but I do know about raising a child alone. Alisha is no more prepared to be a mama and papa to her baby than I was to do the same for Sammy. My daughter needs a mother as well as brothers and sisters. Alisha has agreed to be Sammy's mother. In return, I agreed to be a father to her child."

"What about love?" Hattie said.

"I married Sammy's mother for love and losing her almost killed me. The way I see it, Alisha needs a father for her baby and I need a mother for Sammy. If, in time, love grows, it will be a bonus."

"I ... I don't know what to say," Hattie managed to respond.

"Please say you will be my maid of honor," Alisha replied, coming to Hattie's side. "I have no friends here. From everything Cousin Edna has told me, you are a good person. I would like you to be my friend."

Hattie was shocked by the turn of events. In a little over twenty-four hours, she'd changed her mind twice about the young woman who was staying at Ralph and Edna's farm. She looked from Alisha to David and realized just how unfounded her assumptions had been. The look on David's face told her Alisha was no more than an acquaintance.

Thad's proposal of marriage was even more shocking than the realization of her own shortcomings. What if Alisha was only playing on their generosity?

"Perhaps Alisha and I should have a moment alone to talk," Hattie suggested.

"What about our talk?" David said.

"It can wait. This can't."

Hattie waited while David and Thad returned to the shop before she turned to Alisha. "Would you like a cup of tea?" She set the kettle to boil without waiting for a response.

Once the water was hot, Hattie put tealeaves into her best china teapot and added the water. While it steeped, she brought out two delicate teacups that matched the pot.

"How old are you, dear?" Hattie said, when she finally sat down opposite Alisha.

"I'm seventeen."

"What do you know about being a wife?"

Alisha looked down at her teacup. "Very little. Mama insisted I know how to embroider, crochet, and knit. She also taught me how to do a few things in the kitchen. Beyond that, I know nothing."

"Then why did you accept Thad's proposal?"

"What else could I do? David told me about Thad's intentions yesterday. I've had a long night to think about it. If you were me, wouldn't you want a normal life for your child?"

Hattie kept her tears at bay. No man had ever so much as touched her body, so how could she, in all honesty, know what this child was going through? "I can only imagine your anguish, just as I can only imagine Thad's pain at losing his wife. I've never had anyone who cared about me that much."

"Haven't you? I only have to look into David's eyes when he talks about you to know how much he cares for you."

"That's funny, it hasn't been obviously to me."

The smile crossing Alisha's lips unnerved Hattie. Did David care? It seemed that way until she let her imagination run wild when she saw David and Alisha together at the church.

"I'd like to ask you to help me," Alisha continued, breaking into Hattie's thoughts.

"How can I help you?"

"Teach me how to be a good wife and mother."

This time it was Hattie who laughed. "I have no children, and I've never been married. How could I teach you things I know nothing about?"

"Your home says you know more than I ever will. Cousin Edna told me how you came here to work, not only in the dress shop but also as Mr. Levens' housekeeper. For someone who has no idea how to be a good wife, you're doing a wonderful job of it."

"But I…"

"There's so much more to being a wife than what happens when the lights go out. I know all about that part of marriage. What I don't know is how to cook and sew and how to keep a house. As for you not being a mother, you've been doing a very good job with Sammy, or so I've heard from Cousin Edna, David, and Thad."

Hattie beamed at the compliment. "I never thought of things that way. I've been cooking and keeping house all my life. I never considered it anything special. I started doing all those things when I was only a few years older than Sammy. My ma took sick not long after my older sister ran away to get married. She never recovered. Once she died, I had to keep house for Pa and me."

"Will you teach me?"

"I will, but I have one condition."

"What is that?"

"Search your heart. I know you don't love Thad and he doesn't love you. It's a shame, but it can't be changed in time for the wedding. My condition is that you do everything in your power to make Thad and Sammy happy. He hasn't had an easy life, but he is a good man. I ought to know, he lives in my house and we work together on a daily basis. His offer of marriage is an honorable one. He needs someone to make his life complete."

* * * *

"What do you think they're talking about?" Thad said once he closed the door between the shop and the living quarters.

"My father always said it was best not to question the conversations of women. They aren't anything men can understand. What I want to know is if you're certain about your proposal?"

"I've given it a lot of thought. When I first came here, I told Hattie I would repay her. She said someday I'd do the same for someone else. I think someday came to town with Alisha. She's not a bad girl, just one in trouble. I think we'll do well together."

David prayed Thad was right. Unfortunately, he remembered what Alisha had been like when he knew her in Philadelphia. Was it possible her present condition turned her from one of a girl who loved to be the center of attention no matter what the cost, to the woman who had just accepted Thad's proposal?

"How soon can you marry us?" Thad said, when David made no comment on his previous statement.

"We should post the banns and that will take a week at the least. I suppose we could plan it for a week from Saturday."

"If it only takes a week for the banns, why can't we be married privately a week from tomorrow?"

"I thought Alisha might want more time to plan your wedding."

"This isn't a social event. It's nothing we want to flaunt. If we are married quietly, it won't draw quite as much attention to Alisha's condition."

David felt ashamed. Ever since he recognized Alisha in church on Sunday, his concern had not been for a young girl in trouble. He'd centered his thought on the impact all of this would have on Hattie and her budding faith. His concerns had also been for himself and how Alisha's outburst could endanger his relationship with Hattie and the church council.

He asked the Lord's forgiveness. He needed *His* help to do what was best for everyone, not just himself.

"Can we be married next Tuesday?" Thad said, when David didn't answer immediately.

"Ah, I don't see any reason not to have the ceremony as you suggested. I'm only worrying about such a hasty decision. You hardly know each other, so how can you be certain this is for the best?"

"Marriages have been entered into for far less reasons. Before I moved to Ohio, I lived in New York. There, I met many couples that were married without ever seeing each other before the event. Arranged marriages have been going on since the beginning of time. My own parents married for love and, yet before the accident that took their lives, their love had grown to hate. Perhaps Alisha and I will grow to love each other given enough time. It's what I've prayed for, a mother for Sammy."

David smiled at the logic this young man possessed. "Just how long have you been praying for this?"

"Ever since I heard of her arrival in town last week. The message I sensed is we need each other. I was pleased when she said you told her of my intentions. It gave her time to consider a future with me."

Before David could reply, the door between the shop and the living quarters opened.

David assessed the women who entered the shop. The strain of the situation showed in Hattie's eyes while Alisha literally beamed.

"David has agreed to marry us in a private ceremony a week from tomorrow," Thad announced.

Hattie's expression was one of total surprise. "So ... so soon?" she stammered.

"It's what we want, Hattie," Thad said coming to her side. "There is enough talk going on about Alisha as it is. Once we're married and settled, folks will find something else to talk about."

David understood all too well what Thad meant. From the look on Hattie's face when he first came into the shop with Alisha, David knew the word had spread about him not getting back from the Mason farm last night. Considering what happened in church yesterday, it was no wonder Hattie didn't want to talk to him.

The thought made David realize everything he worked so hard to achieve with Hattie had been shattered in the blink of an eye. He prayed the only thing she'd lost was her trust in him. That could be regained. If the fragile faith that had started to grow had been destroyed, he would feel like a failure.

Before David could say anything more, the bell above the door jingled. He turned to see Ralph and Edna enter the shop. By the look on Edna's face, he knew she was ready to make wedding plans. He certainly wouldn't be needed for such planning.

With one last glance toward the three women who were busy talking about fabric and weddings, David went out into the cold. He had things to attend to at the parsonage.

Chapter Seventeen

Even though Edna Mason was considered the best cook in the county, Alisha insisted on learning the skills she lacked in Hattie's kitchen Alisha's comment about wanting to know exactly what Thad liked left Hattie more than a bit skeptical.

As Hattie got to know Alisha, she realized it wasn't learning how to make Thad's favorites so much as getting to know the man who would become her husband that brought Alisha to the shop on a daily basis.

Sammy enjoyed having Alisha come as much as Thad. If Hattie didn't know better, she would have thought the two were mother and daughter rather than strangers. When Hattie observed how much they looked alike, Thad admitted Alisha bore a striking resemblance to Sammy's mother. Hattie hoped there would be more substance to the relationship than a physical reminder of his dead wife.

By Saturday, Hattie was more than ready for an excuse to leave the shop for a while. As she walked toward the church, she realized she hadn't seen David since Monday afternoon. Her mind spun with the possibilities as to why he was avoiding her. Could it be he was in love with Alisha and only encouraged her to accept Thad's proposal to save himself the embarrassment of the girl's situation. Was it Hattie's cold response to David on Monday that kept him away?

She contemplated both options as she walked the familiar streets. Beneath her feet the crunch of the snow gave up no answers.

"Good afternoon," Maude called as Hattie passed her home.

Didn't that woman ever stay inside? "Good afternoon to you too, Maude," she replied. "As cold as it, I thought you might be snuggled up in front of the fireplace today."

"I was, but then I saw this rug. It just needed shaking. I don't know how things can get so dirty.

"I know what you mean. I find it harder and harder to keep things clean."

"Well, that shouldn't be a problem for you much longer. The way I hear it, you won't have to worry much about housework at all. I can't believe Thad is actually marrying that girl. I thought he had better sense."

Hattie' temper came to a rapid boil. "Thad is doing what he feels is right. Alisha's child needs a father as much as Sammy needs a mother. He knows how hard it is to raise a child alone. I think it's the perfect solution to both of their situations."

Without waiting for Maude to comment further, Hattie turned and continued on her way, a self-satisfied smile on her face.

* * * *

David sat in the front pew, his hands clasped in prayer. In his entire life, he'd never prayed as much as he had these last few days. Had he done the right thing by agreeing to marry Thad and Alisha? No matter how many times he asked the question, the answer was always the same, Thad's solution to the problem had been the best for both parties.

Behind him, the door to the sanctuary opened. Surprised by the intrusion on his private moment, he turned to see Hattie enter through the side door. He wondered how time had gotten away from him. He'd come just after breakfast and expected to be only a few minutes. Instead, it had been hours.

"Oh, David, I didn't expect to see you here," Hattie said.

Just seeing her bathed in the weak winter light from the stained glass window brought a smile to his lips. "Time slipped away from me. I know how you like to be alone on Saturday afternoons."

He wondered if the pink in her cheeks came from the cold or if his presence caused her to blush.

"You don't have to leave," she replied, as she came to the front of

157

the church. "As I recall, we never finished our talk."

"I thought you … well you have been busy."

"Apparently you have as well."

David watched as she unwound he scarf from around her neck and removed her coat. At least the sanctuary was warmer than it had been when he first arrived. By banking the fire in the stove it would stay relatively comfortable for the rest of the afternoon.

"Have you been staying warm enough?" Hattie said, as she opened her bottle of lemon oil.

David reached out and touched her hand. The gesture caused her to set aside the bottle and look into his eyes. "That's not what we have to talk about," he said, once he had her attention.

"I know. I'm sorry I jumped to the wrong conclusions about you and Alisha. You must admit I had provocation." She paused a moment. "Why did you go to the Mason place on Sunday?"

"Do you think Ralph gave me any choice? He assumed the same thing everyone else did. It took most of the afternoon to straighten things out. By the time we did, the storm hit. Getting back to town was impossible."

David waited for Hattie to respond to what he said. When she made no response, he pondered what his next move should be.

"Alisha confided in me about the child's father," Hattie said. "She told me she knew you in Philadelphia, but only as an acquaintance."

"How do you feel about Alisha and Thad's marriage?" David hoped to prolong their conversation.

"I think they'll make a go of it. It's true, they aren't marrying for the reasons they should be, but they are making an effort."

"Will you be comfortable with another woman in your house?"

Hattie's brows knotted at his question. "We've gotten along quite well this past week, but when it's all the time, things could be different. I must say, with Thad helping me in the shop and Alisha in the house, I will be able to find more time to read. It will make up for the hour I miss on Sunday mornings."

Hattie's comment brought a smile to David's lips. "Since I have always enjoyed a good book, perhaps we could spend one evening a week reading."

"It might be a bit hard with Thad and Alisha at the house."

"I was thinking more along the lines of you coming to the parsonage. I could prepare a light supper and spend the evening reading. Afterwards, it would be a pleasure to walk you home."

Hattie's smile was all the reassurance he needed.

* * * *

All the way home, Hattie smiled. She could easily envision herself and David engrossed in one of her many novels, sitting in front of a roaring fire. For one evening a week, it would be as though they were a newlywed couple like Alisha and Thad would soon be.

"What canary did you swallow?" George greeted her when she made her customary stop at the store.

"I don't know what you could possibly mean," she replied, still unable to stop smiling.

"Oh I think you do. How are the wedding plans coming?"

"There aren't many plans to be made," Hattie answered. She was relieved to think he equated her beaming smile with Thad's wedding rather than David's invitation to spend time in her company. "It's going to be a very private affair."

"Thad is a very generous young man. Not many men would marry a complete stranger to give her child a name.

Hattie agreed wholeheartedly. Thad was a very special person. Although he didn't love Alisha, Hattie had no doubt their union would turn from one of convenience to one of love.

* * * *

Tuesday morning dawned with clear skies. A southerly breeze brought temperatures warm enough to melt the snow covering the area for over a week.

To keep Thad and Alisha from seeing each other, Hattie took the dress she made for Alisha to the church. The soft blue fabric Hattie chose suited Alisha much better than the brassy red she'd worn the first time Hattie saw her. To make the dress more functional, Hattie had added gathers to the full skirt that could easily be removed as Alisha's waist thickened to accommodate the precious life she carried just under her heart.

"This dress is beautiful," Alisha declared. "I can't believe you made it especially for me. I thought I'd have to wear one of the dresses I brought with me from Philadelphia."

Hattie could tell Alisha's words rang true. The dress did look good on her. It was certainly more practical than the satin gown Hattie made for Gertie's daughter, Susan, just a year ago.

She mentally compared the two weddings. Susan's wedding day had been much like today only the church was filled with guests and Hattie's music. Herman gave the bride away and Gertie prepared a lavish dinner for the guests.

Had Alisha not listened to her father and traded her favors for legal counsel for her brother, she might have had such a wedding. Instead, she'd been sent hundreds of miles from home because of her disgrace. Instead of friends and close family, she would be married in front of distant relatives and strangers, including the stranger she would call her husband for the rest of her life.

Tears of frustration ran down Hattie's cheeks. Would she be the only one to cry for Alisha on her wedding day? The question brought to mind Laura's wedding. Surely no one cried for her, Pa shouted 'Good riddance' when she rode away with Caleb. Had the curses that surely rang in their ears cursed their union?

Long after, Hattie remembered Laura told her in a letter how she'd taken the dowry money from Pa. At the time Pa complained bitterly about not being able to find the one hundred dollars he'd hidden away in the kitchen. As an appeasement, Ma told him he'd taken it to town months earlier and squandered it in the tavern. Although Pa accepted her explanation, Hattie soon realized her mother helped Laura take the money, knowing her father would have withheld it as well as his consent.

"Oh Hattie," Alisha declared, coming to Hattie's side. "You cannot cry on my wedding day. I forbid it. Everyone must be as happy as I am."

"Are you happy? Are you really and truly happy?"

"Yes I am. I never thought someone like Thad could become so special so quickly. Even Sammy has wormed her way into my heart."

"I'm so glad. You must know I worried about this."

"Of course I do, but you mustn't worry about us. We will do just fine. All my life I've been pampered and spoiled. If I did anything my parents asked, they gave me whatever I wanted. When Papa wanted to save Willard's sorry hide, he told me to let Willard's lawyer have his way with me. By the time I knew about the baby, Willard's trial was over, and he was in jail. Instead of being rewarded for what I was told to do, Papa said I was a disgrace. To put it mildly, I was sent away because my parents didn't want to have to explain my situation to their friends. They threw me away. If not for Thad's generosity, I don't know what I would have done."

Hattie embraced Alisha. This was her wedding day, and she deserved the happiness every bride expected. Hattie only prayed Alisha was ready to be the wife Thad deserved.

As soon as her silent prayer winged its way heavenward, Hattie realized she'd actually been praying. Was she beginning to believe?

What do you think? A strange voice within her replied.

* * * *

"Do you, Thaddeus, take Alisha to be your lawful wedded wife?" David said.

The young man standing before him took his bride's hand in his. "I do." Thad's voice was strong and steady.

"Do you, Alisha, take Thaddeus to be your lawful wedded husband?"

David wondered if it was his imagination or did Alisha hesitate for a moment before adding her 'I do' to the silence that seemed to hang in the almost empty church.

As soon as she did, David breathed a long sigh of relief. He'd held his breath in anticipation of her answer. The realization made him wonder if he thought Alisha would bolt and run.

It pleased him to see her brilliant smile. Relief filled him as he finished the vows they both repeated. Once they were done, he took both their hands in his before he proclaimed them man and wife.

With no hesitation, Thad took Alisha in his arms and kissed her lovingly. As the two of them embraced, David turned his gaze toward Hattie. The single tear rolling down her cheek made him want to take her into his arms as well. Were her tears those of joy at the new union between Thad and Alisha or for some other reason?

161

* * * *

The small wedding party left the church and went to Hattie's house for the luncheon she and Edna prepared. From the parlor, the buzz of conversation between the invited guests alerted Hattie to the need to put out the food.

"Could you use some help?"

Hattie looked up to see David enter the kitchen. "I'd like that," she replied, brushing away a stray strand of hair from her eyes.

"You look bushed. I'm afraid this has been too much for you."

Hattie pulled out a chair and sat down. "It has been a long week. Once today is over, I'll have plenty of time to rest." Hattie hoped David would believe her explanation. She certainly didn't want her dark suspicions about the marriage that just took place to come to the surface.

"I think it's more than a trying week. I'm afraid you were thinking the same thing as I was during the ceremony. I never expected to have such doubts about the first marriage I performed."

Hattie could hardly believe her ears. "If you had doubts, why did you agree to marry them?"

David's smile seemed to fade as he pondered her question. "Thad and I have had some long talks about it. Although he admits he's being selfish in wanting a mother for Sammy, I think he's acting on a directive from God. I only pray Alisha will be able to adapt to her new life."

Pray! The word echoed in Hattie's mind, Hours earlier, she'd questioned her need to pray about the same situation. The realization brought on a flood of tears. To her surprise, David crossed the short expanse separating them to kneel beside her chair. Even more amazing was the tenderness he displayed by taking her in his arms.

"Please don't cry," he pleaded as he stroked her hair. "I'm sure Thad and Alisha will make a go of it."

"The irony of David's statement was suddenly funny. "I'm … I'm not crying for them," she stammered.

David held her at arm's length. "Then why are you crying?"

Hattie took a deep breath. Did she dare open her heart to tell David the truth?

"Did you hear me, Hattie?" David said when she didn't answer.

Hattie found herself praying again. This time it was for the strength to tell David about the strange voice she'd been hearing within the depths of her mind.

"I will give you the strength you need," the voice seemed to say.

"Just before the wedding I actually prayed for Thad and Alisha to be happy."

David stared at her as though he didn't comprehend her meaning.

"I'm so new at all of this I'm sure I'll never find the proper words to say what's in my heart. In all my life I've never been good enough to pray. I ought to know, because my father told me enough times. I've never prayed before today and yet, before the ceremony I prayed for Thad and Alisha. When I did, I heard a strange voice in my head. I thought it was because I was tired when I heard it on Sunday, but..."

"Are you beginning to find our Lord, Hattie? Are you beginning to believe?"

"I ... I don't know. What I do know is that the same voice spoke to me just now. "I'm not ready to say I believe, but I want to learn more. Will you teach me?"

"You don't need a teacher, just someone to show you the way." He smiled. "I have a feeling we may have to get together two nights a week. One for reading your novels, and the other for learning more about God's love."

Chapter Eighteen

"What would you like to have me fix for supper tonight?" Alisha said, when they finished eating their noon meal.

"Whatever the two of you want will be just fine with me," Hattie replied. "I won't be here."

"You won't? Why not?" Thad appeared surprised.

"David and I are spending the evening with one of my novels."

"Do you think that's a good idea?" Thad cautioned.

Hattie checked her temper before answering.

"Now you sound like Maude," Alisha said before Hattie could speak. "Not only do I think it's a wonderful idea Hattie and David are keeping company, but it will give us some time alone. It will be nice to be a family. We can have a special evening with just the three of us."

"But…"

"But nothing, Thad," Hattie said, finding her voice. "David and I agree you need time alone, as a matter of fact, so do we. Tonight we will be reading one of my novels and on Thursday evening we will be discussing the Bible."

Thad's raised eyebrows made Hattie wonder what was going on within the confines of his mind.

"Novel reading and Bible study sound like really exciting evenings to me. Are you certain the two of you don't need a chaperone? You are a proper maiden lady, you know."

Hattie smiled at Thad's teasing tone. "I've been a proper maiden lady all my life. I was one before David Long came to town and I will be one after he leaves. Not so long ago the church council condemned us for eating Sunday dinner together. David told them we would continue to see each other socially. You of all people should be aware of that. David spent enough evenings in this house after you came to Mortonville."

The smile disappeared from Thad's lips. "That was different. You weren't alone. What will people say?"

"Oh, Thad, you must understand, David and I have heard every bit of vicious gossip this town could come up with. At this point, neither of us care much about what other people say. We enjoy being together."

"Since this is how you feel, you have my blessing as well."

* * * *

David checked the chicken roasting in the oven. It was turning a beautiful golden brown and smelled delicious. On the top of the stove a pan of vegetable he found in the basement sat to the back away from the direct heat. Another pan, filled with potatoes came to a boil. He knew Hattie would be here soon and timing was important.

He glanced at the table he'd set. He regretted not heeding his mother's advice when he told her of the condition of the parsonage's china and flatware. He'd spent the major part of the afternoon sorting through the various mismatched plates in order to find two without chips or cracks. His table, in no way, resembled the elegant one Hattie set for him months earlier.

The rap at his front door sounded more tentative than eager. Was Hattie having second thoughts?

David hurried through the front room to greet his guest. He couldn't suppress the feeling of excitement at the prospect of spending and entire evening in her company. Back in Philadelphia, he'd kept company with many young ladies, but always under the watchful eye of the girls' parents.

Before when he'd been alone with Hattie, it had been by the light of day. Even when they went for their carriage rides, they'd been home in time to eat supper before sunset.

When David opened the door, he was greeted by Hattie's warm smile. In one hand she carried a plate of cookies and in the other her ever present music bag.

"And just what do you have in your bag tonight?" David said, once he helped Hattie with her coat and took the heavy bag from her.

"I wasn't certain what you would enjoy, so I brought a variety. I found copies of Homer's *Odyssey*, Mr. Dickens' *A Tale of Two Cities* and Mr. Shakespeare's *Romeo and Juliet*."

"I would prefer something other than *The Odyssey* or *Romeo and Juliet*. I think *A Tale of Two Cities* would be perfect.

Hattie's smile turned to a more somber expression as she wrinkled her nose at the odor coming from the kitchen It certainly wasn't the succulent aroma of roasting chicken, Before either of them could make a move toward the kitchen, smoke began to fill the house.

Hattie was the first to move. She made it to the kitchen only a few steps ahead of David. To his horror the smoke was coming from the pan of potatoes. Without hesitation, she grabbed the pan and pulled it from the stove before dropping it to the floor. It was evident she'd burned her hand in the process.

"What-what do you think happened?" David stammered.

Although he knew she had to be in pain, Hattie began to laugh. "They boiled dry and scorched. It happens even to the best of cooks. I remember the first time it happened to me. My pa beat the tar out of me. I was afraid to ever let it happen again."

David moved to her side, after picking up the pan, using a pair of potholders, and tossing it out into the snow. He took her injured hand in his and examined the blister already beginning to rise on her delicate palm. Thoughts of how to treat a burn rushed through his mind. He remembered telling his mother how his friend had been burned and the boy's mother used butter to treat the injury. His mother told him the best thing for burns was aloe. When he came from Philadelphia to Mortonville, she'd tucked a pot filled with the plant in his trunk.

"I've got just the thing," David declared. He went into the parlor and picked up the pot he'd nurtured ever since his arrival.

"What in the world are you doing?" Hattie asked. "All this needs is a little butter and it will be just fine."

"You have a lot to learn, Miss Fairchild, and it isn't just about God's love. That butter you want will only drive the burn deeper into your skin. This will be much better."

He broke off one of the leaves and milked the soothing liquid from the piece of it he held in his hand. Gently he rubbed the soothing balm over Hattie's injured skin.

"It does feel better," she admitted, as he made a circular motion to make certain the ointment covered the entire burned area.

"I certainly didn't expect you to get hurt by coming here," David said, once he finished. "I'd planned a nice quiet evening."

Hattie raised her injured hand and pressed her finger against his lips. "Whatever it was you used, it did the trick. I can't believe the pain is almost gone. If we stand here looking at my hand any longer though, the chicken I smell in your oven will be as burned as your beans."

"It can wait for a minute. I'd like to put some gauze on your hand so it doesn't get infected."

Hattie shook her head no. "Tell me where I can find the gauze and you take the chicken out of the oven. I don't know about you, but I'm starving."

David told here where to find the dressing for her hand and busied himself taking the roasting pan from the oven. When he checked the color of the skin of the bird, he realized if he'd waited any longer that part of his meal would have been ruined as well.

"Everything looks delicious," Hattie gushed as he held her chair for her.

"Even without the potatoes?"

Hattie laughed. "Even without the potatoes. I'd expected vegetables from one of the tins George has at his store. These beans taste as good as any I've ever canned. Where did you get them?"

"The basement is filled with canned goods. I guess Mrs. Hall liked doing that sort of thing."

"You've got it all wrong. Mabel didn't like doing that kind of thing at all. More than likely these are from my garden or maybe Maude or Gertie put them up. You know, a contribution to the church. I'm amazed there are any left. We must have done that canning three years ago."

David almost choked on the forkful of beans he'd just put into his mouth. "Do you mean I'm eating three year old vegetables?"

Hattie smiled at his comment. "It doesn't look like you're suffering too much. If you've been using these vegetables since you arrived, I think they're safe to eat."

David felt silly for having such a reaction to the canned goods he'd been using since July.

With supper finished, he insisted the dishes could wait until morning, considering Hattie's injured hand.

"You're making far too much of this," she protested. "I was foolish to pick up the pan without a potholder. Besides, whatever it was you put on it really worked. What do you call it?"

"Aloe. I'm surprised you've never heard of it before. My mother swears by it. I tried to tell her I wouldn't need it, but when I unpacked, I found it carefully tucked in one of my trunks, I guess she did know what was best for me after all. If you'd like, I could start you a cutting from it."

He could tell by the look on her face Hattie couldn't envision someone with the size of David's hands planting the delicate cuttings. "I could..."

"No, I'd like to do it for you. My father liked to relax by working with my mother's plants. He told me all men should take the time to work with the soil, He said it relaxed him after a hard day at work. He even built a hothouse for the plants my mother loves so dearly."

* * * *

Hattie tried to imagine an older version of David doing something so out of the ordinary and special for the woman he loved.

At Hattie's insistence, she helped David clear the table before they went to the parlor. She watched as he built up the fire then seated herself beside him on the divan.

"Shall we begin," David said, as he reached into the music bag and retrieved the copy of *A Tale of Two Cities*.

Hattie nodded. "Would you start reading it? I so enjoy listening to you." She tucked her legs beneath her and curled up catlike in the corner of the divan.

"It was the best of times. It was the worst of times." The opening words of the novel led to more and more words as the story unfolded and came to life.

By the time the clock struck nine, Hattie was completely lost in the words of the book as narrated by David. It made her wantonly wish she didn't have to walk the short distance back to her home.

She admonished herself for such foolishness. No man wanted to be saddled with an old maid. He might enjoy spending time with her now, but when someone younger attracted his eye, she'd be as alone as she had been in the past.

"I think we should call it an evening," David said as Hattie stifled a yawn. "You look like you're about to fall asleep. I hope the sound of my voice doesn't have the same effect on the members of my congregation."

Hattie laughed. "On Sunday morning no one would dare to doze off. Your voice booms enough to wake the dead. Even if anyone might try to sleep through one of your sermons, it would be impossible because they are far too interesting."

"You do know all the right things to say. I hope you'll be as well-spoken on Thursday evening when we begin our Bible study."

Hattie shuddered a bit at the thought of a Bible study. Reading novels was one thing. Matching wits with David over something he understood far better than she ever would was frightening.

"Where do we start?" she managed to ask. "It might be in my best interests if I knew what we will be talking about before we begin."

David looked as though he was deep in thought. "I find it's best to start at the beginning."

"Creation?" Hattie said.

"Not that far back. I was thinking along the line of the first chapter of Matthew. With Christmas so close at hand, discovering the events leading up to the holy birth will be the perfect way to begin. Do you have a Bible?"

"What a question to ask. Of course I do. It just so happens I have my father's Bible tucked away, somewhere."

"I don't want you to use that one," David declared.

The statement puzzled Hattie. "Why ever not? A Bible is a Bible, isn't it?

"Yes and no. From what you've told me, your father twisted the message until it suited his needs. That Bible holds some bitter memories for you. Since you're beginning a new journey, I thought you should have a new Bible. One all your own."

Hattie watched as David got up from the divan and opened the roll top desk on the other side of the room. When he returned, he held out a finely bound black book with the words *Holy Bible* embossed into the leather of the cover. Three quarters of the way through the book, a delicate lace bookmark in the shape of a cross, marked the first chapter of Matthew.

"Oh David, wherever did you get this?"

"I had my father get it for me from a special book store in Philadelphia. My mother added the bookmark for you. I hope you like it."

Of all the books Hattie possessed, none were the quality of this one. It surprised her how warm the soft leather felt against her hands. Staring at the page to which she'd opened, she noticed the exceptional quality of the print.

"Open the front cover," David prompted.

On the flyleaf, in the bold script she equated with the Reverend David Long, she saw the inscription. *To Hattie—Let the adventure begin—David.*

Through tear-filled eyes, Hattie looked up at him. To her surprise, his eyes also glistened with tears.

"I thought the words were appropriate," David said without giving Hattie a chance to comment.

"Appropriate? I don't know. I doubt if anyone would ever call me adventurous."

"Maybe not your neighbors, but I happen to think you're very adventurous. Not many women would stand up to their father the way you did. That's only the beginning. It took guts and courage to sell the familiar and venture into the unknown."

"But Abe offered…"

"How many women would have accepted? Not many I'll wager. Of course not many women catch and clean their own fish for Sunday dinner, either."

Hattie could feel a blush of pride creeping into her cheeks. She'd never seen her life in the light David just portrayed it. The things she'd done had been out of necessity. They'd kept her alive. Looking back, they did have an air of adventure to them. She wasn't fighting Indians or wild animals, but her battles had been just as courageous.

"I'll have to think about what you just said," Hattie replied, not wanting David to know how close to the truth he'd come.

* * * *

David enjoyed the look on Hattie's face. It was exactly the one he'd hoped to produce when he first ordered the special Bible. His anticipation had grown as he wrote the inscription. Both his written and spoken words gave her the chance to examine her life in a new light.

Behind him, the mantel clock struck ten times. As though Hattie became Cinderella, her expression changed. "Oh dear, look at the time. Thad will think I've gotten lost. I'd better get home before he starts searching for me."

David chuckled. "I do believe Thad and Alisha have other things on their minds than where you are. Nevertheless, it is late. I'll get our coats and walk you home."

"That's really not…"

"Necessary?" David questioned, finishing Hattie's sentence. "Perhaps not, but it would certainly be pleasant."

He left her standing in the parlor while he went to retrieve her coat from the closet beneath the stairs. On his return, he held her coat and then handed her the scarf she'd worn earlier.

Just the brush of her body against his made him wish he had more to offer Hattie. As a minister, he certainly couldn't shower her with worldly possessions. Beside the clothes on his back and a few personal belongings, he had nothing to offer. The parsonage, as well as its furnishings, belonged to the church. It didn't matter if he were in Mortonville or some other town. The situation would always be the same.

"Is something wrong?" Hattie said, when he held onto her scarf a moment longer than necessary.

"Not really. I was only thinking how nice it was to have you here tonight. I don't want the evening to end."

"We'll have more evenings, but not if I don't get home to bed soon."

David opened the door and held it as Hattie stepped out into the chill of the night to join him. He hadn't realized how warm the house had been until the north wind hit him square in the face.

"We'll have to huddle together to keep warm," Hattie said, her tone making him wish they could cuddle rather than huddle.

Protectively, he put his arm around her shoulders to draw her close to him so they could share each other's warmth. Although he wanted to prolong the short walk between their homes, he quickened his pace. There was no need to risk frostbite.

When they stood at her front door, David threw caution to the wind and took Hattie in his arms. When she didn't protest his actions, he captured her lips, kissing her tenderly.

If Hattie was shocked by his gesture, she didn't show it. Instead she snuggled closer into his embrace.

"I hope I didn't offend you," he whispered, his lips still dangerously close to hers.

"Not in the least. I rather enjoyed it."

Without hesitation, he kissed her once more before bidding her good night.

* * * *

Once inside, Hattie closed the door to the shop and leaned heavily against it. David's unexpected actions of moments earlier should have outraged her. Instead, she'd welcomed his embrace as well as his kiss. She thought of how the young girls in town were teased about being sweet sixteen and never been kissed. At almost twice that age, this was the first kiss she'd ever received from a man.

David's taste lingered on her lips, causing warmth to spread throughout her body. If one kiss could produce such a feeling, it was no wonder girls like Alisha found themselves in trouble.

"We were getting worried," Thad greeted her.

"Don't listen to a word he says," Alisha declared. "We knew you were perfectly safe with David. Did you have a good time?"

The events of the evening flashed through Hattie's mind, beginning with the scorched potatoes and ending with David's kiss. "It was a pleasant evening. I hope I can say as much for Thursday night."

"That's right," Thad said. "You'll be starting your Bible study."

Hattie thought of the new book in her bag. Even with the lateness of the hour, she was anxious to read the chapter David assigned to her.

"What will you be studying?" Thad pressed.

"The first chapter of Matthew," Hattie replied without thinking.

"If you can get through that list of people Jesus was descended from, you'll do all right. It's hardly a spectacular opener."

"I don't expect the Bible to be as exciting as one of my novels, but I'll make it through."

"Well, you'll have to make it alone," Alisha said. "It's been a long day. Now that you're safely home, I think we should go to bed."

Hattie watched Thad help Alisha to her feet. Hand in hand they made their way to the bedroom. Once the door was closed, Hattie could only imagine the whispered words of endearment and the nervous giggles, which would follow.

How she wished David would consider her special and lead her away to unknown delights.

How could she ever believe David would consider her special? A man like him would never be content with a woman like her. He knew too much about her past ever to want her in his life.

Chapter Nineteen

Hattie could hardly hide her shock over the words she'd read and reread over the past two days. To soften their impact, she read the beginnings of all four Gospels. The only thing she'd accomplished was to add to her confusion.

If Mathew's words were correct, Jesus started his life in much the same way as Alisha's child. Had it not been for Joseph, he would have been branded an outcast. The same was true for Mary. If Joseph hadn't taken her as his wife, the good people of Nazareth might have shunned her, forcing the young girl into a life of disgrace. How different things would have been if Joseph had not done the right thing by her.

Hattie put aside the piece on which she was working, but couldn't concentrate on it. Being close to noon, she excused herself and went to the kitchen to see if she could help Alisha.

"This is how Aunt Hattie sets the table," Sammy instructed. "The fork goes here and the knife and spoon on the other side. The knife has to protect the spoon just like Papa protects you and me, but the fork can take care of itself, like Aunt Hattie."

"Where in the world did you ever hear something like that?" Hattie said, as she entered the kitchen.

"I just made it up. I like to make up stories."

Alisha stood at the sink. She was laughing so heartily, Hattie couldn't help but join her. The sound of Alisha's laughter was in contrast to the somber girl who first came to this house. It warmed Hattie's heart.

"Why don't you go and tell your papa to get cleaned up for dinner?"

Alisha suggested. "Hattie and I can finish here."

"How did you know I wanted to talk to you alone?" Hattie said, once Sammy left the room.

"Just a guess. You look like you have something on your mind."

"I do. How did you feel when you first found out about…" Without saying more, Hattie lowered her gaze to the slight bulge under Alisha's apron.

Alisha's smile turned to a pensive look. "At first I didn't want to believe it and felt dirty. Once it sunk in, I realized I had a precious life to think about. My only concern was how people would treat my child, considering … well you know. The best thing that could have happened to me was being sent here and finding Thad and Sammy."

Hattie nodded. That must have be how Mary felt. It surprised her to have such a thought cross her mind.

"It's time to stop talking about me," Thad announced when he entered the kitchen. "Sammy says dinner is ready and I'm starved."

* * * *

David wanted no repeat of the disaster with the potatoes. To avoid it, he checked the canned goods in the basement. He was pleased to find several jars of canned beef he soon turned into a rich stew. A loaf of homemade bread from George's store, along with a jar of applesauce from the basement, completed the meal.

At precisely five o'clock, Hattie knocked at the parsonage door. "I don't smell any scorched potatoes," she teased once he took her coat.

"I doubt if I'll make that mistake again."

Hattie's laughter filled the parsonage, reminding David of how lonely this house could be.

With supper finished, David again insisted he could do the dishes in the morning so they could retire to the parlor for their discussion.

"Did you find the time to read the first chapter of Matthew?"

"That and more. I read the first chapters of all four Gospels. They're all quite different. I was particularly taken with the story of Mary being with child and not married. The only thing the story said was about her disgrace if Joseph put her aside. What would have happened to her?"

"I asked that same question while I was preparing for the ministry. I found the answer in one of the many books I'd been given to study. I read one theory that she would have been stoned as an adulteress. At best, she would have been sent away in disgrace."

"Things haven't changed much, have they?"

David was surprised by Hattie's comment. "I never thought of it that way. You could be right, though. Customs don't change over the years. A child born on the wrong side of the blanket, so to say, has always carried a stigma."

"From what I read, an angel came to Joseph and told him it was all right to take Mary as his wife. Do you think an angel came to Thad?"

David contemplated Hattie's question. If God hadn't sent the angel to Joseph would Mary have been sent to live with strangers and forced to make up a believable lie about her child's father? Had the same angel come to Thad and open his heart to Alisha and the child she carried?

"God works in wondrous ways. It could be that one of God's angels put the idea into Thad's head."

Hattie's quizzical expression amused David. "What do you mean?"

David took her hand in his and brought it to his lips. "I think I'm looking at her."

"Me? I never put such an idea in his head. If anything, I tried to dissuade him."

"I'm certain you did, but if you recall, you did tell him someday he would befriend someone and repay his debt to you for bringing him here. He felt by marrying Alisha, he could not only give Sammy the mother she deserved, but he could also be a father to Alisha's baby. Therefore, my angel, you might be the one who inadvertently gave him the idea. If you hadn't done the Christian thing by bringing him here, he wouldn't have done the same for Alisha."

* * * *

Hattie could hardly believe what David said. No one ever equated her with an angel, especially not an angel from God.

"I ... I think we've gotten off the subject," she stammered.

"Do you know how pretty you are when you're flustered?" David said, placing his hand against her cheek.

In all her life, only her sister, Laura, had been called pretty. Pa certainly never used such an adjective to describe his youngest daughter. Certainly no man ever confirmed David's opinion, since no man ever paid her court. As Pa said, no man in his right mind would want a brazen red head with a head full of independent ideas when there were petite young dependent women in town.

"I appreciate your flattery. I'm just not used to such things. I know I'm no one's idea of the perfect woman, I should know, Pa told me so enough times to impress the truth of it on me." She turned away from David unable to look into his eyes to see the pity hiding there.

"Beauty, my dear Hattie, is in the eye of the beholder. Perhaps the right man hasn't seen it before. George told me he planned to court you until your father scared him away with his shotgun. Well, now there is no shotgun and, even if there were, I doubt if it would stop me. You deserve a man's love."

"Oh, David, you are so wrong. Can't you see I'm not the kind of woman who will sit quietly in a man's shadow? You deserve a docile wife who…"

To Hattie's surprise, David took her in his arms and silenced her words with a loving kiss. "How do you know what I'm looking for in a wife?" he said once they parted.

"Everyone says…"

Again he silenced her. "I'm a big man, one who could have my choice of any empty headed young women in Philadelphia. Before I came here, everyone insisted I needed a wife to come with me. The Lord knew better. He sent me to Mortonville to find a beautiful brazen red head, who was well educated and not afraid to speak her mind."

Hattie looked up, shocked by his words. They were the ones she'd wanted to hear all her life. "What are you saying?"

"I want you in my home and not just on Tuesday and Thursday nights. I intend to have a proper period of courtship, but in the end, I will ask you to be my wife."

Hattie cursed her ability to blush so easily at his words. David was suggesting she become his wife. Her shop would belong to Thad and Alisha. For the first time in her life, she would be respected, the wife of David Long, the minister of Mortonville's church.

"How can you want me?" she said, the nagging guilt of her lack of faith biting at the back of her mind.

"How can I not?"

"But you need a woman who is more pious in her faith."

"I've watched you grow immensely in the past months. I have no doubt the growth will continue. I'm afraid I'm the one who should be concerned about my worthiness of you. Together we will make a good pair. Will you consider being my wife?"

Hattie's heart leaped for joy and beat so wildly, she thought it would fly out of her chest. David loved her. He wanted her to be his wife. "Oh, David, are you certain?"

His nod was all the confirmation Hattie needed. "I'd be proud to be your wife. I'll do my best to learn to trust the Lord and be a compliment to you."

* * * *

By the light of day, Hattie couldn't stop the smile spreading across her face every time she thought of David's proposal. 'A proper period of courtship,' David's words sang in her mind.

She couldn't help but wonder what he considered proper. With Christmas only two weeks away, she knew the season of preparation would be a busy one for him. Reverend Hall always considered it, as well as Easter, the most joyous times of the year. She knew the music for those times were ones she most enjoyed playing.

"Are you all right, Aunt Hattie?" Sammy said, breaking into her thoughts.

"I'm very all right. Why do you ask?"

"You've got a funny look on your face."

Hattie picked up the child and held her close. "I suppose I'm smiling more than usual. I'm just so glad to have you and your daddy and Alisha here. I can't help but smile."

"Sammy's right," Alisha observed. "You do seem happier today than usual."

Hattie was almost ready to tell Alisha the reason for her inability to keep from smiling, when George burst into the shop.

"I just got the wire from Mabel Hall. Thomas passed away last night. Mabel and her son, Carroll are bringing him back here for burial.

Their train will be in tomorrow morning, I've arranged rooms for them at the hotel."

"Tom's dead?" Hattie was unable to grasp the gravity of the situation. All thoughts of David's proposal left her mind as she came to grips with the death of her longtime friend At least she wouldn't be denied the privilege of saying good-bye to him.

"I'm afraid it's true," George assured her, handing Hattie the wire. "What I don't understand is why they wanted to bring him back here for burial?"

"Can't you? Mortonville was his home for more years than I care to count. Of course he would want to be laid to rest here. I've had a couple of letters from Mabel and she said they left because of Tom's health. I know she's been terribly homesick. Maybe she'll decide to move back here. I can't see anyone in this town turning her aside."

"Don't be silly, Hattie, she'll want to stay with her son in Ohio. Mortonville is no longer her home. Even if she is where Tom wanted to be laid to rest, I don't think she'll ever come back to stay."

Hattie buried her doubts over what George said, just as she did any mention of David's proposal. With Mabel coming back to Mortonville, things could change quite quickly, especially if Maude and some of the others passed on their juicy tidbits of gossip. Hattie could only wonder what her former friend would think of her entertaining the new minister in her home and spending her evenings in the parsonage without a proper chaperone.

"I do have some other news," George continued, pulling Hattie to the far corner of the shop. "I thought it was best if I showed you this privately. You know we don't get news from out west on any kind of a regular basis, but I saw this article and well, I thought you should see it."

Hattie took the paper from George's hand and scanned the headlines that seemed to jump out at her.

Caleb Tyler Gang Charged With Bank Robbery And Murder In Oklahoma Territory.

"Has anyone else seen this?" Hattie gasped.

"No. There was only one copy. I thought it best if I showed it to you first. Caleb Tyler is Laura's husband, isn't he?"

George's question made Hattie's knees buckle, and she reached for the nearest chair. "I'm afraid he is, and the gang they speak of are his sons, Frank, Will, Ed, and Clay. Laura has mentioned her suspicions in her letters, but I didn't realize things had progressed to this."

"What's wrong, Hattie," Thad said, rushing into the shop from the living quarters.

Hattie thrust the newspaper into George's hand with a glance she hoped indicated she wanted to keep the contents of it between the two of them. "George brought me some bad news. I'll be fine. I just need to sit down for a while."

George helped Hattie to her feet and led her from the shop to the living quarters. Once he escorted her to the bedroom, he took a comforter from the closet and encouraged her to lie down.

"Even if anyone would have seen it, I doubt if they would equate Caleb Tyler with you. Laura has been gone for so long, most people don't even remember her to say nothing of the man she married. The only reason the name meant anything to me is that I'm the postmaster. I see your outgoing and incoming mail. I've seen too many letters sent to and received from Laura Tyler. You can trust me not to tell another soul about what this article says. As a matter of fact, I'll burn the paper as soon as I get home."

Hattie looked up into George's eyes. "Thank you for being such a good friend, I can always trust you to keep your silence about this. It could ruin everything."

"Everything?"

"For now, it's a secret, but as soon as it's out of the bag, you'll understand."

"Let me guess, David asked you to marry him."

George's statement shocked Hattie. "How did you know?"

"It's been evident to everyone in town but you for months. I was wondering what took him so long. Your secret is safe with me, at least until you're ready to make the announcement yourselves."

Once George left the room, Hattie closed her eyes against the weak December sunlight. She needed time to think about how and if she would tell David about her connection to Caleb Tyler and his murderous gang. Laura's four boys had taken a path far different from the one their mother would have chosen for them. How would David ever be able to accept her once he knew the truth about her family?

Chapter Twenty

On Saturday morning, the train station was filled with members of the congregation that once belonged to Thomas Hall. David felt out of place as Mabel greeted each of her old friends with hugs and warm loving gestures.

"You must be Reverend Long," a man slightly older than David said.

David nodded.

"I'm Reverend Carroll Hall. Thomas was my father. It was his wish to be buried here. He also asked if you would preside at the funeral. I realize you didn't know him, but I can help you with the sermon. My father knew how much my mother would need my help to get through this."

David agreed. Mabel Hall was indeed a frail lady. Although he knew she would prefer to stay at the parsonage, the arrangements had already been made. At least with them staying at the hotel, he wouldn't have to share his home, He knew it belonged to Mabel for many years, but now it was his. He certainly didn't need the woman coming in and dictating how things used to be when she lived here.

Carroll went back to where his mother stood, leaving David to contemplate the funeral sermon he would be giving on Monday morning. It would be the first such sermon he'd ever given. It was unfortunate a man as well loved a Thomas Hall would be eulogized by a stranger.

On the other side of the platform, David watched as Hattie embraced Mabel. When the older woman moved on to other friends, David made his way to Hattie's side.

With all the excitement generated by the telegram received on Friday morning, David hadn't seen Hattie since Thursday night when he blurted out his proposal. He certainly hadn't expected to ask her to marry him so early in their relationship. One thing led to another and before he knew it the words spilled from his mouth.

Before he could say anything to her, everyone turned their attention to the casket being unloaded from the baggage car of the train. Mabel, as well as several other women including Hattie, wept openly at the sight of the pine box being shouldered by six of the young men from town.

In an attempt to give Hattie some semblance of comfort, David put his arm around her shoulders and pulled her close to him. "It's all right," he whispered into the hair covering her left ear.

"I know. I think it would have been easier if they hadn't brought him back here for burial. I was getting used to him not being here. This has just opened the wound of his leaving again."

"Did you know he was ill?"

"He hinted at it. I could see how he'd failed the last few weeks he was here. Thank goodness Mabel has Carroll and his family."

David look skeptically at Carroll as he mingled among old friends, allowing his wife to care for his mother. For some reason the man's actions raised David's hackles. For someone so supposedly concerned about his mother's welfare, he seemed overly attentive to the members of the church council.

* * * *

Hattie prepared Saturday evening supper for Mabel and her son and daughter-in-law. When she first suggested it, Alisha had been nervous about having such prestigious company for supper.

"They're no different from anyone else," Hattie explained as they set the table. "We'll use the good china and you'll make a great impression. Mabel is a wonderful person. I wish I could say the same for her son, Carroll. Of course, he's older now than when he left here."

"Are you sure you want us here tonight, Hattie?" Thad said.

"Don't be silly. You're part of my family."

"But what about David?"

"Tonight is not the time for him to be here."

"What's wrong between the two of you? Friday you were beaming like a school girl until George brought over the telegram."

"There's nothing wrong. David and I just haven't had much time to talk since Thursday night."

Hattie prayed Thad would let the subject drop. It hadn't been the telegram as much as the newspaper article that upset her. For a few wonderful hours she thought of herself as Mrs. David Long, even Hattie Long. The story about Caleb Tyler shattered those dreams. If anyone who mattered ever found out about her brother-in-law and nephews, David's future would be worthless.

A rap at the door broke Hattie's dark thoughts. She knew she had to put on a happy face for Mabel. Theirs had been a strong friendship. She couldn't allow her misgivings to show through when Mabel needed her strength to get through the funeral and burial on Monday.

"Oh Hattie," Mabel gushed, "your home is always so perfect and the aroma from your kitchen is absolutely delicious."

Hattie escorted Mabel to the seat she'd set for her at the head of the table. "It is so good to have you here, even if the circumstances are so terrible. Was it awful?"

"Yes and no. Thomas just seemed to fade away. It was hard to lose him, but he knew me right up to the end, and he died very peacefully."

"So what's the minister they brought in to take Father's place like?" Carroll said.

Hattie wanted to shout for joy and tell Carroll David was wonderful and he'd asked her to be his wife.

"David is a great preacher," Thad replied before Hattie could say a word.

"Just who are you?" Carroll said as though talking down to some person he considered inferior.

"The Lord has been looking out for me," Hattie declared. "Your father knew how much work I had when Abe died. As time went on I became further and further behind. After a freak accident that really laid me low, Gertie made some inquiries of her sister and found Thad. He needed the work and I needed his help. Now with his wife, Alisha, and his daughter, Sammy, this house is alive for the first time since Abe's death.

"From what I heard, the two of you just got married. So how do you explain your wife's condition?" Carroll accused.

"You have no right to question Thad or anyone else," Hattie said through clinched teeth. "Thad has been raising Sammy alone ever since her mother died in childbirth. As for Alisha, her husband..."

"There was no husband," Alisha interrupted. "I made a bad mistake, and my parents sent me here so I wouldn't shame them. Thad did the Christian thing and married me in spite of my shame. He will be a father to my child, and I couldn't love Sammy more if she was my own flesh and blood. I was very lucky to find a man like Thad and a preacher like David who could explain to me about our Lord's forgiveness of sin."

"Very well put, my dear," Mabel said, giving Alisha a reassuring hug.

"At least this young lady was able to tell the truth," Carroll said, giving Hattie a glance that made her shudder with shame. "You always did have a creative way with the truth."

Hattie fought down the lump in her throat. Things hadn't changed much. Carroll could always make her cringe at his words, just as he was doing now.

"Since you're so interested in David Long," Thad commented. "I'm glad I overruled Hattie and asked him to join us tonight."

Hattie turned to see the mischievous grin on Thad's face.

Thad returned her glance and continued. "Coming to supper tonight should be beneficial for David. I heard you asked him to give the funeral sermon. It's a shame he never got to know your father."

Before Carroll could answer, David's forceful knock at the door interrupted them. Hattie hurried to greet him. The expression on David's face put her fears to rest. No matter how terrible Carroll could make her feel, David's smile put everything in to perspective.

"I'd expected the invitation to come from you," David said, once he stepped into the shop and out of the chill of the late afternoon air.

"I thought it might be awkward for you to be here with Mabel and Carroll. I'm so glad Thad knew what was best. Carroll hasn't changed much over the years. Alisha did her best to put him in his place. Unfortunately, he turned his words on me."

"Then you do want me here?"

"Very much so. More than wanting, I need you here." Hattie resisted the urge to stand on tiptoe to kiss David's cheek. If someone were to catch her, she would soon become the talk of the town, again.

* * * *

David walked through the shop and into Hattie's living quarters. As usual, the warmth of the rooms embraced him. It stood in direct contrast to the cold stare emanating from Carroll Hall's eyes.

"Reverend Long, it is indeed a pleasure to have you dining with us," Carroll greeted him. "I must say, I'm rather surprised to hear you've been keeping company with someone like Hattie."

"I don't know why you should be. The two of us have become close friends."

"Then I must assume you don't know about the novels she carries in that music bag of hers on Sunday mornings. My father told me all about what a joke it was to have the church pianist more engrossed in worldly novels than his sermons."

"Carroll!" Maude shouted getting to her feet. "What your father told you was in the strictest of confidence. No one else was ever to know about that."

"It's all right, Mabel," Hattie said, coming to her own defense. "David and I have come to grips with my faith or lack of such. Over the past few months, David has been helping me to understand the Bible and the way God meant it to be understood. In return I am helping him to enjoy my novels to the fullest."

David silently applauded Hattie's pluck. He knew it took a lot for her to admit to her weakness as well as to accuse Tom Hall of not caring enough about her to nurture the faith that lay just beneath the surface of Hattie's brilliant mind.

Before anyone could make a comment, Alisha and Thad entered the room. They each carried a tray with steaming bowls of delicious smelling soup.

"Oh, Hattie," Mabel gushed. "Your soup is always the best."

David looked at Hattie. "I didn't have time to make the soup. Thad and Alisha did the honors for us tonight. Thad is almost as good a cook as he is a tailor. Of course, Alisha is still learning."

"Whoever made this, it is delicious," Carroll said. "If this soup is any indication of your cooking talents, Alisha is a very lucky girl. At least she won't starve while she's learning to cook."

"Yes, Reverend Hall, I am very lucky. Not only will I not have to starve while I learn to cook from both my husband and Hattie, but I have a wonderful pastor who is teaching me about God's love and forgiveness."

David smiled at Alisha's answer. From the look on Carroll's face, David realized she'd impressed Reverend Hall as well.

"For someone so young, you are very well spoken," Carroll observed. "I can see Alisha is not the only lucky person in the room, Hattie. You are lucky to have found both Thad and Alisha to help you out. Thad is also lucky to have found such a generous benefactor as you, Hattie, as well as a lovely young wife as a helpmate. As for you, Reverend Long, you seem to be the luckiest person of all. To come to a community with an established congregation and find such staunch supporters is quite an accomplishment."

David inwardly seethed at Carroll's change in attitude. It was evident the man was trying to ingratiate himself to Thad and Alisha. Did he have an ulterior motive? If he did, David had no idea what it could be.

* * * *

By Monday morning, David was ready for the Halls to hurry through the day and leave Mortonville for good. Carroll made him uneasy. The best way to describe the feeling was to equate it with a cat eyeing a mouse as a potential meal.

David felt blessed by the sun that shone through the stained glass windows. After he read the requested scriptures, he glanced down at the blank pages in his hands.

"Normally, I would, at this point, give a prepared sermon. Since I didn't know Thomas Hall, I thought it best if I called upon those of you who knew him well to eulogize him."

It pleased David when after a few moments of whispered conversations Ralph Mason got to his feet and came forward. The next twenty minutes seemed to fly by as one parishioner after another came to the pulpit to sing Thomas Hall's praises.

When Hattie played the last note of the final hymn, the pallbearers came forward to carry the casket to the churchyard cemetery. David followed behind it, well aware of Carroll and Mabel behind him.

After the words of burial were said, David watched the first shovel full of dirt hit the top of the pine box. Then and only then did he head back to the church where the ladies put out a luncheon in the meeting hall built behind the sanctuary.

"What time does your train leave tomorrow?" Gertie Kellogg said, once she seated herself next to Mabel.

David wanted to say it couldn't be too soon for him, but he held his tongue.

"I really hate to leave, but we have tickets for the train at nine tomorrow morning. Carroll has to get back to his duties in Ohio."

"You know we hate to see you go," Herman said. "But times have changed. David has instilled several changes within our congregation. He's a good man, different from what we were used to, but good nonetheless"

"From what I've heard," Carroll observed, joining the conversation for the first time. "Your Reverend Long is very different from my father. The talk around town is he's been sparking Hattie Fairchild. Didn't the church council tell him such behavior is totally unacceptable?"

"I beg your pardon, Reverend Hall," David said, turning to his accuser. "There is no reason I shouldn't be keeping company with Hattie, especially considering I asked her to be my wife last Thursday night."

* * * *

Hattie put her hand to her mouth at David's premature announcement of their engagement. The shock she experienced seemed to ripple around the room, as forks clattered against plates. As one after another of the people around her regained their senses, Hattie became the center of attention.

"Why didn't you tell us?" Maude said. "Such joyous news is nothing to keep to yourself."

"There-there were too many other things going on with the funeral and all. David and I haven't and any chance to even talk about things since Thursday night."

"Well, did you say yes?" Mabel said.

The heat rushing to her cheeks brought about the memory of her excited acceptance of his proposal.

"Hattie has graciously agreed to be my wife. On Thursday night, I didn't have a symbol of my love to give her. Saturday's mail changed everything,"

Hattie watched as David dug in his pocket and produced a small jewelers' box. In front of everyone he made his way to where she sat and dropped to one knee.

"I'd like to make this official," he said, opening the box to reveal the most beautiful diamond ring Hattie ever saw. "Hattie Fairchild, will you do me the honor of being my wife?"

Thoughts of Laura's outlaw husband slipped in and out of her mind at David's words. There would be time to talk about Caleb Tyler later. Living in Mortonville, Illinois, it was entirely possible their paths would never cross.

After a moment of hesitation, Hattie began to smile broadly. "Yes, David. Like I said on Thursday evening, I will be proud to be your wife."

The room erupted in applause and shouts of well wishes as David slipped the ring on her finger. Once he did, David pulled Hattie to her feet and embraced her tenderly.

"When will the two of you be married?" Carroll spoke, once the excitement died down to a low roar.

"We haven't talked about it," David replied. "I'd like my parents to be here. With winter coming, it's an easier time for them to leave Philadelphia."

"I was thinking that since I'm still in town," Carroll pressed, "I could do the honors right here and now."

Hattie jerked her head in Carroll's direction. How did he dare suggest such a thing? She'd waited all her life to be a bride. How could he even think of having a hurried affair with none of the preparations of traditions she so desired?

To Hattie's surprise, confirmation of her private thoughts came from an unexpected quarter.

"Hattie deserves the very best," Ralph declared. "It won't be difficult to contact another minister to perform the ceremony. That will give all the mother hens in this town a chance to plan one bang up wedding. As for me, I intend to give the bride away."

Through her tears, Hattie embraced Ralph. Years of mistrust and hatred dissolved in a matter of minutes.

What started with the sadness of a funeral, now turned into the joy of the wedding the entire town seemed interested in planning.

Chapter Twenty-One

Hattie checked the shop for the hundredth time. David's parents were due in on the morning train.

Although she knew he wanted them to come for Christmas, David insisted it was best to plan the wedding for the first of February, rather than rush into anything too early.

It seemed as though every woman in town came to the house with preparations for the wedding.

Rather than flowers that were totally impractical in winter, Maude suggested bouquets of fabric and ribbon fashioned into flowers, which wouldn't fade. Gertie surprised Hattie with a delicately embroidered satin Bible cover with pastel pink love knots forming the flowers. From the sides streamed equally delicate pink ribbons. Edna and Alisha planned the wedding dinner along with a several-layered cake. Hattie smiled to think each layer would be of a different flavor.

Although Hattie designed her dress, Thad insisted on doing the work of making it. She'd chosen expensive cream-colored satin brocade and worked day and night to create the lace to trim the high collar and cuffs of the fashionable tight sleeves.

The jingle of the bell above the shop door signaled David's arrival. "Are you ready to go to the station?"

Hattie took a deep breath to calm the flip-flops her stomach was doing. "As ready as I'll ever be. Oh David, what if they hate me?"

David came to her side and enfolded her in his arms. "They'll love you. Now, let's get you bundle up. It's very cold outside.

Hattie nodded as David held her brown wool coat. Once he helped her put it on, he handed her the warm scarf she'd made last winter as well as the fur muff he'd given her for Christmas.

"You and Alisha will be alone for dinner today, Thad," David said, as he held open the shop door. "My parents want to take Hattie and me to the hotel so they can get to know her."

"Are you certain?" Hattie said, once David closed the door behind them.

"Positive. Ma said so in her last letter. She doesn't want you fussing on their account."

"Is it that or is she afraid I can't cook?"

"She knows better than that," David replied, bending to kiss her lips. "She should, considering the number of letters I've written praising your talents in the kitchen. Now, we have to hurry. The train is due in about ten minutes."

Hattie smiled and allowed David to help her into the carriage. Once she was seated, he tucked the buffalo robe around her legs before he closed the door.

"I'm as nervous as a cat about this," Hattie declared as they drove toward the station.

"I know you are, but you have no reason for it. My parents are no different from anyone else you know in Mortonville. They will love you, I promise."

"I hope you're right. As for being no different from anyone in town, I doubt that. They're from Philadelphia. Big city folks are much different from…"

"You forget, they're from outside of Philadelphia. If Pa had his way they'd never go into the city. He only goes because Ma likes to shop there and attend the theatre."

By the time they reached the station the train was already pulling in. The train whistle announced its arrival, as David helped Hattie down from the carriage. He took her arm and hurried across the platform to where the passengers would be disembarking from the train.

The first people emerged from the passenger car before they traversed half the distance between the carriage and the train Hattie saw a couple step down from the train, and she knew immediately they were

David's parents. The man was a more mature version of David. To Hattie's surprise a fashionable hat sat atop the woman's perfectly styled red hair.

"It's no wonder my red hair didn't scare you off," Hattie whispered.

"I've contended with one red head all my life by chance. When I first saw you, I realized I wanted to spend the rest of my life with a red head by choice."

Hattie warmed at his words. She only prayed his parents would feel the same way about her.

* * * *

"David," his mother called as soon as she saw him standing on the other side of the platform. "It's so good to see you."

She held him at arm's length. "It doesn't look like you're suffering too badly from eating your own cooking."

David watched as his mother turned to face Hattie. "And you, my dear, must be Hattie. You're as beautiful as my son says you are. I was afraid he was exaggerating. Now I see he was nothing more than truthful."

"You know, I never exaggerate, Mother," David said, coming to Hattie's side.

"Did you get me that rig, Son?" his father said, joining the conversation for the first time,

"It will be ready when we finish our dinner," David replied.

"I was hoping to have it now. There's a lot of baggage."

His father's statement surprised David. "How much baggage do you need for a week's visit?"

"It's not all for us," his mother answered. "There are two full boxes of wedding presents."

"Wedding presents?" Hattie said. "We certainly didn't expect…"

"Oh, they're not all from us, my dear. David has many friends and relatives in Philadelphia who wanted to remember him on such a special day. With his position with the church, they thought there would be many things you can use. They were sent out of love and should be accepted in the same manner."

David turned to watch the men unloading the baggage car. 'Crates' would have been a better choice of words to describe the size of the boxes sitting on the platform.

"I'm certain Phil, the station manager, will gladly take your things over to the parsonage while we eat dinner," Hattie suggested.

"That's right, William," David's mother agreed. "I'd hate to see either of you two boys hurting yourselves by lifting those boxes. I'm sure there are several young men around town who can do that for you."

All four of them convulsed in laughter. After Hattie arranged for Phil and his assistant to deliver the crates, they got into David's carriage and drove to the hotel.

While David and his father ordered the large steak dinner, Hattie and David's mother opted for the smaller steaks the menu offered.

"Who is going to perform the ceremony, son?"

"Reverend Case is coming from the county seat. He graciously agreed to do the honors."

David thought about Benjamin Case. Until two weeks ago they hadn't met. By that time, David was getting desperate to find someone to perform the wedding ceremony. With Mortonville a remote farming town, David had found little opportunity to meet his contemporaries in the surrounding communities.

It had been George who solved the dilemma by asking David to ride along with him to the county seat. While George did the business he'd planned, David walked the short distance to the church to meet Benjamin. The man was about five years older than David. When David told him of his problem, Benjamin was more than happy to oblige.

"Isn't that right, son?"

David jerked his thoughts back to the conversation at the dinner table. "I'm sorry, Pa. I guess I was somewhere else."

"I told you so, Ruby. David's mind wasn't on our conversation at all."

"All right, Pa, you caught me. I was thinking about the man who will marry us on Saturday. I want everything to be perfect."

"After meeting your bride to be," his mother declared, "I have no worries about imperfection. I can't believe Hattie, that not only did you run your shop alone before you sent for that nice young man to help you, but you also play piano for church. I won't even go into how well educated you are."

As usual David enjoyed Hattie's girlish blush. "I'm afraid you're embarrassing Hattie."

"Now which one of us is assuming the other's feelings?" Hattie teased. "I'm flattered, but not embarrassed. I'm more interested in what is in those crates delivered to the parsonage."

David agreed with Hattie. He certainly hadn't expected his parents to bring presents in addition to coming to the wedding.

With dinner ended, David drove over to the livery stable so they could get the carriage he'd ordered for his parents to use during their visit.

* * * *

Hattie was delighted when they, at last, headed to the parsonage. "I really like your parents," she declared, once they were alone.

"I can tell they love you as well. How much would you like to bet my mother will insist on opening those two crates of wedding presents as soon as we arrive?"

"Why, Reverend Long, I didn't know you were a betting man. Doesn't that go against the principles of your vocation?"

David laughed. It was a sound Hattie had come to love. "My dear bride-to-be, you must remember this wasn't always my calling. When I practiced law, I wagered more than money on the outcome of every case I took before a jury. I learned to be an astutely good judge of human nature."

Since the crates had been left in the foyer, there was little option but to open each of them to inspect their contents.

Hattie felt like a child on Christmas morning as each package was taken from its resting place and opened. The first gift came from David's parents. Hattie could hardly believe her eyes when the box revealed a china setting for twelve as well as the crystal and silver to go with it.

"I … I don't know what to say," Hattie stammered. "This is far too extravagant a gift."

"David is our only child," William declared, putting his hand on Hattie's shoulder, "On the day he passed the bar, my wife started buying these dishes. She said he'd be hosting extravagant parties as a lawyer and deserved the best. I couldn't agree more. Even as a minister, many people will cross his path, and I hope these few worldly things will make a good impression no matter when God decides to send the two of you."

Hattie remembered the cracked and chipped china filling the shelves of David's cupboards. Their contrast to the beautiful china Abe left her was undeniable. It was the one thing Hattie knew she would miss the most once the shop and living quarters belonged to Thad and Alisha.

"We graciously accept your generous gift," David said, giving his mother a hug. "But what about the rest of these presents. They can't all be from you."

"Of course they aren't," Ruby replied. "If you would have been listening when Hattie and I were talking at the station, you would have heard me say they are from our family and friends in Philadelphia."

One after another, Hattie opened the beautiful gifts. Each was unique. Among the embroidered linens were sheets, pillowslips, and towels of every size and description. Cut glass bowls stood in direct contrast to the latest in cookware. Everything a young couple would need to begin a life together had been packed into the two massive crates.

By the time the last gift was opened, the clock in the parlor was striking three. "Oh dear," Hattie exclaimed, getting to her feet. "I almost forgot I promised to pick up the mail. If I don't get home to supervise supper, poor Alisha will be in a panic."

"I'll take you to the store and then home," David suggested. "That will give the folks a chance to rest a bit before they come over for supper."

Hattie allowed David to hold her coat. After they left the parsonage, they made their way to the general store.

To Hattie's surprise, her mail contained a letter from Mabel Hall, while David's held one from the church office in Philadelphia.

"What does your letter say?" David pressed, once they were back in the carriage.

"It's getting too dark to read it here. I'll fix us a cup of tea when we get home, I can read it while we relax.

"What do you think Mabel Hall wants?"

"Probably congratulations us on our wedding."

The aroma of chicken roasting in the oven greeted Hattie as soon as she entered the shop. Although Alisha and Thad were full of questions about her meeting with David's parents, the letter from Mabel intrigued Hattie more.

My Dear Hattie,

The time we spent in Mortonville for Tom's funeral made me realize how much I miss my life and friends there.

I have become so homesick, Carroll has requested a transfer to Mortonville. I don't know when it will come through, but I'm so excited about coming home I had to let you know.

I can hardly wait to get back home to all my old friends and the house where Tom and I were so very happy.

My sincere congratulations on your upcoming marriage.

Love,
Mabel

"How-how could they consider such a thing?" Hattie said, once she put down the letter. "Mortonville is your church, our church."

"Please Hattie, this is something we can't control. Ministers go where they're told. I had no say when they sent me here, and I'll have no say when they decide to move me on to a new congregation. Would moving be so terrible?"

Hattie took a deep breath. "You know I'd go to the ends of the earth with you. What upsets me is that the Halls would go behind your back like this."

"Carroll is a good man. He's only thinking of his mother's happiness."

Hattie set aside the letter and hugged David tightly. "I was just over reacting. It doesn't matter where we go as long as we go together."

She watched as David fingered the letter he took from the inside pocket of his suit coat. "Maybe this letter from the church office will explain more."

Hattie held her breath while David broke the seal on the envelope.

Dear Reverend Long,

Greetings to you from your friends in Christ. Praises of your work in Mortonville have reached this board constantly since your arrival. You are well liked. The changes you have instituted are appreciated by the members of your congregation.

Those praises are the reason it has been such a hard decision to arrange to transfer you to another church. Reverend Thomas Hall was well established in the Mortonville community and leaving has been a hardship on his widow. Reverend Carroll Hall has graciously asked if he could relocate his family to Mortonville for the wellbeing of his mother.

There is another community further west that has an established church, but has never had a minister. You would be a welcome addition to their church.

The move is not planned until spring, so you will have time to make the necessary preparations. With Easter passed, travel to Clarkston, Nebraska, will be much easier for you.

We look forward to hearing from you in the near future. We have received the letter about your impending marriage and wish you and your bride only the best.

Yours in Christ.

The Church Board

The words Clarkston, Nebraska rang in Hattie's ears. Moments earlier she'd promised to go anywhere with David, How could she tell him the one place she didn't want to be was where people would equate them with Caleb Tyler?

Chapter Twenty-Two

David made the excuse of having to go back to be with his parents when he left Hattie's house. Instead of going directly to the parsonage, he made his way to the general store. If anyone knew Hattie, it was George. Perhaps he could shed some light on Hattie's reaction to the letters they'd received. He realized leaving Mortonville would be harder for her than for him, but she had said she'd go anywhere with him. Why then did her face go almost ashen when he told her where they would be going?

"Is something wrong?" George said, when David walked in just as George was putting the CLOSED sign in the window.

"Yes and no. Carroll Hall will be taking my place here after Easter."

George hung his head, indicating David's news came as no surprise. "He hinted at it when he was here. Everyone on the church council objected, but we don't seem to carry much weight with the church board. We all got letters in today's mail. I'm sorry, David. We really hate to see you leave Mortonville. How does Hattie feel about it?"

"That's what I wanted to talk to you about. You seem to know her better than anyone else. At first she was shocked when Mabel told her of the possibility. Once it sank in, she said she'd go to the ends of the earth with me. My letter contained the call. When I told her we'd be going to Clarkston, Nebraska, all the color drained from her face. I don't understand any of it."

George took David's arm. "Come back and sit down. There's a lot you don't know about Hattie."

David followed George to the living quarters behind the store. "You know Hattie has an older sister," George began. "Laura ran away with a smooth talking stranger named Caleb Tyler."

"The outlaw?" David was unable to mask his shock. "Hattie's sister is married to an outlaw?"

"It didn't start out that way. I think she was so desperate to get away from Hank Fairchild she took up with the first man who looked her way. Things went well until their boys started getting older. Caleb wasn't much of a farmer, so he decided robbing banks was easier. He left Laura alone on the farm with the children, According to Hattie, he comes back to bring Laura money and take another boy with him on a yearly basis, The last I heard, Laura and the two youngest kids were still on the farm in Clarkston."

David could hardly believe what George was telling him. Hattie mentioned her sister, Laura, as well as the woman's two children. She'd also said she wanted to bring the family to Mortonville to live with her. In his wildest dreams, he never imagined the husband who deserted Laura to be Caleb Tyler.

"It's no wonder the thought of relocating to Clarkston upset Hattie," David managed to say at last. "She must be worried about how his reputation would affect my ministry. What can I do to set aside her fears?"

"Don't let her know you came here. If I know Hattie, she'll bring up the subject to you. I just hope she won't call off the wedding. She needs you as much as you need her."

David agreed with George's logic. Cable Tyler was Hattie's personal demon.

* * * *

Hattie took a mental note of her table. The white damask tablecloth looked perfect with her good china, crystal, and silver as did the matching napkins in their sliver napkin holders.

"Are we having a party, Aunt Hattie?" Sammy said.

"Yes, Darling, we are. Reverend Long's mother and father came all the way from Philadelphia to be at our wedding. Tonight your mama and I are cooking them a special meal."

"Mama has been cooking all day. She even let me help shape the rolls."

Hattie looked at the perfectly shaped butter horns and round rolls. In their midst were misshapen little rolls that brought tears to Hattie's eyes. "You did a very good job. I'm certain Mr. and Mrs. Long will be impressed with your abilities. Now, you run along and put on that pretty new dress your daddy and I made for you to wear tonight."

Sammy did as she was told, leaving Hattie to her thoughts.

How could one letter so drastically alter her life? Dear God, she needed help to keep Caleb Tyler from tainting David. At the same time, she needed strength to help her sister and her children.

You have to tell David about Caleb, a voice sounded within Hattie's mind silencing her prayer. *He saw the look on your face when he told you where I was sending him. There is a reason for everything, and I do nothing without weighing all the options first.*

Hattie shook her head. She must have imagined what she just heard. Before when she listened to the strange voice, she equated it with God. Was He again speaking to her? If so what did it mean?

"David, it's good to see you," Thad's greeting brought Hattie's thoughts back to the present.

"Your home is beautiful," Ruby exclaimed, once they came from the parlor to the kitchen "I never expected anything so luxurious behind a store front."

"I can't take credit for it," Hattie said. "Abe Levens and his wife owned all the furnishings before I came to work for him."

"You most certainly can take the credit. It's a woman who keeps this house clean and makes it a home. I've never seen such a high shine on a piano before."

David's hearty laughter put Hattie at ease over the compliments of her future mother-in-law. "Remind me to take you over to the church tomorrow morning. The first time I met Hattie she was at the church with a bottle of lemon oil in her music bag polishing the piano. They had it stuck away in the balcony where no one but Hattie could see it. The first thing I did was to have it brought down to the floor of the sanctuary where everyone can enjoy its beauty."

Alisha's announcement supper was ready ended the conversation that tended to embarrass Hattie.

Once in the dining room, Alisha assigned the seating. After she placed David and Thad at the head and foot of the table, she instructed Hattie to sit next to David and his parents across from her.

When they were all seated, they clasped hands and David said the table grace. "Dear Father, thank you for this bounty spread before us tonight. Thank you also for this reunion between my parents and me. Help them to accept this woman who is the light of my life. A-men."

Hattie beamed at David's prayer and the public profession of his love. Alisha's talents in the kitchen also pleased her. It seemed her patient hours of teaching the girl to cook had certainly paid off.

"It's a shame the two of you have to move on so soon after the wedding," David's father said, once they sat in the parlor with their coffee and dessert.

The statement brought Hattie's worse nightmare to the forefront. If indeed she'd heard the voice of God within the confines of her mind, she needed to tell David of her fears.

"You're very quiet, Hattie," David observed. "Obviously something about this move bothers you." He looked at his parents and then at Hattie. "Would you like to go into the shop and talk about it? I'm sure my parents wouldn't mind."

Hattie shook her head no. "It's best if everyone here knows what's bothering me now that Sammy is tucked into her bed."

After taking a deep breath, Hattie told how Caleb Tyler came to Mortonville and stole not only Laura's heart, but also the money he thought he was entitled to as Laura's dowry. Stories of the abuse Laura suffered at his hands spilled from her lips as though she could no longer stand to keep them inside.

"When you said we would be going to Clarkston, I was concerned my connection with Caleb would taint you in the eyes of your new congregation. While I was praying about what to do, I heard a voice in my mind. It said I should be less concerned with you and me. Once I was able to put things into perspective, I realized we are being sent to Clarkston for Laura and her two youngest children. I can only pray Caleb won't turn the hearts of the people against us."

Hattie could feel the weight of years of hiding the truth about Laura and her family lift from her shoulders. Between David and herself, she knew they would be able to lessen the load Laura carried.

David put his arm around Hattie's shoulder and pulled her close to him "I wondered if you were going to say anything. I noticed the look on your face when I read the part of the letter about where we would be going. I was so concerned I went to the general store to talk to George. He told me the entire story. I have to admit, it will be hard being Caleb Tyler's brother-in-law, but it certainly won't be impossible."

"Here, here," William said. "I always said you could pick your friends but not your relatives. I'm certain you remember the stories we heard about my cousin, Oscar, who was hanged for murdering his wife. I liked him when we were boys, but thankfully no one held the relationship against me."

"I have given the matter much thought," Hattie confessed. "I am looking forward to getting to Clarkston and finally seeing my sister as well as her two youngest children, Gary and Jesse. Perhaps we can make a difference in their lives once we get there."

Chapter Twenty-Three

Hattie paced the length of the balcony. "You're going to wear a hole in the floorboards if you keep that up," Alisha teased.

"You were the one who said I should get here three hours early and dress in the balcony," Hattie retorted.

Alisha giggled. "Only because it's bad luck to see the groom before the wedding. It won't be long now. I heard the back door open a while ago so David must be here."

Hattie leaned against the back wall so she wouldn't wrinkle the elegant dress Alisha slipped over her head a few minutes earlier.

It was so cold today, maybe no one would come. Hattie was unable to keep the dark premonitions at bay.

"You look lovely today," Ralph said, causing Hattie to turn toward the stairs. "Your mother would have been so proud of you."

Hattie ran her hand over the fine fabric of the dress. The thought of her mother brought unbidden tears to her eyes."

"I know I've done you wrong in the past," Ralph continued. "Just for today, let's put aside our differences. I'm so proud of the way you turned out. If we had been blessed with a daughter, I would have wanted her to be just like you."

"Thank you, Ralph. I wish we could have put the past behind us before this. In two months, I'll be leaving Mortonville and I know I'll never come back. After today, you'll always be special to me."

A commotion from the sanctuary told them the guests had started arriving. A hundred butterflies took flight in Hattie's stomach. They didn't settle down until someone else climbed the stairs to the balcony, Even though Hattie knew it was Ruth, she prayed David would be the one to come around the corner and enter her line of vision.

When David first asked her to marry him, she'd asked Ruth to be her matron of honor before she knew David asked George to be his best man. It was only right, George and Ruth had always been there for her. If things had been different, she could have been George's wife. Thank goodness God knew what he was doing by giving her a lonely existence. Had that not been the situation, she would not have been ready for an exciting man like David Long to enter her life.

* * * *

The familiar strains David knew Thad had practiced for weeks filled the church and meeting room with delightful music.

Moments earlier, Benjamin and George joined David in the room where meetings and social events were held. He'd hoped to greet their guests here, but the women who knew Hattie all her life took over the planning.

It seemed as though the entire town wanted Hattie's wedding to be a special occasion. The hotel agreed to open its grand ballroom and each woman contributed her specialties to the food laden table Edna described.

The tone of the music changed, telling David it was time to enter the church and face his future.

"Do you have the ring?" he said to George.

"It's right here," George replied, holding up his hand to show the wide gold band resting above the first joint of the little finger on his left hand. "Take a deep breath, David. It's time. In a few minute you and Hattie will be man and wife."

Man and wife. The thanked God for sending him to this town. God knew Hattie was waiting for him. He wanted to be worthy of her. He needed God's help to make the move to Clarkston one she wouldn't regret.

George opened the door to the sanctuary. For a moment, David held his breath at the sight of so many people packed into the pews. On one side of the church sat his parents. His mother dabbed tears of joy with a delicate lace edged handkerchief. Across the aisle sat Alisha with Sammy on her lap. Along with them, Edna Mason shared the pew.

At the back of the church, Ruth stood ready to take the walk to stand with George and witness the joining of David and Hattie. As the music changed to the traditional wedding march, the entire congregation got to its feet.

David's mouth dropped open as Hattie came around the corner, escorted by Ralph. She was the most beautiful vision he'd ever seen.

Her walk from the back of the church to where he stood seemed to take an eternity. When it at last ended, David turned to face Benjamin and fought the urge to take Hattie's hand before it was offered to him.

"Who gives this woman in marriage to this man?" Benjamin said.

"As the representative of her family as well as the people of Mortonville who love her like our own, I do," Ralph replied.

From the congregation, the women cried at the tender words.

Ralph gently kissed Hattie's cheek, then placed her delicate hand into David's much larger one.

"Take good care of her, David. She's a very special lady."

David nodded. No one needed to tell him about Hattie being special. He'd recognized it the day they met. He'd felt it grow every day since. Within a few minutes she would be his to love and protect for the rest of their lives.

"I, David, take you, Hattie, to be my wife."

* * * *

The words David spoke so confidently raised Hattie's spirits to the rafters of the church. When it came time for her to say a similar vow, the whispered words she'd anticipated were spoken with such confidence they were heard by everyone in the packed church. After vowing to love, cherish, and obey David, a warmth began to spread through her.

"By the power vested in me by God and the church, I now pronounce you man and wife. What God has joined together, let no man put asunder."

Upon the proclamation of Benjamin's words, David took Hattie in his arms and kissed her tenderly. Any doubts about the God who now ruled her life disappeared. It was at last clear to her David was the man God chose to save her from a life of doubt and bring her the love she deserved.

She thanked God. Thanked Him for showing her how to love and be loved, not only by David but also by God.

Chapter Twenty-Four

David stared out of the train window at the moonlit countryside speeding past them. Hattie slept peacefully, resting against his side in the comfort of his protective arm. Unfortunately, the peaceful sleep she enjoyed remained a stranger to him.

He couldn't help thinking about what they would find when they reached Clarkston. Hattie's fears certainly had merit. He'd tried so hard to assure her he wasn't worried about what the people would think of Caleb Tyler's brother-in-law, only to find he was fighting her demon in his mind.

In an attempt to get some sleep, he closed his eyes and tried to relax. To his surprise, he felt the hand of God touch his heart and relax his mind.

You will do your best, David. I can ask nothing more. You were sent to Clarkston to melt the ice of the hearts of your new congregation. With Hattie at your side, the task will be completed.

Secure in the words of his dream, David drifted off to a more peaceful sleep.

"Clarkston, next stop Clarkston."

David awoke with a start. It was evident Hattie had been awake for some time, as her hair was tucked perfectly into the upsweep that so flattered her appearance.

Once the train ground to a halt, Hattie squeezed David's hand reassuringly. "We're here. I know living in Caleb Tyler's shadow won't be the easiest thing we could be doing, but we'll make it."

"I'm certain we will."

As soon as they stepped from the train, they were greeted by many of the townspeople.

"I'm Belle Clark," the obvious leader of the women said as she made her way to Hattie's side. "We were thrilled when we learned our new preacher had a wife. I'm certain you'll want to be involved in not only the Ladies Aid Society but also our weekly Bible Study. I just know you will add a new perspective to our weekly devotions."

Hattie cringed and turned to David for support.

"My wife will be a wonderful addition to your groups. I know you will be thrilled with her interpretation of the Bible."

Outwardly, Hattie smiled, but inwardly she winced. When she had David alone, she would certainly give him a piece of her mind.

"Do you, by any chance know of a family by the name of Tyler, Mrs. Clark?" Hattie said.

"Please call me Belle. Everyone else does. As for that terrible family, they live outside of town, but no one associates with them, if you know what I mean. I don't know the wife very well, but Caleb Tyler is an outlaw, and it's the same with that pack of wild young'uns of his. I had great hopes for Gary, the youngest boy, when the teacher at the school wanted to send him to St. Louis to further his education, but then Caleb showed up and took him away. By now, he's not much better than his older brothers. All of them are cold-blooded killers. Why would you want to associate with the likes of them?"

"Laura Tyler is my wife's sister," David said, coming to Hattie's rescue. "They have been separated for many years and coming here will bring the two of them back together."

Hattie watched as Belle withdrew her hand. "Well, I never. What kind of a minister would take up with the sister of an outlaw?"

"My sister is not the outlaw," Hattie declared. "She has no control over her husband. I assure you when they were married Caleb was not the man he is today. Had he been, Laura would have never agreed to his marriage proposal."

Belle's face turned red with anger as she turned from Hattie and David. In her stead, a man approached them.

"Belle will come around, just don't let her get under your skin. I'm

Joshua Sage, the teacher here in town. What she says about Gary is true, I'm afraid. The night before he was to leave for St. Louis, Caleb returned and took him away. It was a sad day indeed, as that boy has a mind for learning and books."

"Can you tell us where we will find my wife's sister and her daughter, Mr. Sage?"

"I'll stop over after you're settled and give you instructions on how to get out there. For now, I'm certain Belle and the ladies of the church are anxious to get you over to the parsonage."

Hattie wanted to cry but instead thanked the schoolteacher and returned her attention to Belle and the ladies. They were, indeed, anxious to get the new minister and his wife to their new home, even if she did claim to be the sister of Laura Tyler.

* * * *

Hattie spent hours arranging and rearranging the numerous wedding presents that had been delivered to the parsonage as well as the many books she brought from her own personal library. She'd been thrilled to find a piano in the parsonage as well as one at the church. Since the church didn't have a pianist she was more than pleased to take on the role she so enjoyed over the past several years.

They'd been in town almost a week when Mr. Sage came to visit. Hattie was glad she'd done her baking early that morning and was able to offer him a plate of homemade treats and fresh coffee.

"What can you tell us about my sister?" She spoke once they were seated in the parlor and enjoying their coffee.

"I have met your sister on many occasions and have often wished there was something I could do to ease her suffering. From everything I've heard, Caleb is a very violent man. It was evident on the morning I went to get Gary to take him to the train. He was so excited about the trip and being able to go to one of the best boarding schools west of the Mississippi that I was excited as well. Unfortunately, when I got there, Caleb had come the previous evening and taken the boy away with him."

"You said he was violent. Can you explain?" David probed.

"When I arrived at the farm, Jesse was doing the chores, and Gary was nowhere in sight. Jesse invited me to come into the house and there I found Laura. She was in bed and it was evident Caleb had beaten her. Her face was swollen, she had two black eyes, and barely enough strength to lift her head from the pillow. That was two months ago."

Hattie felt sick inside. "Have you been back?"

"Jesse made it quite clear she could care for her mother. I can only assume she has been doing just that, since she hasn't been to school. I know I shouldn't have stayed away, but Jesse is such a delicate child I didn't want to cause her any undo distress."

Hattie dabbed at her eyes with her handkerchief. Now, more than ever, she knew coming to Clarkston was the best thing they could have done. Not only did Laura need her, but Jesse did as well.

After Mr. Sage left, David helped Hattie clean up the dishes. "It's still early. I think we will have plenty of time to drive out to your sister's place before dark."

"Oh David, do you mean it?"

"Of course I do. You stack these dishes in the sink and I'll help you with them when we return. Now more than ever we need to see your sister."

The drive out through the countryside was tense. Hattie worried what they would find once they reached the Tyler farm. It concerned her to learn Jesse stopped going to school. Knowing Laura, an education was far more important than chores and farm work. Something must be drastically wrong for her to allow her daughter to ignore her studies.

Laura's farm loomed on their left. Hattie wanted to cry when she saw the condition of the outbuildings. Their father had neglected his farm, but not to the extent of Laura's home. Shutters hung haphazardly as though the nails holding them in place had long since worked themselves loose. The barn was in desperate need of a new roof as well as a coat of paint, and the chicken coop looked as though it would cave in if it were hit by a good stiff gust of wind.

Out at the pump, she saw a young girl with a bucket. It could be no one but Jesse. Her red hair was braided and her slender frame made her look much younger than her twelve years of age.

"Are you Jesse?" David said, as he got down from the buggy.

"Depends on who's askin'," the girl replied.

"I'm Reverend David Long, and this is my wife, Hattie."

For a moment the girl stood scrutinizing them. Hattie wondered if her name meant anything at all to Jesse. "I'm your Aunt Hattie, dear, your mother's sister," she finally said.

"I … I've heard Ma talk about you," Jesse stammered.

She seemed to cringe as David held out his hand. Shyly Jesse put her hands behind her back as though she was ashamed of them. "I'd shake your hand, Reverend, but I'm all dirty."

"Don't ever apologize for the dirt from honest labor, child," David said.

Jesse hung her head and lowered her eyes. "Where are my manners? I should have invited you in right off. Ma would skin me alive if she had the strength. I have some coffee on the stove and some bread I made yesterday."

She led them into the shack she called home. Seeing the dust, Hattie realized there had been precious little time for housekeeping.

Jesse picked up a towel from the table and wiped out two coffee cups before filling and handing them to her guests. "I hope you don't mind takin' your coffee black," she said. "I've been savin' the cream for Ma and I ain't had the time to skim it off this morning."

"Black will be just fine," David assured her. "How long has your mother been ill?"

Before Jesse could answer, a soft moan came from behind the curtain at the far end of the room. Jesse got to her feet and hurried to her mother's side. "Are you all right, Ma? Can I get you anything?"

Laura didn't open her eyes. "My Bible, Jesse," she whispered hoarsely. "I want my Bible."

Jesse picked up the worn book from the chair where she'd left it and handed it to her mother. "We got company, Ma. There's a preacher in town now. He came out to see you. He brought along his wife, she says she's your sister…"

Before she could finish, Laura opened her eyes. "Hattie? Is Hattie here? I must see her."

"I got chores to do, Ma. I'll go out and do them while you and Mrs. Long have yourselves a good visit."

* * * *

212

David watched as Jesse left the room, He knew it must be a relief for her to have someone else to care for her mother.

"Are you all right?" David said to Jesse once they were outside.

Jesse nodded. "You'll have to excuse me, Reverend, like I told Ma, I've got chores to do."

"Let me help you."

"I can do for myself. Ma ain't got long. I've known it for weeks. I'd like it if you'd read to her from the Bible. The Twenty-third Psalm is her favorite. I read other passages to her, but she always insists I read the Psalm to her first. She likes to say the words with me, so when you read it, don't go too fast. I'll be back as soon as I finish what I have to do outside."

David didn't argue with the girl. He would have time to comfort Jesse later. His duty now lay with Laura. Once he returned to Hattie's side, he picked up the worn Bible.

"I wish we were meeting under more favorable conditions," he said, as he took Laura's hand. "Jesse says the words of the Twenty-third Psalm give you comfort. Would you like me to read it to you now?"

The frail woman on the bed nodded her head.

"The Lord is my shepherd, I shall not want..."

With the first words spoken, Hattie joined him in the rest of the litany while Laura moved her lips without making a sound.

"Take care of my Jesse," she whispered when the Psalm came to an end. "She's all I have left. Don't let Caleb take her. Raise her to be a proper lady, but please, please don't let her forget me."

With the words uttered, she closed her eyes and slipped silently away.

Hattie cried bitterly and allowed David to hold her close. "How can we tell that poor child her mother is gone?"

"We'll find a way, and I'll be proud to call her daughter. She resembles you so closely, she could easily be our child."

"Who could be your child?"

Both David and Hattie turned at the sound of Jesse's voice.

"I'm sorry, Jesse. Your mother slipped away while I held her hand. She asked if we would raise you like our own."

"It's best," Jesse replied. David knew the girl was too hardened from the last few months to cry. "She's been powerful sick. I've known for weeks she wanted to go home to the Lord. I'd best fix us somethin' to eat, then get her ready for burial. She wants to rest out back of the house with Andy."

"Andy?" David inquired.

"My brother. He died right after he was born. Ma said he couldn't get his breath and he died. They buried him out back of the house. She wants to rest close to him."

David nodded. "I'll go out to the barn and see if I can find some wood for a coffin and then I'll dig the grave."

* * * *

With the burial finished, Hattie helped Jessie to pack her meager possession. As the carriage pulled from the dooryard, David and Hattie both knew Jesse was saying good-bye to the only life she'd ever known.

For Hattie, the family she'd always dreamed of was hers. It didn't matter that Caleb and Laura Tyler gave birth to the girl who shared the carriage with her and David. From this day forward and forever more, Jesse would be their child. They would raise her with the same love they shared with one another.

It was clear to Hattie now. God brought David into her life for two reasons. They were to bring her to the Lord and Jesse to them when she needed them most.

The End

Coming Soon!

Outlaw's Son, Book 2 of The Outlaw's Series
Outlaw's Daughter, Book 3 of the Outlaw's Series
Outlaw's Secret, Book 4 of the Outlaw's Series

About the Author

Mild Mannered wife, mother and grandmother by day, Sherry Derr-Wille spends her nights writing and writing and writing. Having been inspired by an English assignment in her sophomore year of high school, she had never quite finished the assignment. New stories pop into her head every day with never enough time to write them all.

A Wisconsin native, she grew up a country girl, but enjoys her "city" home. She and her husband of almost 50 years, Bob, live in a mid-sized town close to the Illinois border, where she works as a receptionist for an insurance office and he is retired. Deeming Bob "A Saint" for putting up with her she has never regretted marrying her high school sweetheart just two days after graduation in 1964.

www.derr-wille.com

216